Early Thursday

A Novel

LINDA S. CUNNINGHAM

ISBN (Print): 978-1-09830-480-5
ISBN (eBook): 978-1-09830-481-2

Cover illustration by Jacqueline Halliburton

DEDICATION

To Pat for his love, support, and perseverance in never giving up on me to complete this mission.

Acknowledgments

I am forever grateful to those who inspired me with their stories, humor, editing, knowledge, and love of the Cajun culture especially: Jean "Muffin" Arnaud, Goldie Ardoin (deceased), Candice Burrows, Patrick Cunningham, Charles Corbello (deceased), Larissa Fahrenholz, Jacqueline Halliburton, Perky and Johnny Janese, Judy Joubert, Yvonne Babineaux Key, Lake Charles American Press, Carol Lynn Loker, Elton Louviere (deceased) and Patricia Louviere. Finally, to JC who gave me the seed of talent to be cultivated and who would never have given me a desire to write if it could not have been realized, but most of all, for the gift of his mother who was always in my corner.

CHAPTER ONE

JUNE 2010

Thinking back after all these years when I try to write about the storm of June 27, 1957, I remember the memories of my life when I was drowning—the meticulous reliving in a dimension with no time. I remember barreling over and over, a storming stone through the waves, and when I managed to come up for a breath, I thought the wind would take my head right off my shoulders. My arms grasped at nothing and everything. My legs were useless against the force of wind-driven water. I had no thoughts, just the sense of a storm in my head that shredded everything that had been important to me. I had no great revelations, no great epiphanies, but I saw the extraordinary. Through all the dirty, swirling water that tossed wooden beams, branches, tires, telephone poles and cattle carcasses, my eyes focused microscopically. I marveled at the intricacies of a single oak leaf with its webbing thoroughfare of veins. I marveled at the leaf as a single, cyclical debris of a greater tree, and then I remembered the tree. I remembered Papa shooting at me in the tree. I remembered my mistake. I remembered that all the good that I had done in my short life was defined by one mistake. Why do humans remember only the bad? I was that human remembering my life, and I knew that I was dying. I didn't want to die. I had to atone for too much. I remember that I had the sense that I had been a witness to miracles like the leaf but did not see them because of the swirling debris of my life. It was a great sin. I needed a miracle, so I asked. I heard a woman's voice calling my name,

1

"Walt, Walt, come up."

I grew up on the northern crescent of the Gulf of Mexico, a body of water in the shape of a human brain with the brain stem positioned at the Yucatan Strait. The Gulf at its deepest is around 13,000 to 14,000 feet and is fed by water from the Caribbean Sea entering through the Yucatan Strait. This fast-moving current circulates in a clockwise loop before exiting through the Florida Straits into the Atlantic Ocean. It forms what is known as the Gulf Stream, one of the most powerful water currents in the world. I lived in a small town in southwest Louisiana by the name of Cameron, originally known a hundred years or so earlier as Leesburg, and the only remnant left of that name is a street. Southwest Louisiana is nothing but a speck on the world map, the button of a ball cap on the head of the Gulf of Mexico. Cameron positions itself almost halfway between the hook of Texas, sporting Brownsville, and the toe of Louisiana's boot where the crescent city of New Orleans lay at the mouth of the Mississippi. For nature lovers and birders, Cameron is probably best known for its nature trails. Its marshes grow giant cattails, maiden cane, and bullwhip that are especially good in trapping silt and preventing erosion. It provides a good environment for a wildlife teeming with alligators, reptiles, muskrats, nutria, and migratory birds.

When I was growing up, the semitropical climate was all that I had ever known, its blanket of humidity smothering my world for most of the year—hot summers, mild winters, mild being relative, though. I thought the winters were cold because I had never experienced snow and real cold. I had never been north of Lake Charles or east of St. Martinville, and I had never been to Texas except in my dreams and the movies. We were isolated with a history of being unwanted. My ancestors were Acadians, an exiled people who were expelled from the Canadian Maritime provinces of New

Brunswick, Prince Edward Island, and Nova Scotia, the land that they had cultivated for close to a hundred years, the land that they called *Acadia*, or *Acadie*, a colony of New France, and the land that was conquered by the British in the early eighteenth century.

During the French and Indian Wars, the British demanded that the Acadians sign an oath of allegiance to the King of England and thus the Church of England. Many of the people refused because they were devout Catholics. Others refused because they feared being forced to fight against their native country, France. Still, others refused to sign because they feared an Indian uprising. In today's world the Indians would be referred to as Native Americans, a more dignified name. If they had signed the oath of allegiance to the King of England, the Indians would believe that they were acknowledging British rule. Because of their refusal to cooperate with those in authority, specifically the King of England, the Acadians were expelled which became known as *le Grand Dérangement*, the Great Expulsion. The British burned their homes and confiscated their land and animals. The saddest of all the events that befell them was the splitting up of their families and their deportation on separate ships to various colonies on the eastern seaboard. Some of the ships were lost in storms. Some of the Acadians were sold into slavery. Some became indentured servants to the colonists. Others were sent to England and France where they made their way back to the new world searching for their loved ones. Louisiana was ruled by Spain who allowed the Acadians to settle the coast of Louisiana where they occupied the swamps and marshes, the lands that no one else wanted. They became known as Cajuns. They were my people.

During the post-World War II years, the windows of the world began to open. Uncle Thib's Admiral TV broadened my horizons, and then, many did not believe what they heard on the news, especially the weather report which was so often wrong. When the weatherman reported a hurricane so early in the season, most people thought it was ceremonious like the opening pitch of the baseball season, but the unctuous warning, a slippery science of weather for its time, became the extreme unction for over five hundred people. Most of the town's people were older and didn't have TVs and did not trust the squawking that came from them. My dream, nightmare, or premonition, whatever you want to call it, had broken the time bubble that had been floating around in space and decided to settle on a reed of grass and burst. It happened and all hell broke loose. I was almost twelve-years-old.

CHAPTER TWO

JUNE 1957

The dreams had begun before the drowning. It felt like my whole life had been hurtling through time and space like a meteor streaking to that one last moment. Is that the way it is? We live our lives for that one climactic moment when we die? That night, I woke up fearful and couldn't sleep. I sat up and leaned against the iron headboard. I blinked my eyes to adjust to the dark. The night was black, but I could see the white frame of the windowsill glowing in the soft light of the stars. Many times, I was secretly afraid. I couldn't relax because I was afraid Papa would come into the bedroom and flip the mattress with me still in it. I listened. My senses pricked to the screaming point. I heard my brother Bobby's steady breathing in the twin bed next to mine. I heard Pooch on the floor, his breath also steady. I heard the gentle, rhythmical snoring of the Gulf that lay in a crater several hundred yards away. The Gulf reminded me of Papa. There was something deep and dangerous underneath, if only I could understand him.

I tried to remember the dream but could only feel the confusion. I threw my legs on the side of the bed. It was the first time I realized that I was the least loved by Papa, if loved at all. Sadness filled me and overflowed into the room around me. I saw the aura of myself turn my collar up and walk away. I got out of the bed and followed, groping through the dark, carefully opening the door and making sure the screen door didn't bang shut. Pooch followed me, or us. It was strange. I stepped across the dew-covered St. Augustine grass, bent down and cuddled him.

"I know, my good old Pooch, you love me the most," I said and felt the rise of tears.

I tried to convince myself of the many reasons that I could come up with for Papa's meanness toward me. There was more than I knew at that time, but back then, I just couldn't put my finger on it. Papa must have known. I resolved to try to do something special for him or to make him proud of me in some way. Maybe then he would love me. This was different. The fear was a different kind of fear. It wasn't about Papa. I didn't know why I was so unsettled with a clammy feeling of foreboding. Was it the dream? I didn't know. I couldn't remember. All I wanted was to sleep under the stars so that I would know that God was still in charge, and my problems were nothing but dust in the wind. A mulberry tree grew next to the front porch, and I had rigged a hammock high up in the tree for those fearful nights. I climbed the tree feeling the rough fuzz underneath the glove-like leaves brushing my face. Pooch curled up at the bottom of the tree. I crawled into the hammock, and it molded around me like a cocoon. I fell into a deep sleep and dreamed of the exact occurrence of what happened to me when I was drowning—the barreling through the waves, grasping for anything, and letting go of everything. I dreamed of floating face down with the incredible ability to focus. I heard a woman calling my name, but as I came to consciousness, I realized that it wasn't the lady in the tree calling me, but this time it was Mama.

"Walt, Walt, *wake* up."

Mama came to the front porch. She was calling me into the world of things to do. I heard the front door open again, and Papa came out and picked up the hoe that lay against the house. High above in my hammock, he poked me in the back.

"Up and at 'em, Boy," he said in his gravelly morning voice not yet tempered by his morning coffee. Papa looked at me as I came down the tree. "Why were you in the tree?" he said.

"Don't know. Scared I guess."

"You scaredy-cat, you can't give in to fear. Dying is dying whether you drown in saltwater or pass out in your beer," Papa, known by everyone in the community as *Man* LaCour, said.

"Or fall off the stupid roof," I said. "A Leeeeeeee," I yelled with all my might, but he didn't hear me. Éli, my friend, the idiot-genius stood astride the pitch of the roof, glorious in his devotion to ritual. "I guess," I said, and my voice cracked—the dead giveaway of a boy entering puberty. "I guess that's why we have guardian angels for all the drunks and idiots." Papa sliced his eyes at me.

"Boy, where'd you come from? You act like an old woman."

Papa left me on the porch to watch Éli's ritual by myself. The door slammed. You would think I would have gotten used to it by now because every morning at sunrise, since Uncle Baby picked him up on Highway 27 going toward Cameron, Éli braved the slick, slant of the roof to stand on top of Uncle Thib's *Laissez Les Bons Temps Rouler* bar and serenade the fleet of fishing boats that lined the dock. The shrimp boats rocked on the dark water, the skeletal rigging black against the sky. Today was no different. Through the overgrown vines and roses on the front porch, I watched Éli's silhouetted figure. His dark jacket flapped in the breeze. His arms stretched out like a tightrope walker. One hand gripped his violin, a world-class violin at that, and the other held the bow. There was a big mystery surrounding Éli's violin that no one had figured out yet. It was a Stradivarius. It was supposed to be a secret, but most of us Cajuns didn't give a big cahoot about that. Just so it worked for the *fais-dodo* on Saturday night. Éli staggered. My body tensed.

"For Pete's sake why do you have to get on the roof? Why not the dock? Why not the stupid dock?" I said under my breath. Éli's total lack of self-preservation was part of his condition. His foot slipped. I gasped. "How can anyone be so smart and so dumb all at once?"

Éli bent his knees to regain his balance, stood upright, his back to the sun, facing the wind, and the magnificent, fog-shrouded Gulf, not letting anything mess up his ritual because change was not part of his small vocabulary or his life. I exhaled. Éli lifted his violin and tucked it under his chin; then he lifted his bow and drew it across the strings, trying to understand the very air and properties of the water. The faint strains of sea-groaning notes filled the air. The sun hovered on the horizon flooding the Gulf and inched up the dark sky. Éli played with freshness, as if it was the first time he had seen a sunrise.

Spiders had been busy in the hours before dawn. Their webs strung up and down the barbed wire fence, netted diamonds of dew and every now and then a mosquito or fly. Spiders and shrimp fishermen had something in common. They both had to cast their nets at the right time of day for a good haul, and even then, they might get lucky or they might not catch anything. The beauty of the morning was nature's irony because the weather could change to threatening in no time. I opened the screen door and stepped into the front room and tossed my leather gloves on a chair. I controlled my voice to hide my excitement that the weather would be too bad for shrimping today.

"It's going to rain. Éli is playing some kind of funeral music."

"That's hogwash," Papa said.

"Éli is a barometer. He knows," I insisted.

"The idiot don't know when to come in from the rain."

"Mama says he's a miracle."

"He's retarded for God's sake," Papa said.

Soft light aproned around the bedroom door where my mama, Mary Effie cooed to the four-month-old Baby Faye. Baby Faye babbled. Mama had heard our conversation because she appeared sleepy-eyed at the bedroom door wearing her faded robe and holding a squirming, curly-headed Faye.

"Miracles come in strange packages. God doesn't make mistakes," she said, and turned her attention back to the baby.

"It will be a miracle if I can put food on the table," Papa said. "Miracle is just another word for hard work."

Mama walked around the room in the opposite direction of Papa, bouncing Baby Faye in her arms, stopping in front of the window, and swaying quietly. Papa paced in front of the window; the radio roiled static. Papa and the radio charged the air with electricity. He stopped at the window, parted the curtains and stared at the gathering clouds, those darkening-by-the-minute clouds, stalling over the Gulf, daring the wind to move them until they were emptied. He squeezed his eyebrows and squinted his eyes as if to will the weather to change. Shrimp fishermen were dependent on the weather, just like the farmers, except the farmers usually wanted rain and the fishermen did not. A little rain never scared anyone, but a thunderstorm and rough seas made everyone sit up and take notice. The radio announcer's baritone voice trailed in and out of the static.

"It has been reported that there is a disturbance in the Gulf that's worth keeping an eye on," the radio announcer said. "News out of the New Orleans Weather Bureau reports that the ship the SS Terrier radioed that it unexpectedly experienced thirty-five to forty miles-per-hour winds, probably a tropical depression developing in the Bay of Campeche in the lower Gulf of Mexico. The depression looks like it is moving northward. We will keep an eye out for further bulletins and forward them to you as they come in."

Mama and Papa paused and looked at each other. Fear held their gaze— their lives balancing on that second of knowing. It was June, a little early for the hurricane season, but storms were real in the Gulf south where we lived. Bobby stepped out of the bathroom sporting a bandaged, stubbed toe—a *Kick the Can* injury. Bobby—with his sleepy, black eyes, face glowing with fresh freckles since his last sunburn peeled off had grown a half a foot taller this year and was a little tougher to beat at arm wrestling. I could still slam the back of his hand on the table for now, but time wasn't just whistling *Dixie;* it was blowing and going. I knew back then that my brain would prove to be my best asset, and I worked at it. I was the older brother, and in Bobby's eyes, I still reigned as king of his admiration.

I scooted into the bathroom for fear of holding Papa up. God knows he wasn't a patient man. When Papa was around, the bathroom was the only place where I didn't have to uphold an all-is-well pretense. I closed the bathroom door and accidentally knocked over the bottle of Mercurochrome that Bobby had left uncapped. Instinctively, I tried to catch it. The red liquid filled my hands and splattered on Mama's white bath rug.

"Darn," I said under my breath. In the dull light from the single light bulb, my hands looked bloody. Murder weapons, I imagined. Papa banged on the door.

"Get a move on, Boy."

"Yes, sir," I said in my meekest voice.

Acting in the LaCour family meant self-preservation. My shoulders slumped when I glanced in the mirror at my anxious face, hazel eyes blinking, fair complexion, and a chin that come hell or high water wouldn't grow whiskers. I looked closely at my chin almost in the same way Papa looked at the weather and tried to will it to change. I tried to will whiskers to grow. Even my name, rather my nickname, for God's sake, was a slap in the face of my manhood. Papa called me *Boy* to remind me that I was nothing special, just an immature male of the human species. I didn't like it, but it was all I had ever known. Papa used that name to lord it over me and to keep me in my place. Mama called me Walt Junior. I didn't much like being named after my old man either. His was a legacy that I didn't care to repeat. I was my own person, yet I was *Boy.*

I rinsed the bath rug as best as I could and laid it on the side of the tub. It was stained for good. Mama wasn't going to be happy about that, but I didn't want to get into it now, especially when Papa was around. When I came out of the bathroom, Papa stood on the back porch taking a leak on the oleander bush. I hid my red-stained hands with my work gloves, and at the first chance I got, I showed them to Bobby, pinching him on the arm, angry because he always got me into trouble. Bobby squealed.

"Don't you two start," Papa said coming back into the house zipping up his pants. The door banged behind him.

I glanced at my book, that lay on the fireplace mantel, and wished I could take it with me, but there was no time for reading on a shrimp boat. The fireplace was emptied of logs and ash for the summer. The mantel always held special things—the things we didn't want to lose like the car key and a framed photo of Papa in his US Army uniform standing squarely on two good legs. It was a mantel of memory. *Grandmère's* books were stacked there. Papa had wanted to bury them with her, but Mama said that Grandmère had wanted me to have them. That was one of the very few times that Papa ever talked about his mother. She never existed in his world. She lived in a smooth world, according to Mama—hands gliding through the yellowed pages of the ancients, Shakespeare, and most of all the Bible, books falling open to the chapters she read and reread as if they had a mind of their own, pages worn from use, but never dog-eared—no, never dog-eared. I suppose to most of the hard-working Cajuns, it seemed like a useless pastime. It surely didn't get the lawn mowed, the garden hoed, or the corn shucked, but it took root in me and made me feel like a little fish in a big pond—the more I learned, the less I knew compared to what there was to know. I loved every morsel of the knowing.

I had little memory of my Grandmère except that when she took the bobby pins out of her hair, it fell past her waist in a gray waterfall, and the one memory that shaped my world—she read to me. In the evenings or late afternoons, she sat in her rocker, pulling me onto her lap, reading in English, her eyes hungering for more, my eyes adopting her hunger for secrets that unfolded like Mama's oriental fan that she used in church on hot Sundays. Even though I didn't fully understand the words then, the lilt of the language imprinted my brain.

Although the grandchildren called her Grandmère, the French name for grandmother, she was of English descent and had married a Frenchman, Alton LaCour. The Cajuns began to adopt the customs and attitudes of the American culture when the oil industry took over the economy of southwest Louisiana. Many Anglos married into French families. Our family was one of them. World War II dumped many Cajun soldiers, like Uncle Baby and Papa, into American patriotism, and with the influences of foreign lands, the pure Cajun culture was worn away. Although I was not a fourteen-carat coonass, I considered myself one because of my accent, and the fact that our family was mostly French and had accepted the French culture.

"Ninety-five percent chance of thunderstorms in the a.m." the radio announcer's voice boomed. I heard Papa curse under his breath.

"Can't fish, can't eat. Can't even piss in my own john. Miracles—hmph," he paused for a minute. "We're going out anyway," Papa said. "This ain't a dying day for us; it's just a kiss goodbye for the shrimp," Papa said full of his macho, gun-slinging self. "Get a move on boys."

He crammed his hat on his head and banged out the front door and down the steps, stuffing his bandana in his back pocket, glancing over his shoulder to make sure that Bobby and I followed. Heading for the boat, I watched Papa's lopsided gait as he walked down the crushed clamshell road.

"*Poo Yie. C'est la vie,*" I said to Bobby low under my breath. "It would take a miracle for me to understand Papa."

All I wanted to do was to stow away in my short story where a war was going on and Finny and Gene were Upper Middlers at Devon school. I identified with war: psychological and physical. That and the need to escape kept me reading. Pooch stood on the front porch and barked.

"Come on, Pooch. We have work to do," I said. Pooch barked and bounded off the porch. I considered Pooch to be a human being in a dog suit. I loved him, and he loved me and that was that. I wished my old man loved me like that, but human love wasn't that simple. There was more to our relationship that I didn't understand. I always felt that I was on the brink of discovery, but it escaped me. I was afraid again and fear twisted my stomach.

"I wish I could follow my own intuition," I whispered to Bobby.

"No way with Hitler in charge," Bobby said.

With Papa in the lead, Bobby and I followed. Pooch tagged along behind. We reached the dock where a Negro man who looked to be older than Papa waited for us.

"Mr. Man," he began, "my given name that my mama give upon birthing me is Hipolite Garfield Mays but mostly deys jus call me Pud cause I's always has a hankering for chocolate puddin. I says my name like dis so you never forget: My name is Puddin and tang, ask me again and I'll tell you the same."

"Good morning, Pud," Papa said.

"Ain't so good of a morning, suh."

Pud looked into the sky.

"It'll clear up," Papa said. "What you want?"

"I's got ice in my truck, and I's uh be puttin it in your hold for one dollar."

"I'll give you two bits." Pud scratched his head. The rain came in sprinkles.

"See hows I got ice dats gonna melt my profit and youz the only boat goin out in dis rain, I guess dat will be alright by me."

"You got yourself a deal," Papa said and stuck his hand in his pocket and jingled his coins. "We surely can use an extra hand this morning seeing how these boys are no count."

Pud looked at Bobby and me and winked.

"Deys mighty fine lookin boys dey is. But no suh, I ain't going out in dis weather. It skeers me."

After I cast off and Bobby pulled in the fenders, which were nothing more than old rubber tires that Papa had scavenged at a dump, Papa maneuvered the old shrimp boat, the *Mary Effie*, around the docked boats and chugged through the dark water, heading out to his lucky shrimping place. When we left the dock, I waved at Éli who was still on the roof. Éli saw our boat going out and stopped playing his violin to wave his hands, still holding the violin and bow, in warning as if to flag us down. It was useless. He began playing again furiously moving the bow although we were too far away to hear him. Papa was hell-bent on proving the weatherman wrong. Bobby stayed in the wheelhouse with Papa. We got to the area that Papa liked to claim as his own and lowered the butterfly nets. We all hoped that we would catch enough shrimp, so we could head in early, but to our disappointment, we came up with a couple of red snappers and enough shrimp for a pot of gumbo. Bobby and I picked them out of the nets and threw them on the ice in the hold. Papa came out of the wheelhouse. He frowned and looked out at the horizon.

"Bobby," he yelled over the rumble of the motor, "take her out further. We'll still be in mid-deep water." Bobby, who loved to pilot the boat, gave it a little throttle and headed out.

"Alright, shut her down," Papa yelled to Bobby.

"Papa," I yelled. "Look. It looks like a person. A lady with dark hair."

The sun glinted off the water in a starburst, and I thought of the picture in our parish church of the Virgin Mary, Star of the Sea who was the patron saint for us Cajuns.

Papa squinted to where my outstretched arm pointed. Bobby ran out to take a look.

"That ain't nuttin. Probably a dolphin. Old sailors saw apparitions like that a lot, probably because they had been out to sea too long. Maybe we will catch us a mermaid," he laughed.

Papa took over the boat and went another mile out. I couldn't see the lady or whatever anymore, so Pooch and I sat down and felt the boat rise and fall. The waves were higher, and the boat fell into a galloping rhythm, the bottom of the boat slamming the trough between waves like my butt hitting the saddle when I galloped Mr. Doguet's horse, Belle. I glanced over at Bobby who was holding on. Bobby gave me the thumbs-up sign. I felt a little puny, and I'm sure I looked green, but I nodded back at Bobby. I surely didn't want to get sick. That would also be a slap in the face of my manhood. Papa slowed the boat, and settled in, and cast the butterfly nets again and again and finally, coming up with a small, net-belly of writhing shrimp and a few fish—an okay catch. Bobby and I worked the nets while Papa shoveled the shrimp in the hold. I was slowed down by the shrimp stink that made me want to puke. Papa frowned at me for being slow, and he joined in to help, so we could hurry. When we finished, I sat down and held Pooch. Bobby stood up and saw a band of dark clouds that gathered further out.

"Papa," he yelled and pointed toward the sky.

"Let's bring her in," Papa said. When he turned the *Mary Effie* toward home, a wave caught us just right, and I lunged sideways losing my balance. My already sick stomach made my legs and arms so weak that I couldn't grab on to anything. Pooch went flying out of my arms, and in a flutter of a heartbeat, he was overboard.

"Papa," I yelled frantically over the engine noise. "Pooch is overboard!" Pooch dog-paddled keeping his head above water.

"We ain't got time to stop," Papa yelled back. "The storm will be upon us any minute. We will all drown!"

Lightening ripped across the sky. Thunder boomed. In a flash, without a second thought of danger, I dove into the water and swam toward Pooch. When I reached him, I came up sputtering salty water and looked around for the boat. Waves came crashing in on us, and it was all I could do to keep my head and Pooch's above water. Bobby ran to get Papa's attention. Papa stopped the boat and grabbed a lifesaver. Although I tried to swim toward the boat, I floated further away with each wave that surged over us. I held on to Pooch. The clouds let go of a hard, pelting rain and made it impossible for me to see the boat. I was terrified and realized that the foreboding feeling that I had last night was real. Papa had turned the boat to get closer to us, and I saw it emerge from the downpour. He sprinted from the wheelhouse and climbed out on the nets and hurled the white lifesaver toward us. I saw the white disc through the rain, flying overhead like a halo in slow motion—coming closer and closer to me.

"Keep coming, a little more," I said, but it fell short. My heart caved in my chest. With Pooch under one arm, I gave a desperate, spirited kick that pushed us toward it, and I grabbed it with my outstretched, free hand. Papa leaned with all of his weight and pulled the rope. Pooch and I paddled as hard as we could.

"Give me your hand," Papa yelled. I reached out and he grabbed me, lifting me up until I got a hold of the nets. Bobby grabbed Pooch and pulled him over the rail into the safety of the boat.

"That was a close call. Are you okay?" Bobby said. I nodded, breathing heavily.

Papa pulled himself back onto the deck and gave me a trembling hug. I cringed, expecting a wallop, but Papa was too tired and scared himself.

"Don't you ever pull a stunt like that again. You good for nothing," Papa yelled more out of fear than anger, but I was unaware of it. "Get your life preservers on, the both of you. We got to get the hell outta here if we ever want to see dry land again."

Wet and shivering, Pooch and I curled up under a tarp. I listened to the train of blood roaring through my veins, and my lungs pumping like bellows, bringing air in and kicking it out all in a superb and delicate balance like walking a tightrope, or like Éli on the roof. The rain fell in torrents just as Éli had predicted. I listened to the sound of the rain that beat harder and harder on the tarp. A crack of thunder made my heart quake. Hidden under the tarp, I cried.

CHAPTER THREE

LATE AFTERNOON, SAME DAY

When I was drowning, I could see myself floating face down; then, I remembered the tree. I was fascinated by the details of color, texture, and emotion. I understood that my brain was impressed every day by my experiences and what I made of them, but when they presented themselves to me, as they say, "your life flashes before your eyes," they were all out of sequence. They were scattered, each in their own beauty, hunting the tail of the previous experience to attach to. It was sort of like arranging words in a scrambled sentence so that it would make sense. The memory settled on me, and I gazed up into the light. I stared at the live oak tree stretching high into the sky, that oak tree holding my efforts of the day, firing my imagination. That oak tree seemed sacred. It knew that it was important to me, even before I knew it. That oak tree, for a coastal boy, was my Mount Everest that left me shaking with fear, my stomach in a knot as the rope around my waist was tied in a knot. I mounted the ladder nailed to the trunk. Hand over hand, I climbed higher and higher into a higher perspective. I looked out at the horizon, over the coffee-colored rooftops, the watermelons bulbous and bloating in Mama's garden, and the clothes drying on the line. I looked out at the salt grass of the distant marshes where egrets and *poule d'eau* searched for food. I looked out at the sun going down over the pearl-gray Gulf, and suddenly, the earth shook when I looked down at the upturned faces of my brother and friends.

"Don't look down," they yelled up at me.

I looked down, gasping. I couldn't understand how I could be driven to do something so stupid. I remembered Uncle Baby's quote from Emerson, "Fear defeats more people than any one thing in the world." I closed my eyes and took a deep breath, belly-inching my way out on the highest limb and looped the rope, tied and knotted it again. I got a little braver and sat up straddling the limb. I tried to give the rope an extra tight pull, but when I yanked on it, I slipped. My friends below gasped. Instinctively, I lunged forward, bear hugging the limb and wrapped my legs around it. I felt the gnarled banks and rivulets coursing the bark of the tree. I thought I could hear the sap rising. I felt my body tremble and clung tighter to the tree; I felt the wilderness of death giving up its secrets. I squeezed my eyes shut and felt the whoosh of my own blood in my ears and knew that if I became dizzy, I would fall for sure. I had flashes of scenes when Papa hurt his leg and was in traction in his bedroom—the white cast on his leg in a stationary Heil Hitler march step. I couldn't let go or sit up, so I scooted—my only option.

"Don't fall, Boy. Papa will kill you," Bobby yelled. I slowly inched my way back down the limb.

"*Merci, Mon Dieu,*" I whispered when my feet touched the solid boards of the platform. I could no longer hear the rush of blood in my ears.

"Way to go, Boy," Al, better known by us kids as Potted Meat, yelled.

I heard cheers from below. I tied a big knot at the bottom of the rope to sit on and took a deep breath. I straddled the rounded knot with its long tail of unraveled rope.

"A fiery horse with the speed of light!" I yelled and whooped shoving off the platform amidst the groan of rope rub and wind whistles in my ears. I sailed to the point where I no longer went up and the point I returned down, briefly suspended like my heart between beats and floated in the evening air. My excitement shattered with Papa's thunder-thickened call.

"Boy, Bobby, suppertime."

"Hurry up, Boy," Bobby called and took off toward the house.

The other kids scattered. They didn't want to be around when Papa was in one of his moods. Only Pooch stayed waiting for me. I stretched my legs out to land on the platform only to bang my shins. I flew back out feeling the pain pulse up to my knees. Time was running out. Papa waited. I hit the platform again. This time I had to do it. I swung back out and turned with determination to land on the platform. If I were late, Papa would take the hide right off my back.

"Boy," I heard the thunderclap call for the God-forsaking second time.

One more time out and I landed on the platform. I let go of the rope and shimmied down the makeshift ladder nailed to the tree, so fast that the bark scraped the skin off my knees. I landed with my two feet on the ground. Good old Pooch grabbed the unraveled end of the rope. He growled and shook it furiously like he did when he got a hold of Baby Faye's rag doll and shook it so hard the stuffing went all over the yard.

"Come on, Pooch," I said, and we took off full speed to the house.

The white-framed house glowed in the fading light. Bobby and I had spent last summer scraping paint and repainting it because Papa had wanted to make men out of us and thought that we should learn to do a man's day of labor, which took us most of the summer vacation. We didn't mind the painting so much, but the scraping covered us with bits of dried paint that made us itch. The closer I got to the house the higher it loomed, and in my mind, it had lost its luster because I remembered the reason for my hurry—Papa. The fear of being late wrenched my stomach. When Pooch and I reached the steps, we took them three at a time. I bolted through the screen door. It slammed behind me. I smelled sauce piquant when I entered the yellow light of the kitchen where Papa sat at the head of the table with his back toward me. The table was set with Mama's blue and white plates that she had dug out of boxes of washing powder. Mama stood at the stove. She stirred a black, cast-iron pot, set the spoon down, picked it back up, peeked under the lid of the rice pot, stirred the sauce piquant again, and wiped her hands on the white apron with the bright red cherries. Wisps of dark hair that had escaped from the combs that held them back floated around her face. Mama glanced at me, and then at Papa. She filled the teakettle with water and sat it on the stove for Papa's after-dinner coffee.

"Where you been, Boy?" Papa said never turning around, sitting so very still and staring at his plate. I could tell that Papa had been drinking.

I looked around the room searching for an answer or a lie that would get me off the hook. I stared at the shine bouncing off Papa's bald spot at the crown of his head. Papa had a way of making me feel as different as a green pea in a pot of red beans. I stared at Mama's buffet with the wood-carvings of a hare and a fish that was given to her when her mother passed away. Mama's one and only china cup and saucer with the pink roses on it, which she had also inherited from her mother, sat on display. When Baby Faye slept in the jaundiced afternoons of summer, Mama sat out on the front porch and sipped her demitasse cup of Seaport coffee. It was her favorite time of day to sit, usually alone. Her dreamy look turned sad, eyes stared out at the watery horizon, not seeing anything but the landscape of her own memories.

"Answer me," Papa said.

I nearly jumped out of my skin.

"Come around here, so I can get a good look at you."

The water in the teakettle crackled. I shuffled around to face Papa. My young mind jumped from the catalog of lies in my brain, of which none would work in this situation, back into the tension of Papa's tirade. I mumbled under my breath.

"What did you say?" Papa said.

When I got nervous my ears drowned with every sound: the refrigerator's hum, the rhythmical rasp of Mama stirring the pot, the distress of my feet changing positions, the clicks of the clock, and the kettle building steam.

"What was the question, again?"

"Where have you been?" Papa asked more forcefully.

"Outside."

I looked down at my dirty feet and bloody shins. Bobby looked at me with huge eyes. I could hear Bobby pop his fingers under the table. Baby Faye who had been banging her spoon on her highchair stopped its flight in mid-air. She sat quietly with her thumb stuck in her rosette mouth and a sock hanging off her left foot.

"Where outside?"

Here we go again, I thought. Papa was the fisherman that cast hard questions—questions that led me on a crooked path like the question mark itself, a hook that would snare me. Yellow light from the hanging light bulb enclosed us, trapping me on center stage. I felt that I wasn't really the source of Papa's irritation. I was the neck he slapped instead of the mosquito.

"In the tree house," I said, staring at a hair on Papa's eyebrow—a conductor's baton that waved with the ups and downs of his facial gestures. The red web of veins on his nose glared a signal to stop. The kettle boiled.

"What the devil is so important in that tree house? Ain't you got better things to do? You could have helped me paint the rails on the shrimp boat or given your Mama a hand, hoeing the garden or the like. You lazy, good-for-nothing. I ain't never seen anyone like you in all my thirty-eight years. Always dreaming and reading some damn, old book like a little sissy or doing what you ain't supposed to be doing."

"But Papa—"

"Watch the slap, Boy," Papa said holding up a threatening hand.

"Mr. Daigle came by and said that Walt Jr. made all A's on his report card," Mama said in an attempt to change the subject. "He said the Bookmobile was coming next week and that I should encourage the boys to read."

Her voice seemed to soften the air like wind chimes. Bobby hung his spoon on his nose and stuck the handle end of his fork in his ear letting it hang. I was the only one who noticed. I clinched my jaw to keep from smiling. The kettle rocked a rhythm of boiling water and lisped a whisper of a whistle.

"I guess I am supposed to be proud of that," Papa said. "But grades don't make a man. Being a man means to sacrifice your precious pleasure to make a living, and you boys don't want to do that. You don't want to help when things get tough. You just want to play in your fantasy world."

Papa slammed his fist on the table accidentally smashing a slice of white bread. Bobby's utensils clattered on his plate. Papa continued in his rolling, sermon voice.

"Books don't amount to a hill of rice hulls. You and your Mama always dreaming of being somebody you ain't."

The kettle finally blew its whistle like a referee.

Mama's eyes smoldered. She turned back to the stove. Her face was steaming as much as the kettle that she took off the burner. The tyrant continued his ranting. The kettle continued to whistle.

"Dreams are like a fire that burns everything to ash and what's left floats off in smoke. So, what's the use of dreaming?" Papa said.

Mama jerked her head up with a stern look at Papa. I wanted to protect Mama like I've always tried to protect her, but I remained silent. I knew which line in the sand I could cross, and this wasn't one. The kettle's shrieking whistle began to fade when she poured the water into the coffeepot.

"Go to the sink and wash your hands," Mama said to me and looked crossly at Papa.

"Don't pass me a pair of eyes, woman," Papa said.

I walked to the sink trying to be invisible. Poo yie! The flowers on Mama's shirtwaist dress trembled when she reached out to serve each plate. I sat down glad to be out of the limelight and watched a fly struggle against the sticky fly-strip hanging from the kitchen light. It fluttered its wings, but it couldn't get airborne. I pitied the fly because I knew that we were both born to a sticky fate. At Mama's lead, we mumbled and made a swipe at the sign of the cross. At last, the table was quiet except for the chewing. At first, I nibbled at my bread and took a bite of the rice and some kind of sauce piquant while the butterflies settled in my stomach. Then, I ate like I hadn't seen a morsel in a week.

"What is this?" I said.

"Rabbit sauce piquant," Mama said.

My jaws stopped in mid-chew. I stared at my plate.

"Rabbit?" I asked.

I looked into Mama's eyes. They darted from mine. I looked down and dabbed my napkin at my mouth. I bolted to the back door and threw up on the oleander bush. Wiping my mouth on my sleeve, I ran behind the garage to the rabbit cage. Thumper twitched her nose and nibbled on a lettuce leaf, but Foot-Foot was gone. I remember sobbing when I picked up Thumper, her ears alert and twitching—the inside of them thin as onionskin and pink with blood glow. I nuzzled her and cried in her soft, gray fur. The back door slammed, and I heard Papa's heavy boots stomp down the steps with the weight of one foot heavier than the other. I squeezed my eyes shut and let Thumper go free. Papa rounded the corner of the garage at the very moment that I let Thumper go. He started to chase her, but the rabbit took off in a panic. Papa chased her around the pecan tree and under the oleander bush that I had just thrown up on. He slipped down on his good knee but got up and continued to chase the rabbit.

"I'm gonna snap your neck when I get a hold of you," Papa yelled at the rabbit; at least, I thought he was talking to the rabbit.

Pooch rounded the corner and joined in the chase.

"Go get him, Pooch," Papa commanded.

Pooch and Thumper took off under the mustard greens, crossed the row of bell peppers and banana peppers while Papa hopped over the rows on his good leg in pursuit. I whistled.

"Pooch!"

Pooch stopped to look at me.

"Come."

"Pooch get the rabbit," Papa said.

Pooch looked at Papa and then looked at me.

"Come Pooch," I said again.

Pooch came to me with an awe-shucks-you-spoil-all-the-fun look. Papa cursed, kicked at Pooch, but missed and slipped on the damp St. Augustine grass. Thumper got away. If I hadn't been so upset over losing Foot-Foot, I would have laughed out loud, but Papa raised himself up on his big arms and hunched his neck and shoulders. The laughter turned sour in my throat.

"That was Foot-Foot, we ate," I said right before Papa backhanded me in the face.

Later in the evening, Bobby and I holed up in our bedroom and listened to Mama and Papa argue.

"*Je m'en fichu*," Papa said from his bedroom where he and Mama were having it out.

Bobby and I knew that meant "I don't give a damn" in French. Bobby grabbed a Mason jar from the dresser that contained the lightening bugs he had caught right after the supper dishes had been washed and put away. He opened the window, unlatched the screen and let them fly free to blink their mating call in the dark. The arguing continued. I rolled my eyes not sure if I could handle another drama. Bobby put his ear to the jar and held it against the wall. He stared listening while he picked at a dingy rose on the yellowed wallpaper.

"What are they saying?" I said, leaning against the iron headboard of the bed and staring at the ceiling in concentration. I ran my fingers over the tufts of the brown chenille bedspread while my right hand held a piece of ice wrapped in a dishrag to my nose. I wasn't up to writing in my journal, which was nothing more than a Big Chief notebook that lay safely tucked away along with my baseball cards in an old, tin breadbox that I kept under my bed.

"I don't know," Bobby said. "Papa is talking in French."

I remember wishing like everything that I could still speak French, but I could only pick up a few words here and there.

"Come on, what are they saying?" I asked again.

"Shh," Bobby said as he strained to hear. "They're talking in English now. I can hear Mama talking."

"What is she saying?"

"Mama says, 'Why are you so hard on Walt Junior?' Papa says. 'I gotta toughen him up. He's too tenderhearted, crying over every animal that dies. It's just too sissified. I gotta make a man out of him,'" Bobby repeated, then paused and listened. "Mama's says, 'What kind of man are you that would hurt a child?'" Bobby continued. "'Spare the rod and spoil the child,'" Papa says.

"Since when did Papa ever have any religion?" I said.

The thud of a flying shoe hitting the wall could be heard from their bedroom. Mama had been known to throw shoes at Bobby and me when we crawled under the bed to escape her. Bobby jumped in bed with the Mason jar and pulled the covers over his head. Baby Faye started bawling. We heard Papa yell.

"I ain't a wife beater, but this is just about as close as it gets. Don't you ever talk to me about being a man again."

A crash came from the kitchen, then the heavy stomp of feet across the wooden floor of the living room, the front door opened and then the house-shaking slam. Baby Faye wailed. Bobby and I sat still in the dark and listened. When we thought the coast was clear, we crept out of bed. I opened the bedroom door and peeked in the kitchen. Mama knelt on the floor holding Baby Faye and picked up the pieces of her china cup. The one with the pink roses on it—her one luxury that made her feel special. It was a memory of her people. Mama and Faye cried. I started to come out of the bedroom because it was in my nature to protect Mama, but when she saw me, she waved me back.

Bobby and I jumped into our beds. At last, Baby Faye hushed. Lying still in the darkness, I smelled Papa's cigarette smoke that floated through the screened windows. I heard the rhythmic clunk of the whiskey bottle on the porch steps until it stopped, and his snoring was steady. When I thought he was sound asleep, I tiptoed to the back door to let Pooch in. During sad times, I hugged Pooch's neck and buried my face in his soft fur. He was wise for an animal and sensed my feelings. Pooch and Bobby fell asleep, but I stared at the moonlight. I felt so alone in the world, even though Bobby and Pooch lay next to me. It wasn't enough. I had difficulty speaking about my confusion, my anger, and my frustration of not being allowed to be who I was.

The lace curtains came alive with the evening breeze, inhaling and exhaling through the window. They whispered for me to close my eyes. Mama once said to me that people create their own spaces in this world by the threads they weave. I thought that souls must slip through those spaces when they died and went to heaven. I worried that if I died tonight, my soul would struggle to get around the knot hanging on the fabric of my being. That was Papa. I couldn't understand why Papa had it in for me. He certainly didn't treat Bobby the same way. It was a mystery why Papa couldn't love me. I made plans to run away. Just when I was almost asleep, I heard the most beautiful voice. It was mama singing, but it sounded different in the night air. I crept through the kitchen, through the back door and sat on the back steps to listen to the music. The moon filled the night with light.

Mama was in the vegetable garden, her white nightgown blowing in the breeze. I had never heard of the song she was singing.

Everywhere I turn there is a memory of you.

I breathe the air that you breathed

I see the moon that you knew.

I close my eyes. I feel your embrace.

Your words in my heart that time will not erase.

Walk me through the storm in this glitch of time.

You said you would return and be mine.

I believed you, I believed you from the depths of my soul I believed.

The waves surround me, swirl around me.

I am lost without your love.

I believed you, I believed you from the depths of my soul I believed.

The waves surround me, swirl around me.

I am lost without your love.

When Mama finished, her voice faded to a hum. She walked, touching the leaves of the corn stalks that were bathed in liquid moonlight. I felt an anguished cry rise in my throat. I was an intruder on my mother's personal sorrow, yet we were prisoners. We were stuck, Mama, the fly, and me.

CHAPTER FOUR

For the most part, time slipped upon me so subtly that it was here and gone leaving me looking around and wondering what happened. When I look into the mirror, I am dismayed at the white-haired stranger looking back at me because most of my memories nowadays are about my youth. Today, time felt different like a warm, old coat, but as I continued to write about the memory of drowning, I felt that I was an observer following myself around. I was impressed with the little things that gave me so much pleasure. I was very much aware of the importance of my senses that I used to evaluate and judge my world. I felt the experiences of when I was twelve as if time had not passed, and I was once again that boy. As much as I tried to get away from Papa, he was still central in my thoughts when I was drowning.

Pooch thumped his tail and licked my face with a wet kiss. My eyes creaked open that morning to see Pooch sitting up and staring at me. I put my arms around his neck. I stared at the light and shadows on the ceiling. The sun reflected off the antique mirror of the dresser making it look new. I looked out the front bedroom window and saw Papa stretched out on the front porch clutching his whiskey bottle; then I remembered that it was no longer my physical senses that I dealt with, but it was my anger. My hopes for that morning to begin anew melted away.

"Bobby," I said, "you awake?"

"Yep. What are we gonna do about Papa?"

"Let's go to the garden. He will never think to look for us there. Besides, we can hide in the corn rows."

We put our clothes on and crept from the bedroom into the kitchen when Papa startled himself with his own snoring. Bobby and I froze in mid-step, daring not to move a muscle. Papa's hangovers were as bad as his behavior during his drinking sprees. Papa held his breath a moment and settled back into a rhythmic snoring.

I crept to Mama's bedroom and peeked in the crack of the door. Baby Faye curled in the crook of her arm—mother and child—like Mama's cameo brooch. They had a rough night. Bobby and I left her sleeping and sprinted out of the kitchen on our toes with Pooch at our heels. Bobby caught the screen door before it slammed and roused the beast. Breakfast was a promise to our stomachs. We grabbed the hoes that leaned against the side of the house and headed for the garden. The sunlight and the dew on the corn leaves glistened. The beauty of the morning helped me to forgive my bad temper and get over it. The aged hoe handle felt smooth and cool to my grip. I started the earth turning with a fury. In the stillness of the morning, we hoed around the squash, shallots, and eggplants, listening to the quiet rasp of the hoe. Bobby broke the silence.

"Why is Papa so mean?"

I paused and reflected on the word *mean* and how a life could funnel down to a single label.

"'Cause he was a cook in the army," I said.

I wasn't sure where that came from. It just popped out. Bobby dug his hoe into the soil under the squash leaves and turned to me with a quizzical look.

"What's that got to do with anything?"

"Uncle Thib said that in World War II, Papa wanted to be a big war hero—a real fighting man because he was so mad at the Japs for bombing Pearl Harbor, but the army made him a cook. He had to peel potatoes and sling slop while his cousins and Uncle Baby joined the Marines and fought at someplace called Iwo Jima," I said.

I stopped my hoe in mid-air, dug it into the earth like an exclamation mark that screamed for attention. It had just occurred to me that Papa could have ever had a dream of being somebody and look what he became—a mean drunk. I thought of the word fisherman, but that gave him far too much dignity. He fished and shrimped because he never had the money for an education. He wasn't doing what he wanted to do, whatever that was. I don't think he knew himself. Papa had lost his passion for living.

"The military awarded Uncle Baby the Silver Star for bravery under fire for action on Iwo Jima," I said. "He took it, but he said that he didn't need a medal because he carried a scar on his chest as wide as a stripe on the flag. That was his medal. He would do it all over again and not whine about it. America was the mother he fought for, not the sugar daddy that he expected to take care of him. That was a quote from a newspaper article about him that I found folded up in Grandmère's Bible."

I paused and remembered reading the article and feeling my heart swell with pride for Uncle Baby.

"He may be a war hero, but Uncle Baby is a big baby when it comes to the *National Anthem*," Bobby said. "He cries at all the ball games."

"Nanan said that Uncle Baby gave a speech and dedicated the medal to all the support troops like the cooks. 'If we didn't eat, we couldn't fight,' he had said. She said it embarrassed Papa because he didn't want anyone to know that he had been a cook in the army."

"Why didn't Papa join the Marines?" Bobby said.

"Don't know. Never figured it out. There must have been some important reason."

We fell silent and continued to hoe.

My stomach growled, and I realized that I had never taken a sip of water much less eaten any breakfast.

"I got a big *envie* for fried eggs and a slab of bacon," I said.

"Or pancakes with Steen's Pure Cane Syrup," Bobby said.

"What about some good old *couche-couche?*"

"I know. How about biscuits and gravy and some grits with butter on top," Bobby said.

They heard the familiar sound of Mama banging a spoon on the cast-iron pot.

"Mama must have read our minds," Bobby said. "She must be as smart as God."

We dropped our hoes and ran to the end of the row. Mama had a skillet full of hot cornbread with milk poured on top of it. She handed the spoons to us and we ate straight from the skillet.

"You should have woken me up," she said.

"Nah. You were sleeping too sound," I said.

"Besides it may have woken Hitler," Bobby said.

"Bobby, don't you disrespect your Papa. I won't have it," Mama said.

"Yes, ma'am," Bobby said.

"He's still sleeping, so you two keep on working out here. You can come back to the house when he leaves," she said.

Mama walked back carrying her iron pot by the handle. Her shoulders slumped with loneliness and the weight of Papa's drinking. Bobby and I hoed around the pole beans, shallots, carrots, and all the good things Mama cooked in her gumbos, jambalayas, and sauces piquant.

"Sauce Piquant!" I said out loud.

"Is that a new cuss word?" Bobby asked.

"No, goofus. I just remembered that I let Thumper go last night, so Mama wouldn't cook him."

"The traps!" Bobby said.

We hoed quickly so that we could head for the marsh to spring the nutria traps before Thumper was snared if he wasn't already snared. The neighborhood kids, Cracklin Bilbo, Potted Meat Miller, and his pest of a little sister Snukie, came along shortly and helped with the hoeing, so that we could hurry to the marsh. When we hoed the last row, we raced back to the house. The plan was to head straight for the marsh except it was delayed because of a little altercation with Snukie. She started to follow us until Potted Meat stopped her.

"Snukie, this isn't a chore for girls. You know how sweet you are on rabbits. Besides, I heard the *Loup Garou* in the marsh last night, and he's waiting to chew on your bones," Potted Meat said.

Snukie was only a year younger than us, and she wasn't that dumb to believe him, but she was a girl.

"Al, you know there is no such thing as a Loup Garou, werewolf, or anything else out there in the marsh that your pea-brain can think of. That's just caca to scare me, and I'm not scared," she said.

Snukie turned her back to them and headed up the clamshell road. I heard her sniffling. Then she got mad. She wheeled back around, slinging her brown pigtails like whips, dried her eyes with her sleeve, and glared at us. She stomped her foot.

"Y'all can go to H E double you know what!"

She slung her pigtails back over her shoulders with a *so there!* attitude and took off running.

"You dumb girl," I yelled.

"You little *bebette*," Potted Meat yelled.

We picked up a few rocks and threw them at her, but I wasn't aiming.

"Girls are a pain in the butt," I said shaking my head in despair.

Everyone mumbled in agreement.

"Come on, let's save Thumper," Bobby said.

We took off for the marsh on a mission. I knew that we, especially me, would get in big trouble with Papa if he found out that we had sprung his traps. Once again, I faced the dilemma of obeying Papa or listening to my own heart. I decided on the latter; besides, my nose didn't hurt too much anymore. It was just swollen, and I had already forgotten about the pain in my determination to keep Thumper from ending up in mama's cast-iron pot, yet a part of me envied his freedom.

The salt grass flushed with amber light; the familiarity of the beauty bred a lack of appreciation in me. Besides, we were bent on a mission. When we reached the marsh, a couple of snapping turtles dove off a log into the ditch water scaring up hundreds of redwing black birds that had settled in the grass. They flew up in a huff at the intrusion. Nature had its own rhythm. The marsh teemed with a day-to-day survival of the fittest that I understood.

"I wonder why they don't run into each other," I said. "They all fly up in one direction like they have one mind."

"They must have some kind of antenna," Potted Meat said.

"It's probably the same reason bees don't fly into the rose thorns. They can see 'em," Cracklin said.

"Maybe there was a cute female that took off first. If I were a bird, that would get me to flapping," Bobby said.

"You are part bird—birdbrain," I said.

"But," Bobby said, "everything is about the birds and the bees, so there will be more baby birds and bees in the world."

"What about fear and self-preservation? Maybe they flew off because they're scared that something was gonna get 'em," I said. "Maybe, we scared the hell out of 'em."

We sloshed on through the salt grass toward the traps, scaring up a muskrat and a few frogs. I knew where all the traps were because Bobby and I had been out with Papa a thousand times. When we came upon a trap, I was extra careful not to get the stick caught when I sprang it. Papa would have known for sure that we were the culprits if he had found sticks in his traps. I was determined not to get caught. I took a branch from a hackberry tree and dragged it across the marsh grass to bend it back up to cover our trail. When the last trap was sprung, we headed back toward the road. I threw the hackberry limb out into the marsh, and it hit something solid.

"What was that?" Potted Meat said

"Let's take a look," I said.

We sloshed through the briny water to investigate. Muck sucked our boots, and grass clung to our legs. An old boat, half buried in the muck, but still in fairly good shape, lay hidden in the marsh grass.

"This is as good as buried treasure," Cracklin said. "There ain't no tree with an X carved on it, but this ain't a trifling thing."

"*Garde donc ça*. Ain't this a lucky day," Potted Meat said.

"It must have gotten washed up here from the last flood," Bobby said. We inspected the inside.

"Looks like it's okay to me," Potted Meat said. "We'll have to put it in the ditch to see if it takes on water."

"We can hoist it up in our tree house. It'll make a great pirate's fort," I said.

I secretly thought it would be a good place to hide when Papa was on the rampage from too much hooch. He would never look there; besides, he wouldn't be able to climb the tree.

"Yeah, right, Einstein. How are we even going to get it home, much less up that oak tree?" Potted Meat said.

"Look, it has a chain. Two of you can pull and the other two can push. It'll work, boys. It should slide okay across the marsh grass, and when we get it to the ditch, we can float it down as far as we can. Then we will have to drag it the rest of the way," I said.

"And how are we going to get it up in the tree?" Cracklin said.

"Papa's got some pulleys and rope that we can use. It'll work. Have faith, y'all," I said.

They looked at me with wide eyes but decided to give it a whirl. We got behind the boat fired up by our own imagination. It was stuck, so we all got behind it and pushed and pulled it back and forth until the mud gave way, and it slid out. We slipped and sloshed all the way down to the ditch where it got stuck on what was once a rice levee. It hung there like a teeter-totter, and before we could shove it again, something heavy hit the side.

"What the heck was that? It sounded like a log hit it," Cracklin said.

We walked to the bow of the boat to take a look.

"That ain't no log; it's a gator!" I yelled.

An alligator turned its tail so fast it nearly knocked me down. Meat and Bobby took off running across the marsh. Cracklin and I jumped in the boat, and I grabbed the oar.

"Look out, Boy!" Cracklin said.

The gator was gnarled like an old tree trunk. It opened its huge mouth, its teeth ready to tear flesh. It rushed us. I hit it a couple of times as hard as I could with the edge of the oar, hoping it would take off. I knew that one leap and it would be in the boat with us. I lifted the oar as high as my arms could stretch to hit it again, and it leaped into the air with a flash of pale underbelly. It grabbed the oar out of my hands, and I fell backward in the boat. When the gator came down, it landed on the bow of the boat, which was balancing on the rice levee. It was so heavy that it tipped the boat and pitched us in the air. We tumbled over the gator screaming and landed in the ditch. I swam like hell before my head ever came out of the water. I knew that a gator would grab you, pull you underwater and roll until you drowned. When I got to the other side and climbed up the bank, I saw Snukie pelting the gator's snout and around its eyes with rocks slung from her slingshot. She kept the gator at bay, until Cracklin and I were safe on the other side. Snukie was a hell of a shot. The agitated gator slipped into the ditch, and we watched its nose make a vee in the water all the way down as far as we could see. Potted Meat and Bobby crossed the ditch farther down and ran back up the bank toward us. Before we could say anything to Snukie, she turned on her heel and took off with her slingshot swinging from her back pocket. We sat on the bank and tried to get over the shakes. I stretched out and breathed the smell of the earth and the marsh water, glad to be alive and to have all of my limbs.

"Holy smoke!" Cracklin said. "I nearly caught a heart attack. I ain't never seen a gator that big!"

"I ain't either. That was the *grandpère* for sure," Bobby said.

"It must have been thirteen to fourteen feet long and weighed as much as a horse," I said. "I didn't know something that big could move that fast."

"Maybe, this ain't such a good idea," Potted Meat said.

"Don't be chicken," I said. "It won't bother us anymore. He has already skedaddled."

"But what if his old lady is around and she's got some babies. Ain't no mama gonna leave them babies now," Cracklin said.

"Your imagination is making chicken feed outa your brain. Come on fellas, let's swim back across the ditch and get that boat moving," I said.

When we got to the other side of the ditch, we clamored up the bank and turned the boat back over. We strained with all of our might to push it to the bank and into the ditch. We floated it all the way down to the road where the hard part began. The boat was fairly sound and took on very little water. When we pulled the boat out of the ditch and turned it over to drain, a blue truck pulled up, and a man rolled his window down. He stuck his head out of the window and blew cigarette smoke in the air.

"Excuse me, boys. Do you know where the Laissez Les Bons Temps Rouler bar is?

Bobby walked up to the truck to talk to him.

"Follow this road on down toward the water and turn right. You can't miss it."

"Do they have a band?" He took a drag on his cigarette.

"I reckon we do. Every Saturday night. Ain't a fais-dodo without music."

"Do y'all have a fiddle player?"

"Does Howdy Doody have wooden balls?" Bobby said.

The man laughed.

"I guess we do! He's the best," Bobby said.

"What's his name?"

"Come on Bobby. We gotta get going," I said.

"Éli Dunneaux," Bobby said.

"Okey doke, boys. Thanks for the scoop. I'll look into it," the man said and turned the truck in the direction of the bar, the tires crunching on the shell.

"Bobby, you're always yakking it up and telling everything you know. You don't know those men. Well, just forget it for right now. Let's get this boat to the tree," I said.

The clamshell road proved to be another obstacle. We pushed and pulled, cussed and cajoled until we got that stupid boat across the road, down into the ditch water on the other side, then up the bank and all the way to the oak tree. What a racket that metal boat made on the shell road. We lay sprawled out like Papa had been on the front porch last night, not from brain-dumbing whiskey, but from the sweetness of tired muscles and the excitement of our find. I looked toward the house to see if Papa had seen us. I had a gut feeling that he wouldn't like that boat in the tree. I knew my life or at least the skin on my back would be in danger. Papa would use his belt or the hose or anything handy to beat his will into my back. That thought made me more determined than ever to get the boat in the tree so that I would have a place to hide.

"Later, gator," Potted Meat said.

"Fine with me, *cocodrie*" Bobby said.

"Don't test fate and be alligator bait," I said.

"A little late for that, Boy. If my mama finds out about that gator, she would bust my head." Cracklin said as they walked along.

Cracklin started singing:

"My old Lady done told me today,"

"Yeah? What she say?" Bobby jived.

"You know that gumbo I made yesterday?" Cracklin sang.

"Uh huh," Bobby continued.

"I saved them feathers from that guinea hen," Cracklin sang.

"Hm Hm, ain't that bad." Bobby said, pretending to hold a microphone.

"You come home staggering drunk again,

I'm gonna tar and feather you

with my household glue," Cracklin sang.

"Oh, no, awe, honey," Bobby said.

"Gonna tar and feather you,

"Boo hoo, boo hoo," Bobby said.

"Gonna break yo' plate, 'cause you've been late

again, and again and again.

Gator gonna think he ate

a guinea hen. Uh huh uh huh," Bobby, Potted Meat and I chimed in on the chorus.

We parted ways in a trail of melody singing, "Gonna break yo' plate 'cause you've been late."

CHAPTER FIVE

When I was drowning, I realized it was the easiest thing I had ever done. I wasn't dealing with my ego or my pride. It was simply like letting a kite string slide through your fingers and releasing it to be cast upon a greater wind. Frustration seemed to be a big part of my life. I was no longer frustrated with living a life of square pegs in round holes, but I remembered my frustration. I remembered the daunting task of putting a boat in a tree, and I wondered why I had put myself through such stuff. It was the dumbest idea that I had ever had. I remember doubting my own sanity. But I was driven to do it to prove something to myself. It was one of those times that my dreams and my big mouth made my ego walk a tightrope. I had to save face in front of my friends. Somehow, someway, by hook or crook, I had to get that boat up into the tree. I was a hardheaded coonass, and I believed that where there was a will, there was a way which was what my Gammy with the Dress, my Mama's mother, used to say.

"Boy, I think you got hit in the head one too many times," Potted Meat said.

"What else can we do with it? It ain't any good; it's all beat up. Come on, just wait, you'll see," I said.

I headed straight away to the garage to get Papa's pulleys, hammer, and ropes. I thought if I could to do something to impress Papa, maybe I could show him that dreams don't always go up in smoke—you can make things happen. The truth was that I wanted a place to hide and the boat was perfect. I could lie flat in the bottom when Papa was out looking for me. He would never think to look up there. Besides, with Papa's bum leg and being liquored up on hooch, he wouldn't even try to climb the tree. He probably wouldn't even remember that I wasn't around or what he was ticked off about. When I got back with the pulleys, Potted Meat, Cracklin, and Bobby stared up into the tree. We sat on the ground in a circle each of us with a stick in hand. It seemed that we could think better when we poked the ground with a stick like we were digging in our brains to find the answer. Pooch walked into the middle of our circle and sat down.

"I'll be a monkey's uncle if we get that thing in the tree," Potted Meat said.

"Oh, ye of little faith," Cracklin said.

"We can do it," Bobby piped in.

Under the canopy of that old oak tree, a life decision was made. The power of never giving up floated above us like campfire smoke while we powwowed all the ways to get a boat into a tree.

"We could hang it like a hammock," Bobby said.

"Yeah, but it might loop-tee-loop and flip us all out on our heads," Cracklin said.

We sat quietly staring up into the tree.

"We can hang a pulley over this limb and then one over that one," I said while pointing up into the tree. "We gotta hook one rope to the pulley for the stern end and the other one for the bow end. Then pull it up and wedge the bow in that crook between that big limb and the trunk, and then rest the stern end on that big limb over there. Easy as pie. Ta daa."

"Okay, wise guy. These smaller limbs are going to be in the way. How are we going to get the stern end around them? They're too far out to cut them off," Potted Meat said.

We sat there and stared into the tree, again. Snukie had overheard our conversation.

When she came through the trees, she looked up and said, "If you pull the bow up vertically, higher than the limb you want to rest the stern on,

41

you would be past the lower limbs; then, you can start pulling the other pulley to make it horizontal. But the other pulley has to be around that limb there," she said and pointed to an even higher branch.

We nearly dropped our teeth. We didn't know Snukie knew words like horizontal and vertical much less anything about tree house engineering.

"I'll be danged," we said in unison.

Snukie had a walkie-talkie that she had made from two tin cans and string that we used for crabbing. She put it to her mouth and looked back and waved at Mama. Mama was standing on the steps and put the tin can to her ear. Snukie said,

"Can you hear me, Miss Mary Effie?"

She moved to stretch the string tighter and spoke again.

"Can you hear me now?" she said. Then she put it to her ear.

We could see Mama speaking into her can.

Snukie turned to us and said, "She wants you to come inside in about thirty minutes."

"Let us try," we said and gathered around Snukie hoping to get a turn with the walkie-talkie.

"Nothing doing," Snukie said. "Well maybe, if I can be the first one in the boat when you get it in the tree," she said. We looked at each other and groaned.

"Maybe," Potted Meat said, "if we get the boat up there in the first place." He turned back to us. "We gotta get the pulleys up there on the limbs. Boy, since it was your big idea, you are elected."

"I second that," Cracklin said.

"I third it," Bobby said.

I looked up into the tree and took a deep breath. I climbed hand over hand up the trunk and scooted out on the limb on my belly. I wasn't nearly as scared as I was the first time that I climbed that high. I attached the rope with the pulley on it to the limb and inched back down to the trunk.

I looked up at the higher limb. Fear punched me in the gut. I hesitated and then started climbing to the higher limb. I wanted to do it more than ever since Snukie was watching.

"Wait, Boy," Snukie said. "I've got an idea. Come down."

When I got on the ground, Snukie had already tied a length of crabbing string to the end of the rope. She tied the other end of the crab line around a rock several times and put it in her slingshot. She took careful aim and slung it over the limb. She had to stand on my shoulders to reach the crab line. Then she pulled on the string, and the rope snaked up over the limb. We hooked the pulley to it and pulled it back up to the limb.

"*Voilà*," she said when it was all said and done.

I couldn't believe it. We all whooped, and I grabbed Snukie in a bear hug, lifting her off the ground. I swung her around and put her down real fast. I felt my nose and face Rudolph over my outburst. Snukie was as smart as Mama!

Bobby and Cracklin tied the ropes to each end of the boat, and I climbed back up into the tree.

"Okay, let her blow," I yelled.

Bobby, Meat, and Cracklin started pulling on the rope tied to the bow end.

"I don't think we can do it," Bobby said. "It's too heavy."

I could see their muscles straining and the boat teetering over their heads.

"I can't hold it anymore," Bobby said. "Look out."

It came down with a crash.

"Geez, Louise. We were nearly smushed into grease spots with that thing," Cracklin said.

"Boy, come down and help us pull," Potted Meat said.

"If I come down from the tree, how are we going to guide it into the crook of the limb?" he said. "We need more help."

We all looked around at Snukie. She stood with her hand on her hip enjoying her new-found power.

"Okay," I said. "Snukie, if you will help us pull it up, you can be the first one in."

"But you gotta let us try out the walkie-talkie," Potted Meat said to his sister.

"Okay," she said, "let's give it a whirl."

Although Snukie was an average size for her age, for eleven that is, she was strong and added just the strength we needed to get the boat into the tree. I had to admit that Snukie was also smart, for a girl. With Snukie's help, the bow end of the boat was pulled up until the stern was past the smaller limbs, and Snukie tied the rope around one of the rungs on the ladder to secure it. Gradually they lowered the other end of the boat until it was horizontal. When I gave her the ok, Snukie loosened the rope, and I guided the bow into the wedge between the tree limbs. It slid down into the crook of the limb so hard that it was stuck for good. I was ready for a hard bounce of the limb and held on. I wrapped the chain around the limb several times for good measure. The gang let out a whooping cheer.

"So far, so good," I said making my way down the limb. I took a deep breath and climbed the other limb to guide the stern.

"Lower her down real slow," I said.

The stern end hit the big limb with a bounce and shook me up for a minute. I bear hugged the limb until it stopped swaying. Was that the way Finny felt before he fell? Was he the only stable object when the earth moved? When the boat rested snugly, I wrapped the rope around the limb several times. Well, what do you know; it worked.

"Hot diggity dog," Cracklin yelled.

"Way to go, boys," I said. Snukie scorched me with a glare. I quickly bowed and added, "and girl," I said. I looked at Snukie and grinned. She smiled back. I couldn't risk messing up again and insulting her.

"All we need now are some old sheets with a skull-and-crossbones painted on it, and we have us an honest to God pirate's ship," Cracklin said.

With a dramatic flair, Snukie climbed the tree. Cracklin pretended to roll a drumbeat. Snukie got into the boat and tested its steadiness.

"Ta daa," she said as she took a bow.

"Okay, Snukie, send the walkie-talkie down," Potted Meat said.

She dropped one of the cans of the walkie-talkie.

"It's okay. Come on up," she said into the can. Even though I had a basic understanding of the sound waves coursing the tight string, I was still surprised to hear a voice in the can. The rest of the gang climbed up and gathered in the boat. We were amazed at how sturdy it was. I untied the pulleys and dropped them to the ground and climbed down with the others following.

"Bobby," I said, would you put these back in the garage?"

"Boy and Bobby, time to come in," Mama called.

"Yeah, later," Bobby answered me.

They stopped briefly to stare at the boat in the tree. I felt a surge of pride in our success.

"Come hell or high water, it ain't going anywhere," I said.

"You can say that again," Potted Meat said.

"Come hell or high water, it ain't going anywhere."

"Can it, Boy," Meat said.

Pooch had to get his two cents in. He growled and shook the frayed end of the rope swing like it was something that needed a neck breaking.

CHAPTER SIX

Bobby and I headed back to the house, hot-footed it behind the garage and listened.

"I don't think he's in there," I said. We crept to the side of the garage and peaked around to see if Papa was still on the porch.

"Coast is clear," Bobby said.

We sprinted the short distance from the garage to the house and listened at the window. Mama was singing *My Blue Heaven*.

"He ain't in there. Mama never sings when Papa is home," I said.

Bobby and I let out a sigh of relief and took turns with the hosepipe, washing the marsh stink off from head to toe. We bolted up the back-porch steps and stripped down to our underwear, dropped our clothes in a washtub and went in to change. Mama stood at the ironing board and stopped singing, holding the iron in the air over Baby Faye's christening gown. She glanced at us when we walked through the room toward our bedroom.

"How did you two get so wet?" she said.

"We just hosed down 'cause we were stinky with swamp water," I said.

"Boy had to swim the ditch to get out of the way of an ole gator," Bobby said

"Shut up, big mouth," I said to him in a low voice.

"You boys gotta be careful in that ditch and the marshes," Mama called after us. "There are alligators and moccasins that could really get you in trouble."

"We keep an eye out for them. Don't worry," I said.

"But I do worry. I know your Papa wants you to grow up and be able to handle yourselves in the marsh. I just want you to grow up. You boys keep my knees raw from praying," she said.

I came back into the kitchen in fresh clothes and rooted through the icebox for something to eat. Mama turned her attention back to the iron. She was being super careful with the tatting because her mother had made the christening gown that Bobby and I had also worn. Mama sat the iron on its end and unplugged it from the wall. She wrapped the gown in a pillowcase to be saved in the event another baby came along.

"Walt Junior, after you've eaten, would you put this gown back in the trunk in the attic, please?"

"I surely will, little Mama," I said. Teasing always got her in a better mood.

"Second thought, Walt. Take this sack to Uncle Thib's first. When you come home put the gown away. You know what I'm talking about. I'm going out with the baby for the afternoon," she said, lifting Baby Faye from her crib.

"Will do," I said.

Mama grabbed her umbrella.

"It's starting to sprinkle, but it'll blow over in no time. Bobby, mop up that mess on the back porch before your Papa sees it,"

"Yes, Ma'am," Bobby said, and she and Baby Faye left out the front door.

By the time I finished lunch, the thunderclouds had exhausted their heaviness of rain that glazed the grass and roads, filling ruts with mirroring light. I carried the sun on my shoulders; I carried the wind billowing in my tee shirt, and I carried the special thought of owning the day's minutes to be spent on anything my heart desired, and at that moment, I was heading toward Uncle Thib's Laissez Les Bons Temps Rouler bar with a special package. Bobby caught up with me.

The red paint on the Bons Temps of the sign curled and peeled in distress from the ravages of the Gulf Coast climate, but the good times still rolled in the good, old, foot-stomping heel of Louisiana's boot. The weathered, gray building with its pitched roof was rather large on the inside but appeared small from the outside with the Gulf in the background. A wide front porch wrapped around the side of the building so that you could sit on the porch and still see the Gulf and catch a breeze. At the Laissez Les Bons Temps Rouler, Buddy Holly's *That'll Be the Day* shook the windows and weatherworn walls when I be-bopped up the steps carrying Mama's sack. I took my ball and glove, tossing it on the porch floor and entered through the screen door, wearing my school-is-out, ragged, cut-off jeans. I felt the grit of my bare feet leaving sandy footprints over the worn, wooden floor where the shuffle of two-stepping couples joined the lilting complaints of Cajun music at the fais-dodo on Saturday nights. I sat the sack that I had guarded with my life, on the floor next to the bar. My footprints scattered when in tromped Potted Meat and Snukie. Cracklin hung outside the screen door because his tan was too dark. He shielded his eyes from the glare and pressed his face to the screen to see if there were any other white folks in there besides us. A tail-wagging Pooch kept him company.

Uncle Thib, who was my mother's brother, had an attic fan that created a draft that kept the bar tolerable. He glanced up from hunching over the sports page, took his black reading glasses off, and folded the newspaper. His fingers were smudged with the news of the day. He ran them from his bushy eyebrows through his graying hair, and back to his pipe, spilling cold ash on the bar next to the paper. He turned to the back counter where a large mirror doubled the size of the liquor inventory. He turned the radio down a bit and belted out his famous belly laugh.

"*Mais garde donc ça.* Just look what the cat done drug in. If it ain't Walter Manley LaCour Jr., alias 'Boy', alias the 'I wonder boy' and gang. *Comment ça va?*"

"*Ça va bien, Parrain,*" I said.

"Bobby, *Mon neveu.* How is my man? And the gang?"

"*Bien,*" they chorused.

"What's the word today, Boy?"

I looked down at my feet and drew circles on the sandy floor with my big toe while churning up a thought that would amuse Uncle Thib. I glanced out the window at a gull perched on the shed that housed Papa's almost completed shrimp boat. Stripped to the waist, his back glistening with sweat, Papa varnished his big ambition in life—his dream boat that he was building. He stopped and took off the red bandana from his head and wiped sweat from his face. The gull lifted off the shed, wings dipping up and down slowly and flapped away gaining speed. I turned to Uncle Thib with mock seriousness.

"I wonder if gooses get gas when they fly north with a hard wind from the south?" I said. Uncle Thib started his rolling belly laugh. He held on to the edge of the bar and braced himself against the wave of laughter that threatened to wash him away. He laughed so hard that he passed gas.

"Loose board here," Uncle Thib said and pretended to be surfing. We doubled over from laughing so hard, and when Uncle Thib could talk again, he dried his eyes. "Put your nickels away boys, this one is on the house."

"Cracklin's got a powerful thirst too," I said.

Uncle Thib glanced at the door and saw Cracklin peeking in.

"Come on in here, Ti Maurice. Ain't nobody in here but the ducks," and he started laughing again. Cracklin opened the door and came boogying inside to the music with a grin the size of a crescent moon.

"Much obliged, Mr. Thib." Everyone laughed at Cracklin's jiving, which was just the appreciation he wanted.

"How's it going, Cracklin?" Uncle Thib asked while he poured root beers for each of us.

"Best day of my life, Sir. Couldn't get any better."

"Well, I think it just did," Uncle Thib said and passed him a mug of root beer with froth trickling down its side.

"Icing on the cake," Cracklin said. "Thanks, Mr. Thib."

"Merci, Parrain," Bobby and Boy said. Snukie and Potted Meat chorused their thanks.

"Cracklin, they tell me you can walk on your hands as good as your feet."

"I rightly can, Mr. Thib. I can walk down dem steps on my hands."

"You don't say. I gotta see that."

We all turned toward the door, carrying our mugs, Potted Meat's little sister Snukie leading the way. *C'est la vie.* She used to be a bebette and still was according to her brother, but I wasn't sure how I felt about her. I really noticed her and wondered when the gritty grain of sand became a pearl in progress. She headed for the door and everyone followed her except me. I held back for good reason.

"Parrain," I said in a hushed voice, "you know the problem we've been having with Papa—you know—when he drinks too much hooch." I lifted the sack and set it on the bar.

"Yep, know what you mean. Do you want me to talk to him?"

"No, it would only make things worse, but Mama and I have a plan if you can help us out. Maybe you could have a special bottle for him—watered-down. It's wrapped in a dishrag at the bottom of the sack."

"You think that's gonna help?"

"I gotta do something. He's gonna end up killing us or at the least, beating the heck out of me."

"Don't you worry about that, Boy. I can take care of that. I'll give him full strength on the first couple, and then give him the watered-down stuff. He'll never know the difference."

"That will make Mama and me happy."

I stuck my hand out to Uncle Thib, and we shook hands on our conspiracy. A shadow passed in front of the door when I turned to leave. The door opened, and Papa walked in. The screen door slammed behind him. I froze and wondered if Papa had heard our conversation.

"What you lookin for in here, Boy?" he said.

"Nothing. Mama sent me to deliver some fig preserves."

Papa glanced in the sack. I held my breath. He took a mason jar out and unrolled the dishrag that Mama wrapped it in so that it wouldn't break. He held the amber jar up to the light and unscrewed the lid, sticking his finger in and tasting the sticky, sweet preserves.

"Hm, um. Let me try some of this, me. I was looking for a little snack," he said. "Thib, give me a couple of shots to wash it down."

Uncle Thib poured him a shot of whiskey and Papa downed it. He poured another and while Papa was downing that one Uncle Thib took the sack off the counter and put it behind the bar.

"*Allons y*. Let's go outside, Man. Cracklin's gonna walk down the steps on his hands," Parrain said.

"*Mais* Nah. I ain't got no time to look at that. I gotta get back to work on that boat and get it ready to float before them hurricanes start up out in the Gulf."

He took the jar of fig preserves and left. Uncle Thib and I glanced at each other with a sigh of relief. Uncle Thib clapped me on the back. We went outside, down the porch steps to the dirt parking lot when Uncle Baby drove up in his old Chevy pickup in a cloud of dust. Papa's brother, whose real name was Édmond LaCour, was known to everyone as *Bébé*, and to us kids, *Noncle Bébé* or just plain Uncle Baby. He got out of the truck whistling while he unloaded supplies from the back. Uncle Baby was a few inches taller than Papa which made him appear slimmer in his Levi jeans. His white tee shirt showed his bulky shoulders, just like Papa's, but he didn't have the gut that Papa had.

"Look what I got, y'all," Uncle Baby said.

He lifted an American flag to show Uncle Thib that he had bought a replacement for the old one with the stripes that flapped like ragged kite tails on the flagpole outside the bar.

"Ay, tear her tattered ensign down! Long has it waved on high, and many an eye has danced to see that banner in the sky," Uncle Baby quoted.

"What's that from?" I said.

"*Old Ironsides.* Oliver Wendell Holmes, my Boy Oh Boy," Uncle Baby said.

Uncle Baby wasn't just a flag-waving patriot, but one who could quote Thomas Jefferson and parts of the Constitution. It didn't rattle Uncle Baby if someone considered him to be an ignorant coonass because of his Cajun accent. He knew who he was. "The fool doth think he is wise, but the wise man knows himself to be a fool," he would quote from Shakespeare. He was a *méli-mélange*, mish-mash soul, who was also swayed by his mother's love of books. His mother was my Grandmère.

Uncle Thib's wife, Althea, or Nanan to Bobby and me, got out of the cab of the truck while Éli scrambled from the bed. The wind gusted and wrapped Nanan's plump legs with her skirt printed with tiny green flowers. She grabbed her straw hat with the fake roses on the brim with one hand and wrangled with her skirt with the other. Her purse flopped on her elbow. Nanan always dressed the part of a lady when she went to town in Lake Charles.

"Nanan, you got to watch Cracklin," Bobby said.

"Mon cher (Sha) bébés. Of course, I will."

Nanan always spoke sweetly to us kids, probably because she never had any of her own to drive her crazy. She was a saint, especially when she took Éli in.

"Bébé, thanks for running them up to Lake Charles for me. Did you forget to get that man to fix that violin for Éli?" Uncle Thib said.

"Nah, Thib. I did that the first thing. It's fit as a fiddle," Uncle Baby said. "That man said he would give Éli one hundred dollars for that violin. Me, I think that was a good deal, but Éli threw a screaming and hollering fit. That man told me to get that crazy idiot outta there."

"That was his old man's violin. Éli would die before he gave that thing up. He don't like that old fiddle that someone left in there; besides, we sure need him to play Saturday night," Uncle Thib said.

They continued talking in French, but I didn't understand too much anymore.

"Cracklin, I want to see you walk on your hands," Uncle Thib said.

"Ladies and gentlemen, I present to you the one, the only, Ti Maurice 'Cracklin' Bilbo," I said in my best circus master voice.

Cracklin moved through life with the ease of putting on a bright, yellow coat that fit him to a T. He was a born performer, hoping one day to be a singer, a preacher or a rodeo clown. Stretching his arms up and pretending to acknowledge a circus-tent filled audience, Cracklin kicked his feet up in the air, bowed his back and walked on his hands to the edge of the step. He teetered and paused to catch his balance and took one step at a time all the way down to the last step where he turned half-way around, lowering both feet down, pushing off the step and doing a back flip to land on the parking lot. He came up with his arms in the air and bowed with a big smile. We clapped and cheered.

"Mais garde donc ça, if that ain't the cat's meow," Uncle Thib said as he stood in the doorway. We took our drinks off the porch and sat on the steps. We made mustaches on our faces from the root beer foam and laughed and giggled over Uncle Thib's farting. We felt slaphappy with giggles that were useless to try and stop, much like trying to stop the hiccups. Drunk with laughter, root beer and sun-drench over the Gulf of Mexico, we fell silent, engulfed in our own thoughts. Uncle Thib came back out on the porch with his accordion and sat down. His real name was Alcide Thibodeaux, but Cajuns have a whole slew of names for each of us. I used Uncle Thib and Parrain each in its turn, but most of the time, I called him Parrain because that was the French name for Godfather.

"Parrain, I said, "I can't understand when you talk that French anymore. You know that old teacher I had in the first grade, old Mrs. Wallace?"

"Oui, I surely do," Uncle Thib said and nodded.

"That old lady wouldn't let us talk that French in school. Now I can hardly talk it."

"Yeah, that's right," Potted Meat said. "Boy had to hold his nose in a circle on the chalk board for the whole recess for talking French."

"You don't say," Uncle Thib said frowning.

"Yeah, and I slipped up again. *Cre boucane*! Holy Smoke! That crazy old lady, she made me kneel on rice in the corner for the whole recess. I think I still have a grain of rice stuck under the skin of my knee," Boy said. "Then, I messed up one more time, and she put a clothespin on my tongue. I hollered so loud that it scared her, and she took it off. But I got to tell you, I ain't never spoke that French again."

"Why she don't want you to speak, French?" Uncle Thib said.

"She said that we were living in a cocoon of the Cajun culture, and it would isolate us. She said that Cajun French wasn't the same French spoken in France, and we got to speak English if we are to make it in this country."

Uncle Baby began, "Me, I think she should let all you kids speak that French. It's a good thing to know both, but to speak that English honors America and our forefathers, you know, George Washington, Thomas Jefferson, and those fellows. It ties us together, you know. It shows that you want to be American, but don't ever forget that Cajun French because that is your heritage. Here in America, we are like one big gumbo, and it taste better for all the differences.

Sure enough. Um hm. Just don't take yourself too seriously. You gotta laugh a lot," Uncle Thib said and squeezed his accordion, running his fingers over the keys to warm up. A cool breeze blew off the water and tormented a Fudgesicle wrapper until it found refuge under the building.

"Well speaking of laughing, I ain't gonna be laughing if I don't mow the grasses for my Pop," Potted Meat said.

Uncle Baby excused himself and one by one the kids had to leave and do chores before they got in trouble. It ended up just Uncle Thib, Éli, and me.

"Parrain, I think you're the happiest man I've ever known. I wish Mama was as happy as you," I said.

"Your Mama used to be just as happy," he said.

"When did she become sad? What happened? Why?"

Parrain smiled and never gave a complete answer.

"Hmm. I forgot my remember," he said. "Life, I suppose," he continued and turned to hook the bellow strap on his accordion.

Sometimes in church, I remembered watching Mama's face through the spaces of her black, lace scarf while her fingers remembered each bead of the Rosary. Her straight nose and dark lashes with her chin tilted down made her look like the Madonna. She blinked a tear out of the corner of her eye, and I watched its progress down her cheek and wondered about the sorrow it carried.

Uncle Thib ran his fingers over the accordion and squeezed. The air wheezed and resounded over the reed, making a lingering, lonesome melody that his soft voice picked up as he sang in Cajun French about a long, lost love. Éli picked up the tune and played along. He understood all that there was to know about the meaning of the song from the melody itself that echoed through his ears and to his heart. Éli was not exactly retarded, but he was not normal either. Sometimes, I felt that we were the ones that had lost our normalness that somehow, we were short-circuited from a deeper understanding and connectedness. Most folks didn't think of it that way; they just saw the Éli who couldn't tie his shoes, couldn't speak complex sentences, couldn't stop repeating things, and couldn't understand things like eating ice cream with a fork instead of a spoon. He didn't like the melting texture; he didn't like change. The remarkable thing was that he could play that violin like a master, and everybody loved him for it. He was a mystery that the whole town took pride in.

Uncle Thib set his accordion down and rocked in his rocker. The rocker squeaked the seconds away. Uncle Thib was the most present person I knew, having a sixth sense about people. He knew when they were ready to listen, when they needed to talk, or when to be quiet.

"Parrain, you ain't never said anything bad about nobody," I said.

"Ain't supposed to judge folks," Uncle Thib said. "You gotta listen and know when to shut up and be silent. Silence is simple. Silence is when the mind listens to the voice of the soul. You can't hurry silence."

That was why Uncle Thib was a good bartender. He allowed people to be who they were and that was why Éli was so calm around Uncle Thib. Although Uncle Thib gave everyone the benefit of the doubt, Éli sensed good and evil in people.

Not long after Uncle Baby, Nanan, and Éli had come back from Lake Charles, a white, two-door sedan drove into the parking lot. A dusty, blue Ford pick-up truck that looked like it had followed the sedan was parked across the street. Two men sat inside. It was the same men that stopped Bobby and me on the road and asked about our fiddle player. Uncle Baby was sitting in his usual seat at the bar, and Uncle Thib was standing at his usual spot behind the bar. As usual, I was all eyes and ears while I swept the floor. Éli sat back where the band played, messing around with his violin. We heard a car door slam. I glanced up and saw a stranger heading for the bar.

"I've seen that fellow before. He's the owner of the shop where we had Éli's violin fixed," Uncle Baby said. "Wonder what he wants."

"Mais oui, we're about to find out," Uncle Thib said. The man, dressed in a suit, came in and went to the bar. He turned to Uncle Baby.

"Good to see you again, my friend," he said. "Turner's my name," and he held out his hand to Uncle Baby.

Uncle Baby had a beer in his hand and didn't make a move to set it down to shake hands with this Turner fellow. The guy put his hand in his pocket. Uncle Baby eyed him up and down.

"What's your business, man—to come all the way to Cameron from Lake Charles.

"Well sir," he said, "I've come to make another offer to buy that violin from your friend over there."

Mr. Turner jingled the change in his pocket. Éli stopped playing and watched the man as suspiciously as Uncle Baby had.

"I thought we told you it wasn't for sale," Uncle Baby said.

"Yeah, that's what you said, but maybe I didn't make you a good enough offer," Mr. Turner said. "How about $500 for that violin."

Uncle Baby choked on his beer.

"You want it that bad?" Uncle Baby's voiced trailed off. "It's not my violin; you'll have to talk to Éli."

They all looked over at Éli who was clutching the violin to his chest.

"I'm Éli's guardian," Uncle Thib said. "It don't look like he wants to sell it. That violin belonged to his dead papa."

"I see. Do you mind if I look inside the violin?" he asked.

"Ain't you seen it once before?" Uncle Baby said.

"Yes, sir. I just want to double check my own vision,"

"Éli brought yourself over here and bring that violin with you," Uncle Thib said. Éli put his violin in the case and brought it up to the counter. The Star of David and the Christian cross that were tied to the handle of the case clinked together. Mr. Turner reached out to open it, but Éli caterwauled a big one, grabbed the case, and held it close to his chest. Everyone jumped.

"What do you want to know, Mr. Turner? Éli will let me look in it," I said.

"Very well."

I opened the case slowly and ran my fingers over the green velvet lining. With the light at the right angle, I saw writing in a language that I was not familiar with.

"*Antonius Stradivarius Cremonensis Faceibat Anno___,*" I spelled out. "There's a handwritten number, but it's kind of scribbled. Sorry, I can't make it out. There is a circle with a cross and the letters A and S inside of it. It looks like it may have been stamped," I said.

"Care if I take a look if you hold it?" he asked.

I looked over at Éli and lifted it out of the case and held it so Mr. Turner could look inside.

"It begins with a 1 and a 6, I think," he said. "Can't read the rest of it," Mr. Turner said.

"Why is that so important? Uncle Thib asked. "Now, don't piss on my leg and tell me it's raining."

"It means that it is a very old violin," Mr. Turner said. "A collector's item. I have some sources that may want to pay a couple hundred more, but I would have to check first."

"Well sir," Uncle Thib said, "we'll have to study on it. I'll let you know if Éli changes his mind."

Mr. Turner left out the front door and got into the sedan. It roared off in a cloud of dust, and the truck that was parked across the street followed it.

It was still early since the incident with Mr. Turner. The after-work crowd had not started coming in, so Uncle Thib picked up his accordion and headed for the door. On cue, Uncle Baby and I went outside with him. Éli followed with his violin. He opened the case, and I pointed to a little compartment at the end and he lifted the lid. A chunk of rosin lay on top of a folded piece of paper. Éli took it out and showed us the letter.

"What's this?" I said and opened the letter.

A picture fell out on the porch. Uncle Thib bent over and picked it up.

"Oh, I think that's the letter Éli's mama wrote when she sent him to live with us," Uncle Thib said.

He handed the picture to me, and I squinted at the black and white photo of Uncle Thib, and a dark-haired woman with a shy smile standing between two men, one with blond hair the other dark. The shadow of the man taking the picture was in the foreground, and in the background was an old Ford tractor in a cane field.

"Those were German POWs," Uncle Thib said. They worked in the cane fields because all the young men went off to war.

"German POWs in the United States?" I said.

"You bet your bottom dollar there were. Italians too. There were probably eight or nine thousand POWs come through south Louisiana. That's your Papa's shadow there, taking the picture. He was a guard at the POW camp there in Franklin. He had hurt his knee and had just come back from the war, so they made him a guard before he was discharged."

"Mama said he had first hurt his knee in the army, and the oilrig accident was injury on top of injury."

"That's the way I remember it," Uncle Baby said.

"Were you in the war?" I asked Uncle Thib.

"Nah. By the time the war broke out, I was too old. After Pearl Harbor was bombed, I sure wanted to go. Everyone was fighting mad. Those Japs stirred up a hornet's nest for sure."

"You got that right," Uncle Baby said.

"I guess I was needed to man the home front," Uncle Thib said. "I stayed busy with all kinds of odd jobs, but mostly supervising the German POWs in the cane fields. They always had a guard there too. The guard sat on a chair on top of the cab of the truck with his shotgun when they were working the fields. There were about three hundred prisoners in all. They were a friendly lot. Most of them didn't want to escape because they liked all that Cajun cooking."

Uncle Thib squinted at the picture. "I was the supervisor for that job."

"Mama," he said. He then pointed to the older looking dark-headed fellow and said "Papa."

"Yeah, that's Éli's Papa, Jakob, before he escaped," Uncle Thib said.

"Escaped?" I said.

"Well," Uncle Thib said. "He skedaddled—got the hell out of that POW camp. He was afraid he would be sent back to Germany like Johann, the guy on the right. He fell in love with that pretty little gal, and he wasn't going nowhere. He was wanted over here too, so he went into hiding."

"So why did his mama send Éli to you?"

"Well, she explains it in that letter to me and Nanan. Read the letter, Boy," Uncle Thib said. I began.

Dear Alcide and Althea,

I have come on hard times and need your help in a mighty big way. As you probably know by now, Jakob passed a year ago of a heart attack. It was all of a sudden. Please take my Éli. He is a good boy. I can't cook or take care of him no more because I am sick with the cancer. He can't do many things, but he is a master violinist. He never had lessons. He was born with this gift. I don't want him to be in an asylum. He has too much talent and soul to be caged. Since Jakob's name was in the paper telling about the funeral, someone

tried to steal the violin. I think they know, and I'm afraid of Éli getting
hurt. He loves that violin. I love my son, and I want him to be happy.
I don't want him to remember me being sick. I don't know what it
would do to him. I will see him again one day. I have no one to turn
to. My parents passed many years ago, and I am the only one left. I
will not be long in this world. God bless you.

> *Your dear friend,*
> *Yvette.*

"I was dumbfounded when Éli first gave me that letter. I read that thing real slow, and then I said, 'I had to sit on that one; sitting made my brain work,'" Uncle Thib said.

"Éli, I remember when anyone asked you your name," I said turning to him. "You would say your name. When we asked you your last name, you said '*dunno, dunno,*' so voilà, we called you Éli Dunneaux. Uncle Thib, you knew who Éli was all along," I said glancing at him.

"Yup. Sure did. I was just trying to protect my friends and Éli himself," Uncle Thib said.

I remembered the first time Éli sat down on the top step of the front porch and opened his violin case. No one was prepared for the type of music he played. It was a classical piece that no one had ever heard before. Of course, none of us knew anything about classical musicians. The only one that I had ever heard the name of was Handel, and that was only because of Handel's *Hallelujah Chorus* at a church in Lake Charles one Christmas Eve. Éli didn't have any idea of musicians either. He didn't know a major chord from a minor chord. His music was pure inspiration. Éli closed his eyes and played the saddest song. When he drew the bow over the last note, a tear ran down his cheek. In my mind, it was a goodbye song to his mama. No one said anything for a few minutes until Uncle Thib broke the silence and said that he could live upstairs in the storeroom over the bar. We later found out that Éli could play anything he heard with his eyes closed. If you hummed it, he could play it. If he heard it on the radio, he could play it. He could imitate any style of music. Everyone was sure glad when he joined the band that played for the Saturday night fais-dodos.

Uncle Thib ran his fingers over his accordion and gently squeezed and began chords that were unfamiliar to me, but Éli picked up the tune and joined in. Uncle Thib sang.

Oh, my maman

Save me with your prayers.

My tongue is tied,

I cannot pray.

I have cried

day after day.

Oh, my maman

Save me with your prayers.

Touch my face

with your cool hand

slow my heart's pace

Amen, amen

Save me with your prayers.

I sat silent, feeling the vibrations of the music and breathing the scent of salt and sea. I leaned against a post and stretched out my legs. My thoughts clouded. I thought of Mama's sorrow and Papa's drinking. I sat and thought about all that Uncle Thib said and about the violin. I began to smell something fishy. I didn't know what, but something wasn't on the up and up.

CHAPTER SEVEN

Mama wasn't back yet, and I remembered that she had asked me to put the christening gown away. I climbed the rickety stepladder that I had put under the attic opening and banged on the door with the hammer to loosen the dried paint that kept it from budging. The ladder swayed. Holding on to the molding around the opening, I steadied myself. I banged again and finally loosened it, pushing the door open and putting the gown, hammer, and flashlight inside. I pulled myself up into the dark. Breathing the stifling air, I groped over to the old, leather-strapped trunk. Strips of light and a little breeze came in from a vent. I hung the flashlight on a nail over the trunk and opened it. The trunk was so neatly packed that I sensed its importance. I dug around being careful to put everything back in just the right place. It was a trunk of history: a trunk filled with secrets of a world that I knew little about, a world that didn't want to be forgotten, a world that Mama surely wanted to remember. I felt like a snoop; hell, I was a snoop, but it was my history too.

I had often speculated about Mama's broken heart until that afternoon; I made a discovery that brought up more questions than it answered. I rummaged through the stuff and wondered what happened to all of those memories and experiences? Is the world alive only for a day? I knew that memory wasn't unique to humans because Pooch would surely get out of the way of Papa after being kicked a few times. On a larger scale, I thought of memory. Does the earth and sea remember? Nah, I answered. I lifted the layers of baby clothes and found Mama's wedding suit, as well as her mother's wedding dress. At the bottom of the trunk, I found the wooden shoes that Gammy with the Dress used to call *sabots*. She had told the story of how they had been passed down in Mama's family for generations—all the way back to the first Acadians who were exiled from Nova Scotia. I picked up a sepia, wedding photo of Mama's grandparents, my great grandparents. The couple sat erect and stared at the camera with stern, unsmiling faces. I wondered why people didn't smile in pictures back then. Probably because they had bad teeth, I thought. I tried to read the look in their eyes to discover what happiness, if any, that they may have had on their wedding day. I noticed that their hands were placed palm down on their thighs, but his little finger and her little finger touched. That was the only clue that there was any love or passion between them. I looked at their eyes and thought that I could detect a slight look of amusement over the secret the two of them kept from the photographer. They didn't know that their secret would be noticeable to everyone who saw the picture. Gammy with the Dress's wedding photo looked like something out of the roaring twenties. I barely knew my Grandpère, Gammy with the Pants, because he had passed away when I was about six years old. In the photo, Gammy with the Pants looked like a riverboat gambler, and Gammy with the Dress had a veil that wrapped around her head and was crowned with a wreath of flowers low on her forehead. She looked like a flapper which was the style then in New Orleans where she grew up.

Mama and Papa's wedding picture was different. She wore a tailored suit, and Papa wore his army uniform. I remembered that Mama had told me that she and Papa married when he was discharged from the U.S. Army, but he didn't have his official papers yet. There was no time to plan a big wedding even if money had not been a problem. They were poor, but so were 90 percent of the rest of the town. Their faces looked so young and eager. I could see a glint of sorrow in Mama's eyes even then. The energy from Papa's smile, frozen in black and white gloss, said that his heart was on fire. They appeared to be happy, at least Papa did. I put the picture back and dug around in the trunk again. I discovered in the corner of the trunk an old family Bible that contained a packet of tea-colored letters tied with red ribbon. I could tell that they were important, so I carefully untied the ribbon and leafed through the papers. They were love letters written by a German POW who had been in a hospital in Franklin where Mama worked, before she married Papa. Most of them were posted from Germany, addressed to her and written in French. The only way that I knew they were love letters was by the x's and o's and hearts drawn under the signature. Mama had told me one time that many of the German POWs spoke French, so she was asked to translate in French and write letters for those who couldn't write. She would send their letters back home to Germany for them. I couldn't read French, but the signature, which I couldn't make out either, was the same on all of them except the last one where there was no signature— just a line beginning mid-sentence and streaking limply down and off the paper. Was it the gravity of a last motion? Was there a full moon shining through his window, lighting his letter? I understood gravity when I was in the tree, but I didn't understand the moon. Since the moon affects the gravitational pull of the ocean's tides, I supposed that it could affect the tides of our own blood.

The letters only made me more curious. I dug through the trunk some more and found a diary that had a broken latch and lock. I opened it carefully and discovered Mama's diary written in her hand. I thumbed through it looking at the dates and settled on the first page. The first entry began.

Monday, December 4, 1944

Dear Diary,

I entrust you, my dear friend, with the news of my day and the secrets of my heart. The war goes on still and everyone, including myself, is so tired. I think the whole world has gone crazy. I wonder if anything will ever be normal again. I haven't had any nylons or combs for my hair in so long. Only people with plenty of money can afford such luxuries. Even though we still have a car, Papa can't drive it anywhere because the gas is rationed. We all have to sacrifice for the cause. It is our duty and an honor to do so. Forgive me of my complaints. I ride my bicycle to Aycock's Clinic every day, rain or shine. I like to ride by the high school at noon when the gym doors are open. I can hear rhumba, tango, or cha-cha music being played depending on what dance the gym teacher is teaching. I miss having fun. All of this is nitpicking stuff compared to what I've seen in the clinic. We have about fifteen beds and lately they have been filled which keeps me busy. There are people suffering and in far worse condition than me. I am ashamed to complain. I've been working as a nurse's aide now for three months. I'm so glad to have the job. It's hard to think about the future, but I have hope in my heart.

My friend Yvette is in love with a German POW. It's a big secret because most of the folks in town do not associate with them and frown on those who do. The POW camp is where the Civilian Conservation Corps camp was once located—about a mile west. Although it has been here for about a year now, I don't know too much about them, except that they were captured German soldiers of the Afrika Korps. I remember when they marched to the camp from the Southern Pacific train station. I was sitting on Aunt Feliciane's porch on Adams Street when they marched by. Aunt Feliciane has the cutest dachshund named Saucisse, that means hot dog, but we call her Sauci for short. Sauci barked her little head off when the POWs marched by. She ran among them and the POWs laughed and spoke German to her. One POW couldn't resist bending down and petting Sauci until one of the guards told him to move on. The POWs are mostly blond and pink-skinned compared to most of us. They are handsome men. My brother Alcide supervises them in the cane

fields. He made friends with Yvette's boyfriend, Jakob Leitz. Yvette
says Jakob has a friend that she wants me to meet. Love seems out
of the question for me right now. For one thing, there aren't many
young men around. I know I'm getting kind of old, and I certainly
don't want to be an old maid, but right now, I'm just trying to earn
and save a little money.

Your friend,
Mary Effie Thibodeaux

Guilt nagged at my conscience. I felt bad about reading something not
meant for my eyes, but to discover who my mother had been at twenty-four
years old nudged me on. I decided to take the diary downstairs before the
sweat from my forehead dripped on the pages. I straightened the contents
of the trunk and carefully closed the lid. With the diary under my arm, I
groped over the rafters and climbed down from the attic. Once I was in the
bedroom, I reminded myself that I must be extra careful that no one, and I
meant no one, could know that I was reading Mama's diary, not even Bobby.
I vowed to put it back as soon as I finished reading it. Although no one was
in the house, I decided to crawl under the bed and read just in case I fell
asleep. I just didn't want to get caught. It was bad enough having your father
hate you, but much worse having your mother hate you as well. I read on.

Tuesday, December 5, 1944

Dear Diary,

Today began as an ordinary day, but after lunch it became rather
eventful. A prison camp truck pulled up and several German soldiers
from the POW camp got out of the back dressed in their blue prisoner's
uniform with large PW letters on the back of their shirts. A soldier
with a rifle guarded them while they carried one prisoner in on a

stretcher. Some of them had cuts from cane knives, which are typical for this time of year because the sugarcane is still being harvested, even though it is nearing the end for this season. The farmers want to get the crop in before freezing and the cane turns sour. I know they are working fast to finish before Christmas. After everything settled down, my supervisor asked me if I would write letters for these prisoners, since many of them are illiterate. Several of them can speak French but can't write it. I was delighted to do so. It was a much easier job than carrying bedpans. I try to be cheerful around them and encourage them. Most of them are lonely and just want to go home. One prisoner named Johann Sebastian Wilhelm was brought in with a shattered tibia and his right hand was broken. It appeared that he was in a fight, but I was told that he had been driving a tractor, and it flipped over on its side, pinning his leg underneath. The doc put his leg in traction. He moaned in his sleep. When he was fully awake and the fog of pain lifted, his eyes looked like pools of blue water. I have never seen eyes this color. After work, my brother told me that one of the guys he supervised flipped a tractor and broke his leg. He had to get the mules out as a backup because the wheel on the tractor was bent. I wonder if this is the guy Yvette wants me to meet. I will find out tomorrow.

Yours truly,
Mary Effie

Thursday, December 7, 1944

Dear Diary,

Today is a somber day since it is the anniversary of the bombing of Pearl Harbor, December 7, 1941. Twenty-four hundred men were killed. Everyone talks about where they were when they got the news. I was in our kitchen drinking coffee and eating syrup cake with Maman and Papa when the door flew open and one of Papa's friends, Anatole Duplantier, said, 'Hey y'all, America has been attacked by the Japanese.' We were shocked. 'Who are the Japanese?' Mama and Papa said at the same time. I told her that they were people from Japan and that it was an island country next to China. 'Where did they attack?' was the next question. 'Pearl Harbor,' Anatole said. 'Where is Pearl Harbor?' Mama and Papa asked. 'The Hawaiian Islands,' he said. They turned the radio on, and it explained the rest. Mama and I cried when we heard how many of our sailors were killed. In spite of all the sadness of the day, I am beginning to feel like I have more energy. There is lightness in my step and in my thoughts, even though I'm always on the go. I spoke with M'sieu Wilhelm in French today. He asked me to call him by his Christian name, Johann. Although, I have many duties, I look forward to taking care of him. I think I could drown in his eyes. They are arresting. I must keep my resolve. I talked with Yvette today and yes indeed that's the guy she wanted me to meet. She said that she would ask Alcide if Jakob could visit him in the hospital. She would come too and formally introduce us. Johann is a handsome fellow, but he is a German soldier! He is the enemy that our red-blooded American boys are fighting. He is the *enemy that killed husbands, fathers, brothers, sons, and uncles. How can I forgive this man? Why does war exist?*

Yours truly,
Mary Effie

Friday, December 8, 1944

Dear Diary,

It rained cats, dogs, and little frogs this afternoon. I usually don't mind the rain. It seems to slow the world down, but I just don't like to ride my bicycle home in it, even though I have on my raincoat and galoshes. The rain brought a nice surprise because the prisoners got off work early. Alcide brought Yvette and Jakob by the clinic to visit Johann. They formally introduced me to Johann. Jakob and Johann talked in German. I knew they were talking about Yvette and me, so I piped in and told Jakob that he would have to interpret the German or speak in French; better yet, they should both learn to speak English. Jakob and Johann both apologized in broken English that they had learned in school. Yvette doesn't seem to be bothered about dating a German. She told me that he really wasn't German or a Nazi; he was Jewish. She said that he escaped from one of the death camps by stealing a German soldier's uniform, putting it on and walking out of the gate with a group of new recruits that didn't know who he was. He walked out as big as you please with his violin close to his side. Jakob had more freedom than most of the prisoners because he was a virtuoso violinist. He played for the Führer and other German officers and their wives. The violin that the officers (at the request of Hitler himself) had given him is the same one he plays

*today. After he escaped the death camp, the Americans picked him
up thinking he was a German soldier and sent him here to Louisiana
to the POW camp along with the POWs from the Africa Korp. She
says that he hates the Nazis and so does Johann. I can't think any
more about that. I'm really tired now. Had a long day at the clinic.
Will write more later.*

Yours,

M.E.T.

Monday, December 18, 1944

Dear Diary,

*Today I bent over to help Johann lean forward, so I could adjust
his pillows, and I felt his breath on my neck. A thrill like a shot of
adrenalin went through my body. He said he liked my perfume. It
was just cheap dime store rose water, but I didn't tell him that. His
gaze held mine, and I held my breath. When I could breathe again,
I said, 'thanks.' I continue to write letters to his mother and father
for him. He is a good son. He worries about his mother's health
and all of the chores his father has to do. I can't stop thinking about
Johann. Mama is calling for me to help her chop nuts and fruit for
her fruitcakes. Must go for now.*

Yours,

Mary Effie

Thursday, December 21, 1944

Dear Diary,

Christmas is almost here. I haven't much money for gifts and I have racked my mind to think of something for Maman and Papa. Also, I want to do something for the POWs that are still here in the clinic, especially for Johann. I've kept my guard up, but when you write letters to someone's mother, father, and family, you really get to know the kind of person they are. "Honor thy father and mother," the good book says. Johann is a nice man and he loves his family. He is so lonesome for them. I'm sure the holidays have something to do with it. I asked Johann if he had a girlfriend that he may want to write, and he said that in Germany during the war there was no time for love. Love was only a dream. Johann has no malice toward the American soldiers. Although he has not said this directly, I think he is really cheering the Americans on to win the war. He has to be careful. He is very courteous and grateful for anything I do for him. I hope our soldiers received the packaged goods that I helped pack for the Red Cross. I know they will appreciate warm socks and undershirts. I hope some German girl is being kind to American soldiers and boosting their morale with the Christmas spirit. I must go. We have so many preparations to make. Auntie La La, Uncle Dub, Phoebe, aka Fe Fe, Alcide, and Althea are coming for dinner on Christmas day. It won't be like Christmases past with all the gifts, but we are grateful and happy to be together. Yay!

Merry Christmas,
Mary Effie

Friday, December 22, 1944

Dear Diary,

I finally figured out what to give Maman and Papa and the POWs at the clinic. I talked with Alcide to get permission for Jakob to come to the hospital on Christmas Eve and play some Christmas carols for the patients. Jakob can play anything he has ever heard. I talked with my supervisor and she talked with hers and we have the A-OK to go ahead with our plans. I invited Maman and Papa to come to the clinic to hear Jakob play. I'm so excited to have a world-class violinist play in our little town. We decorated a Christmas tree up front. I had some of the patients, the ones that could, string popcorn to put on the tree. That didn't work so good because most of them ate the popcorn. The paper chains worked just fine.

Merry Christmas,
Mary Effie

Sunday, December 24, 1944

Dear Diary,

I have never heard music played so beautifully. Maman and Papa and everyone at the hospital enjoyed the music. We all had tears in our eyes. Jakob's talent is truly a gift from God. The German POWs wanted to give us a gift too. Jakob played Silent Night or Stille Nacht *and they sang in German. It was so beautiful that I couldn't wait to go to midnight mass and thank God for sending his Son and allowing enemy soldiers to share their talents with us. They did it in the name of love.*

Happy Birthday Jesus,
Mary Effie

Monday, January 1, 1945

Dearest Diary,

It is 1945! It sounds so peculiar on my tongue, but I will get used to it. I had to work today even though it was a holiday. People die on holidays, and I know our soldiers overseas are lonesome and some are probably dying. I wake up looking forward to going to work. This evening I helped Maman make jambalaya for supper. We also had black-eyed peas for good luck and cabbage for plenty of money in this New Year. Maman noticed that I sing more often, and she has commented on my cheerfulness. I must tell you a wonderful secret. I'm in love. Johann and I are growing in friendship and love. He says he wants nothing more to do with war. He didn't have a choice. He was forced into the German army. These Alsatian recruits were known as malgré nous which means "against their will." He is not a Nazi. He never joined the Nazi party. He was born in the city of Kolmar in Alsace which was a part of France until the Germans took over. He considers himself to be Alsatian where French was his native language. He said that when the Germans took over that they were no longer allowed to speak French. If a simple word like bonjour or bonne nuit was spoken, you would have to pay a fine. He misses his homeland terribly, but he says that if he had to go home, he would

miss me more. He likes my hair when strands fall from my nurse's
cap. He begs me to take it off and let my hair fall freely. I dare not.

Happy New Year,
Mary Effie

Entry after entry, I read of the budding romance between Mama and
this German soldier. It surprised me that Mama could have loved anyone
else but Papa. It embarrassed me, but I couldn't stop reading. I had long
felt that I was about to discover something really big, but now I felt that I
had stumbled into it. I flipped through the entries giving them a kiss and
a promise to read them in detail later. On a gut level, I searched for clues—
clues of what? My mother's past? I didn't know, but I felt driven to read on,
desperate to have some answers.

Wednesday, January 10, 1945

Dearest Diary,

I woke up this morning happy to go to work. I hurried through
the drudgery of making beds and emptying bedpans so that I could
spend more time with Johann. I bathed Johann's back and chest today.
Ever since he has been here, he has refused to allow me to help him
with the bedpan. Rufus, the guy that sweeps and cleans helps him.
Rufus wasn't too keen to help, but I promised to bring him a piece
of Maman's sweet potato pie. I keep him supplied with cornbread
and other stuff that Maman makes. I have seen many men only in
the course of my duties as a nurse's aide. I am most curious about
Johann.

Love,
Mary Effie

Wednesday, January 17, 1945

Dearest Diary,

It has been six weeks now since Johann first came to the hospital. Doctor Robicheaux took the plaster cast off of his hand and leg. Johann was so glad to have his leg out of traction. Dr. Robicheaux encouraged him to practice standing with my help. I was thrilled to put my arm around him and his around me. I felt his ribs. He must eat more. I will see to it that he gets an extra portion.

Love and Kisses,
Mary Effie

Friday, January 19, 1945

Dearest Diary,

I take Johann out in a wheelchair every afternoon when the weather cooperates. Luckily, we have had a mild winter. Johann is getting stronger but still can't walk more than a few yards at a time. His wrist has healed but, he pretends he can't write so that I will continue to write letters for him. I stroll him to a grove of pine trees where we talk. He enjoys the sun, but not for long. He is so fair. We speak in English because he wants to practice. Today, he kissed me, and I kissed him back. I am deliriously in love. I pray the war ends before he has to go back to the POW camp where he will be sent to work. I would not be able to see him very often and I don't think I could bear it. I worry that his barracks would not be warm enough. He is still thin as a slice of bought bread and he has not gotten his strength back. Maman is knitting him a sweater to go under his work shirt. I pray the guards will not take it from him.

> *Love,*
> *M.E.*

Wednesday, January 24, 1945

Dear Diary,

Time is running out. Johann pretends to the doctors that he can't walk very well. I know he is stalling. Mrs. Trahan, my supervisor, asked me today to take the night shift since the night nurse quit. Johann was surprised. When everyone on the ward was asleep and the curtain was drawn, Johann took my cap off. My hair fell across his chest. I kissed him passionately. I was so nervous that I didn't stay long.

> *Love,*
> *M.E.*

Monday, January 29, 1945

Dear Diary,

Johann was discharged today. He will return to the POW camp and resume his duties. I will miss him so much, but Alcide said that he would arrange for us to meet. I miss him already. I am really in the dumps. In fact, I got off early today and rode by the POW camp. There are four guard towers around the compound. One of the guards whistled at me, but I didn't care. I was hoping for a glimpse of Johann, but no such luck. I don't know which barracks he is in. The barracks are long and a weathered, gray color, just like my mood.

M.E.

Wednesday, February 14, 1945

Dear Diary,

I have only gotten to see Johann when he is out working. He writes me sweet letters and gives them to Alcide to give to me. Alcide said that even though the camp is considered low security, they got a new guard. The last guard fell asleep under a tree while the prisoners were working. One of the prisoners kicked him and said 'Wake-up. You're supposed to be guarding us.' Alcide lets me know when and where I can meet him. Today is Valentine's Day. Alcide arranged for Johann and me to have dinner at their house. Althea cooked a pork roast with potatoes instead of the usual rice and gravy. I was so thrilled to see Johann. It was like a real date. When we were finished eating, Johann and I washed and dried the dishes. Alcide and Althea left to bring a plate of food to a neighbor who has been under the weather. Johann took my hair down, and we ended up in the spare bedroom. I am no longer curious. I am thrilled!

XXXOOO

M.E.

My head was spinning; my heart was thumping. My emotions were a multiple-choice question. Wow! Angry? Shocked? All of the above! My mother? My mother went all the way with some German Soldier! Had S-E-X? I continued to read.

Monday, March 19, 1945

Dear Diary,

I received a note from Johann, and he said that the Americans were going to release him early because of his leg. He still limps and can't work very hard. They have given up on him and will send him to another camp near New Orleans next week. He may be released early in anticipation of the war being over soon. They will ship him back to Kolmar. I am in shock. I can't think enough to write.

M.E.

Tuesday, March 20, 1945

Dear Diary,

I met Yvette after work for a Coke. We had a very interesting talk. She whispered that she and Jakob were eloping tomorrow. He will be working in the Bernard fields near the bayou. Alcide does not supervise that crew, thank God. Jakob plans to take off and Yvette will meet up with him. They will go into hiding until the war is over. Her parents don't know because the Military Police will probably talk with them about Jakob's whereabouts. She gave me a letter explaining the situation. I am to give it to her parents, so they will not worry. I am to give it to them when the MP's have given up looking for Jakob. I think that would be in about two weeks. Yvette also made me promise in the name of Jesus Christ that I would not tell Alcide or anyone! I hugged her and wished her much happiness. I will see you after the war, she said. I pray that they will be safe.

M.

Wednesday, March 21, 1945

Dear Diary,

They made it, thank God.

M.

Friday March 30, 1945

Dear Diary,

I begged Alcide to let me have one night with Johann and he made the arrangements. (Maman and Papa would kill me if they knew, but my brother is my closest confidant. He knows that Johann and I are in love.) It wasn't for the whole night because Johann had to sneak back to the camp, but we had several hours. Alcide and Althea were conveniently not at home. Johann asked me to marry him and I said "YES!" I am thrilled. He took out a ring that he had hammered and worked on for weeks. He made it out of silver dimes that he had melted down. It fit perfectly. He said that he would do better later. It will be the only thought that makes life bearable when he leaves. If we could have gotten married today, we would have done so. Johann

said that he would come back for me and that I should make plans.
We had the tenderest lovemaking ever.

Love,

M.

My surprise turned to dismay when I figured up the days on the calendar. I tried to remember when Baby Faye was born. It took nine months. If Mama had gotten PG by Johann, I would have been born before Christmas, but I was born on December 30. Mama always said that I came early, or was I really a few days late if the German was my father? I couldn't stop my hands from trembling. Everyone thought I looked like Mama, but my eyes were hazel. I had brown hair rather than black like Mama or Papa and my skin was not as dark as Mama's, Papa's, or even Bobby's. Mon Dieu what a Pandora's box I had opened. I was compelled to read on.

Saturday, March 31, 1945

Dear Diary,

I think today was the hardest day of my life. Johann and some other German POWS were sent to a camp near New Orleans. They were put on a train for Baton Rouge and then in a few days they will go to the port of New Orleans where they will board a ship that will take them back to Germany, so they were told. They don't tell them too much. I went to the train station to see him off. In spite of the guards, he kissed me and held me and cried unashamedly. I cried, too. "I'll be back for you, my darling and I will marry you. I can't live without you. This war was the best thing that ever happened to me because I met you," he said. "I love you." The last thing he said as he hoisted his duffle bag up and got on the train was, "I'll come back to you. I promise." I ran alongside of the train waving my handkerchief, until he became a small dot in the window. I turned around crying and walked back. Tears filled my eye. I wasn't watching where I was going and tripped over someone's luggage. A soldier, who was one of the new guards at the POW camp, named Walter LaCour helped me up and carried me to the street. He flagged down a car and rode with me to the clinic. Doctor Robicheaux said that my ankle was broken, and he put it in a plaster cast. My broken heart hurts far more than my ankle.

M.

Thursday, April 12, 1945

Dear Diary,

There is more sadness to burden my heart. President Roosevelt died today. The news reported that Roosevelt said, "I have a terrific pain in the back of my head." He then slumped over in his chair unconscious. He died later during the day. Our vice president Harry S. Truman is now our president. The world is a dark place. But I am hopeful that the war will be over soon, and the troops will be home. I miss Johann so much.

M.

Monday, April 16, 1945

Dear Diary,

I have cried in my pillow every night since Johann left. I know how Longfellow's "Evangeline" must have felt. I haunt the mailbox every day. I finally received letters today—seven letters in all! Two of the letters were mailed before he left the States. The rest were written from Kolmar, Alsace-Lorraine and posted from there. Dear Diary, now that he can write for himself, he writes such beautiful letters. I will treasure his letters forever because my heart cries for him. He wrote: "Moi, j'ai pris le grand chemin de fer avec le coeur aussi cassé"— I took the train with such a broken heart." "We have a love that the world can't stop," and "I'll close with all the love I can bestow on the most precious part of my life." "Sweetheart you have captured my heart." And "You are my conquistador." He signed a letter "I send oceans of love and kisses to the most beautiful girl in the world. Love Eternally, Johann." The last letter that I read was frightening. He has suffered another fall. His leg is shattered again, compound fracture. The bone broke through the skin. He was in the hospital, but now he is at home and in traction again. I am so worried. I am so tired that I can hardly write. Walter LaCour visits me every day since Johann left on the train. He is so persistent. He brings me flowers and peppermint candy. We sit out on the porch and talk. It is so strange that I am still in a cast and now Johann is in a cast again. I have sympathy for him. Now I know how a cast feels and how hot it is and how much it itches. I pray that Johann and I will both get well and be whole again. I pray that Johann will return to me. He said that he would come back to me. He promised me that. I have to have hope in that statement. I am so anxious.

M.

Wednesday, April 18, 1945

Dearest Diary,

I went to work today for just a short while. I saw Mrs. Trahan my supervisor walking down the hall toward me. She looked at me so focused. I stood against the wall and looked at her. She carried something in her hand. Her look was serious. I looked away and then back at her. Somehow, I knew. She handed a telegram to me. I stared at it, afraid to open it, because it was from Alsace-Lorraine. I trembled when I finally managed to open it. It was from Johann's father. "Johann sleeps eternally. Blood poisoning. Nothing the doctors could do. He loved you," it said. I dropped the telegram and crumpled on the floor. I am numb. I have died too.

Wednesday, April 25, 1945

Dearest Diary,

Sometimes I wonder if I can go on. I have not been back to work since the news. I can't face the memories at the clinic and do my job properly. Papa and Maman have not pushed me to go back. They look at me with sorrowful eyes. Maman tries to make me eat and cooks my favorite meals, but hunger has escaped me. I go to the grove of trees behind the clinic, where Johann and I talked and kissed. I listen for him, I look for him, I remember, and I sing, "Everywhere I turn there is a memory of you. I breathe the air that you breathed, I see the moon that you knew. I close my eyes. I feel your embrace. Your words in my heart that time will not erase. Walk me through the storm in this glitch of time. You said you would return and be mine. I believed you, I believed you from the depths of my soul I believed. The waves surround me, swirl around me. I am lost without your love." My voice trails off and I cry again. I force myself to stand and walk home. I look forward to sleep because I dream of Johann and that he is alive. His beautiful eyes are holding my gaze. I feel his breath on my neck. We are together and so in love. My heart swells with happiness, but I wake up and feel warm and loved, and then, I remember, and I am completely broken. I had so many air castles and dreams built for our future. I have spent every day in the chapel and pray before the Blessed Sacrament. I light a candle for Johann. His memory will be forever alive in me. I know I must be resurrected from this misery. Walter came. He said that he knew he would find me before the Blessed Sacrament. He knows that I grieve for Johann. Perhaps Walter doesn't know the depth of my relationship with Johann. Then again, maybe he does because I am completely devastated, yet he continues to be there for me. Walter will not let me die. He loves me. How can I ever love again?

May 1, 1945

Dear Diary,

I read in the newspaper today that Hitler committed suicide yesterday. The war will be over soon.

M

May 8, 1945

Dear Diary,

President Truman declared today as VE day, which stands for Victory in Europe. The German high command surrenders all land, sea, and air forces unconditionally to the allies. I wish Johann were alive to witness this day. He hated war. The war goes on against the Japanese in places I've never heard of. My heart still cries for Johann.

M

Saturday, June 1, 1945

Dearest Diary,

I will never stop loving Johann, but I choose to love Walter. We will make our life together.

M.

I wiped the tears from my eyes. I felt her pain. I was confused over my own pain. When were Mama and Papa married? June 1, 1945 must have been the date. I was pretty sure that that was the date. Why did she marry so soon? The burden of not knowing for sure weighed heavily on me. I took a deep breath. I had a lump in my throat that wouldn't go down. I turned the page and read the final entry.

Sunday, September 2, 1945

Dear Diary,

I *am delirious. Today the Japanese surrendered! The war is over! The headlines in huge print in the newspaper today was* JAPAN SURRENDERS TO ALLIES. *The war is officially over. The Japanese surrendered on board the ship the USS Missouri in Tokyo Bay. Mama saved the whole newspaper. The people in town went crazy. They blew their car horns or bugles or anything that made noise. Some drove down the main street throwing watermelons out of the beds of trucks. Some went to church in thanksgiving. Others went to the liquor store to booze it up. Everyone is ecstatic! There is hope that happiness will return to this world.*

M

CHAPTER EIGHT

I put the diary back in the trunk and walked hunched over along the rafters to the opening. Heavy with questions, and drowning in confusion, I lowered myself down from the attic. I folded the ladder and put it away in the garage and had just walked into the kitchen when I heard the screen door open and close. It was Mama returning home much earlier than I expected. She tiptoed in and put Baby Faye to bed. I took a deep breath and tried to forget what I had read, but I brooded. My mother in my mind was pure and good and to think a German soldier! In my mind's eye, I could see his arms around her, her lips pressed to his. I could see the very stirrings of myself coming into being. I've got to stop thinking or Mama's going to read my mind. I opened the refrigerator door and stuck my head in so Mama wouldn't see my face. I poured myself some Kool Aid and covered my face with the glass when Mama came into the kitchen.

"What's wrong, Walt?"

"Nothing. Except for being hot."

Mama read faces and body language with a sixth sense. She looked me in the eye, and I worked at pretending that everything was hunky-dory.

"Yes, something," Mama said.

"Oh, the short-story that I'm reading is sad. One of the characters bounces on a tree limb that he and his best friend are standing on and his friend, who is the star athlete, falls and breaks his leg. I suppose that I'm just bored," I said.

I was glad that statement was true, but not the real truth. I had a hard time lying to Mama.

"Summer-time blues," she said and busied herself with the dishes.

Later in the afternoon when Baby Faye woke from her nap, Mama dressed her in a white dress with yellow chicks and orange ducks on the collar that she had embroidered under the lamp by her chair in the late evenings. She was trying to create a fairytale for her little princess. She wanted nice things, but it was only through the work of her hands and her imagination that she could create a different world for her. One of my favorite memories was of Mama bending forward squinting at tiny, accordion folds of fabric and sewing them with white thread, the needle streaking through the fabric, like a shooting star. Bent over her work, she reminded me of her mother, my Gammy with the Dress.

Gammy with the Dress was an old lady when she passed away. The striking thing about her was that she curled inward. I was curious about old folks and wondered if you grew into yourself when you grew older. Do you curl back up the way a fern is curled before it opens? Do you go back to a fetal position the way Baby Faye slept right after she was born? Do you grow into yourself? Do their hands curl inward the way Baby Faye closed her fists like she was holding onto an invisible hand—her guardian angel's? When Gammy with the Dress visited her sister, Auntie La La, there wasn't much visiting going on. She sat curled up in a chair, and Auntie La La was curled up in her wheelchair. I told Gammy with the Dress to "look up, look out, and ask Auntie La La how she is doing." I guess I was really telling her to uncurl; don't shrivel up; don't die. She looked up at me and said, "She's fine," and curled back down to stare at her hands. After a short time, Gammy with the Dress said that her hands looked like her mother's hands.

Auntie La La said, "No Marie, my hands look like *Maman's*." They argued back and forth in French. That's when I could understand their French, but what I understood more was that old people curled back into a fetal position before they died.

Mama tied the ribbon of Baby Faye's matching bonnet and settled her in the baby buggy. Faye was the cutest baby that I had ever seen. She was the spitting image of the baby on the Gerber Baby food jar. Her big, black eyes jumped with excitement as if she wanted to jump right out of herself and tell everyone who she was. Bobby and I could make her laugh with the funny noises we made. When she stretched out on her back, we thought that she would run in the Olympics one day because she moved her legs so fast like pistons propelled by a little motor whirring inside of her.

"Bobby, will you please stroll Baby Faye to Nanan's?" She is going to look after her tonight while we go to the fais-dodo."

"Sure. I like to play race car driver with the buggy."

Mama gave him a stern look.

"Well, okay. I'll just go ten miles per hour instead of fifty."

Mama raised her eyebrow at him.

"Okay, okay, I'll go two miles per hour."

He grinned and pushed the buggy to the front door and backed it down the steps. He made racing engine and squealing brakes noises just to get a rise out of Mama. I walked to the front porch and said quietly to Bobby when Mama wasn't looking.

"Bring Nanan's wishbook back."

Mama didn't like for us to dream of material things because she knew that we would be disappointed. When I was younger, I flipped through the pages in the toy section of the Montgomery Ward catalog for hours. I prayed for a miracle. I prayed that Papa *Noël* would bring me an erector set and toy soldiers for Christmas. He didn't. Later, I prayed that he would bring me a new bike or skates. He didn't. I gave up on Papa Noël and miracles to boot which was why I had a hard time in church. It seemed like miracles only happened in Biblical times. I wanted to believe, but it just felt like I was fooling myself. I still liked to dream though, and I knew Nanan wouldn't mind loaning her book to me because I always took good care of books.

If Uncle Thib was the happiest person I had ever known, Nanan was the sweetest. Nanan said that it takes three people to make a marriage and that being the two of them and Jesus Christ. I knew Jesus resided in our house because Mama talked to him all the time, saying "sweet Jesus" this and "sweet Jesus" that. There was a big battle going on between Jesus and the devil. Papa's whiskey bottle could surely bring the devil out.

After Bobby and Baby Faye left, I gathered the pieces of Mama's demitasse cup and saucer and arranged them on the kitchen table so that I could get a good look at the edges. It was as difficult as gluing the stars and sky together to make the shape of the universe. Slowly but surely, I glued pieces here and there and the shape of the cup began to take form. Mama busied herself with cooking chores at the kitchen counter, even though she didn't consider cooking a chore. She peeled the parchment-like paper from an onion, quartered the onion, and wielded her knife over them. She usually lit a candle when she chopped onions because she said it kept her from crying so much. I dug around in the junk drawer and found the box of matches and scratched one against the box. The flame burst into life. I held it still until it gained strength enough to move and tipped it to the wick of the candle. The flame held on. I blew the match out and sat back down to the smell of sulfur. Mama continued her furious onion chopping, and I finally realized that she wanted an excuse to cry.

"How can people live with meanness?" I said. Mama stopped chopping for a minute and looked at me and said immediately.

"Love," she paused. "Love looks for the goodness in people."

She put the knife in the sink and washed her hands, turned around and leaned against the counter, drying her hands on her apron. She took a deep breath.

"Do you remember that old gray cat, Smokey, that we used to have?" she said.

I shook my head, no.

"I guess you were too little. One day in the late spring, I was walking on the beach looking for shells and old bottles when I came across a gunnysack that had washed up. I got closer to it and saw it move. I untied the twine and opened it up very carefully. I thought a snake was going to jump out at me, but I found this little gray kitten that almost drowned. Cher bébé, he was so cute. There were four other kittens in the litter, but they were all dead. Smokey was the only one that survived. Someone had put a rock in the sack to deliberately drown those cats. I took Smokey home and nursed him back to health, but I got to tell you cher, that he was the meanest cat I had ever seen. He clawed me and he clawed you. He swatted at my eyes. Your Papa told me to get rid of that cat before it blinded us, but I kept feeding him. I gave him milk and petted him while he lapped. I loved on that cat and even kissed the tips of his ears. He became the most adoring cat that I had ever seen. Never again did he scratch or hurt me. Love did that. Love changes things. You see Walt, I didn't take away his weapons; I took away his desire to use them."

Mama turned back to the stove and began chopping celery and bell pepper. Then she scraped all of them off the cutting board into the black cast-iron skillet and shook it to spread them out.

"Did Hitler's mama love him?" I said. Mama could read my mind, and she knew where I was going with this.

"I don't know, Walt. I don't know when a person becomes evil. I do know that Smokey was striking out at us because he was scared. There's a big difference. I'm not an educated woman, but Hitler meant to get rid of a whole race of people because they didn't think like him or look like him. He thought he was smarter and more powerful than anyone else. They said that he was doing the devil's bidding and that he was evil through and through. Well, I'm not going to judge people, but I know right from wrong. People have the right to defend themselves. We are our brother's keeper as the Good Book says."

"Didn't Hitler love his mistress, Eva something or other?" I asked. "If someone can still love, is he completely evil?"

"Hmm, she said. You always keep me on my toes. You could be right because a lot of sin can happen in the name of love, but then again, maybe he loved himself in her presence."

I went back to work on the cup thinking about what Mama just said. She picked up a wooden spoon and returned to sautéing the onions. Even though Mama said she was uneducated except for high school, she was the smartest person I knew.

"Is Papa evil? Because he sure is mean. I think he hates me."

I held my breath. I wanted to ask her about her diary and the German soldier, but I didn't have the nerve. Mama would have been so disappointed in me, and what if the German soldier was my father? It would break her heart all over again.

Mama bent over to examine the flame; then she turned the gas on low. She moved to the sink and washed her hands with a deliberate slowness. The welcoming smell of onions cooking filled the kitchen. I felt comfortable talking about my thoughts with Mama, something I could not do with Papa. Papa didn't care to know about things and the thoughts of other people. Mama turned around and wiped the tears with the corner of her apron.

"Those durn onions," she said and sat down in the chair next to me.

She grabbed my arm with both hands. I stared at her work-worn hands for a minute. They were warm and small. The pink and white ovals of her fingernails were the color of wet seashells and so frail, but her grip said that she was strong and determined. She held on to me with a fierce love, as if she was never going to let me go.

"Son," she said and paused.

She thought of all the right words and put them in the right order so that I would believe her. There were some things in life that words could not hold their meaning. There were no words big enough. I paid attention to the art of arranging words, but I never could get it right in order to convince Papa of anything.

"Your Papa loves you and all of us very much. When he hurt his leg in that oilrig accident, it seemed like the lifeblood of his ambitions drained out of him. He started drinking because he was in so much pain. His pain was not only in his knee and leg, but also in his mind. He lost control. His body betrayed him. Life betrayed him."

Mama paused for a moment to let me breathe in the light.

"He's disappointed in life because he can't provide for us like he thinks a man should. He made good money in the oil fields, and now we scrape by. He's frustrated because the whiskey snared his willpower, and he can't get out of its grips. He feels helpless." She paused. "He's just sad and scared." She paused again. "Son, he deserves our love."

I picked up a piece of the broken cup and globbed a dab of glue on it. I put it in place while I held the tip of my tongue between my teeth. I thought and thought about what Mama had said. I felt her eyes on me like the eyes I had felt late at night when sleep wouldn't come—Loving eyes. I glanced up at her. She sat very still and watched me put the pieces together. She gave me time to put all the pieces of our conversation together in my mind. Mama knew when to use words and when silence was the best unspoken word of all.

"I just want to live a rightly life," I said.

"My sweet-spirited boy," she said kissing me on the forehead and holding my face in her hands. I could smell the faint mixture of lemony soap and onions. "I am so proud of you," she said in the soft, rounded sounds of doves.

I knew she had said that to make up for Papa's meanness because he certainly wasn't proud of me.

For many nights after that conversation, I thought of Mama's hands. I could feel the pressure of her warmth and see the hurt, anger, and want in those hands: hands that clawed a soap bar to protect her seashell colored nails before she worked in the garden dirt or picked bell pepper and okra— hands that chopped onions, cooked, and cleaned—hands that touched your cheek when you were sick or sad, and you knew that she loved you—hands that would never see the inside of a lady's gloves. Poor little thing. *Pauve tete bete.*

CHAPTER NINE

As I wrote page after page of my memoir, I remembered how connected we all were. I remembered that when one person had a problem, it became the entire family's problem. At that time, our household had become a battlefield. It had become a war of the booze. Papa himself was the enemy and the casualty. He wasn't the only victim of his drinking; we all were. I was alone in the house when my already strained relationship with Papa took a different twist. I became the adult, and Papa was the child. Papa had a chip on his shoulder, and it grew bigger as he grew unhappier. Alcohol was kindling his anger. I was under the bed reading when the screen door sounded like it was torn off its frame. I knew it was Papa because of the sound of one footstep heavier than the other. I heard him stomp into the kitchen. I heard him banging pots and breaking glass. If Papa knew that I was in the house, he would vent his anger on me. Curiosity got the best of me, so I crawled out from under the bed. I crept from the bedroom but froze in my position when I heard a crash against the wall. I hid behind the door and peaked into the kitchen. Papa ripped through the kitchen with the most crazed face I had ever seen. His jaw clenched, and his eyes glazed in desperation. The kitchen was a holy mess.

"Damn it," he said. "Where does she keep it?" Papa said.

I knew that he was looking for Mama's egg money that she had saved for a rainy day—or for special occasions. I feared for my life if Papa saw me, so I watched quietly. Papa rummaged among the contents of the freezer. Flour flew everywhere when he emptied the canister, then the sugar canister, rice was next, then cornmeal and finally, the coffee canister. Papa found a wad of cash in a small brown paper bag at the bottom of the coffee canister. Mama had hidden it there with coffee grounds covering it. He took the money and rushed out the door with a wake of trailing flour dust as fast and as furiously as he had come in. I crept out of my hiding place, glad that Papa was gone but cautious in case he came back. I thought about cleaning up the kitchen before Mama got home, but then maybe she should know Papa's desperation. A short time later I heard Mama calling me.

"Boy? What happened to the screen door? It has been pulled off the top hinge," her voice faded when she walked into the kitchen. "Oh my God," she said.

I stood in the kitchen with a broom in my hand. Her eyes swept the shambles of her kitchen. She sat down in the middle of the mess and cried, rocking back and forth.

"Mama, it was Papa. He took your egg money."

"I know," she cried, "I know."

After I helped Mama clean up the mess, I went out on the front porch to read when I saw Papa drive up in front of the garage. Papa didn't see me sitting on the porch, when he lifted a box from the trunk of the car. He carried it inside the garage, and a few minutes later he came out carrying a whiskey bottle and unscrewed the top. He stopped, threw his head back, and took a long swig from it and shook his head like the burn was so good. He hopped in the car and took off, never noticing me watching. I wondered about watching. There was power in observation. Out of curiosity, I went into the garage to see what was in the box. I dug around in the junk and found Papa's stash of whiskey hidden under a pile of old, horse harnesses, a saddle and a faded blanket in a corner of the garage. I was furious. I lifted the box of booze and carried it out of the garage and sat it by the front fence.

I ran inside the house, into Mama's bedroom, and got Papa's pistol that he kept for rabid raccoons and skunks and went back outside. I took every one of the leather-smelling, amber bottles and lined them up, one by one, on the fence and used them as target practice. Mama came to the door when she heard the shooting.

"Walt Junior, what has gotten into you?"

She glanced at the whiskey bottles and surmised that her egg money was spent on booze.

"Pick the glass up when you're done," she said and went back inside.

When Papa came home, I watched him from the front window stop and sniff at the fence curious about the smell of whiskey. He went to the garage and uncovered the saddle, but his stash was not there. You would have thought World War III had broken out. He charged into the house hunting for me and chased me around the room.

"You are always talking to me about life lessons, why don't you learn one?" I yelled.

I got on the other side of the table.

"That whiskey is causing a lot more damage than the oilrig accident ever did," I yelled. Papa charged around the table, knocking the kitchen chairs over. He caught me and lifted me by my shoulders and nailed me against the wall.

"That was a hundred and twenty dollars, you little shit," he yelled in my face with his whiskey breath.

"It was well spent to keep you sober," I yelled back. I kicked Papa in the groin, and he let me go. Papa doubled over, and I crashed to the floor. I scrambled up and started to take off, but Papa's long arm reached out and grabbed me by my foot. I tripped and fell headlong across the kitchen floor, skinning my elbows. I scrambled up again and took off, stumbling down the back-porch steps. It had started raining, and I slipped on the wet grass in my hurry to get to the tree. Seconds later, Papa came out the back door with his pistol and headed to the tree. I climbed the tree with Papa in pursuit.

"Come down here, you good for nothing," Papa yelled. I jumped in the boat, crouching down and breathing hard. Papa stopped short of the tree. He stared up into the tree.

"Stupidest thing I ever saw, sort of like making a planter out of an old toilet."

I lifted my head up over the edge of the boat.

"What the hell were you thinking? Where did you get that boat, anyway?" he said in a drunken rage.

I sat in the boat, rounded my shoulders and huddled. The rain dripped off my head and into my eyes and down my nose, my voice squeaking with effort, my mind scrambling for answers to stupid questions.

"My friends and I found it in the marsh. It was no good, beat up and all. It must have washed up in the last storm. Didn't think it was good for anything but a fort seeing how we ain't got lumber for a tree house. Nobody's name was on it, so I named it *Pooch*."

I dismissed the hope that Papa would say what a good, ingenious job that we all had done, and everything would be all right, but Papa didn't say anything I wanted to hear.

"You little shit. You're always messing in my business. I'll show you who's boss," he yelled and staggered in his drunken tirade. Papa lifted the pistol and cocked it. With his arm extended, he swayed back and forth trying to focus. I ducked down into the boat scared out of my mind. He fired shots into the air and tree. He hit the bottom of the boat and made a hole in it. The bullet just missed my head. I curled down into the boat and trembled over the close call of nearly having my brains blown out. Papa exhausted the ammunition and himself. He staggered back to the house. I wouldn't come down the tree, even though Mama begged me. I spent the night in the boat until Papa cooled off. Papa did vow to Mama to try to give up whiskey because she threatened to leave him. Poor Papa, he lived such a blistered life.

I stayed a few days at Uncle Thib and Nanan's until the storm blew over in our house. Early on the last morning that I was there, Uncle Thib sat down at the breakfast table. Nanan had made her good biscuits, and I was relishing them with some syrup. Uncle Thib buttered his biscuit slowly, set his knife down and looked at me.

"Boy, I'm your Parrain, right? I nodded my head wondering where this conversation was going.

"I wouldn't lead you wrong, no?" he said. I nodded my head. "Me, I've learned a lot working in a bar for all these years. That old bar is a great teacher. Life itself is a great teacher. Me, I learned that you never want to leave this world hating nobody. I believe that God will judge us by the measure of our love. How much we love other folks, you know. What you think about that?

I hung my head and wiped my fingers on my napkin.

"I think I hate Papa," I said.

"What do you think you should do about it?"

"I think I will meet him when his boat comes in this morning and help him unload the shrimp and clean up his boat."

"By doing that, what do you think you are saying?" Uncle Thib said.

"I'm saying I forgive him and will ask him to forgive me."

"Ok, then. I think that's a right smart thing to do, son."

I left out of the house and got my leather, work gloves. I waited on the dock for the *Mary Effie* to come in. I heard the water lapping at the boats. I heard the gulls call. I watched them dive. I saw Papa's boat coming in. Sea gulls were following it knowing that they might get some shrimp. Bobby was at the wheel and Papa was on deck. Papa stood there wiping his face with his red bandana. He looked at me and I looked at him. I mouthed, "I'm sorry." He mouthed back, "me too." Papa clapped me on the back when I came on board. We got to work unloading the shrimp and my mood improved as we worked. When we were done, Papa left in the truck. Bobby and I had intended on going home, but we changed our minds.

"Bobby," I said, "if we go home, Mama's gonna put us to work. Let's go to Uncle Thib's. I got to tell him how things went."

"Okay by me," Bobby said. I took off like a bat out of hell, and Bobby was keeping up with me. When we got to the bar a blue truck was parked in front.

"Ain't that the truck with those men asking about Éli's violin?" I said.

"Yep, it sure is. Wonder what they want."

"I think they're up to no good," I said. Let's sneak in the backdoor, so we can hear what's going on."

We crept in and hid behind the door to the office and listened. I could see the guys through the crack of the door. The two men sat at the bar drinking beer. When they finished their bottles of beer they stood up.

"I am Jack Stovall, and my partner here is Tanner McHughes. We are federal marshals and we're here to check on a violin that we suspect doesn't belong to you."

"What you talking about? That old fiddle that somebody left? I don't own no violin," Uncle Thib said.

"Are you Éli Dunneaux's guardian?" Jack said.

"First of all, I want to see your badges or some kind of identification," Uncle Thib said.

They both pulled out a badge from the inside pocket of their jackets and laid them on the bar.

"That don't tell me nothing. You could have stolen those as far as I know. Second of all, you would have to have a court order to take anything from here, and last of all, I ain't never heard of a government man working on Saturdays and drinking beer on duty," Uncle Thib said.

He started sniffing his nose like he smelled something bad. I thought he smelled the shrimp stink on Bobby and me, but he stopped.

"I think I smell vermin," Uncle Thib said.

"Now listen here, Mr. Thibodeaux, there's a tropical storm that may turn into a hurricane out in the Gulf, and we come to get the violin before it gets lost in the storm," Jack said.

"We can strong arm you into giving us what we want," the other one said. They sucked in air and lifted their chests to make themselves look bigger.

"Me, I don't think your arm is strong enough. I have two weapons," Uncle Thib said. He pointed in the direction of the door. The men turned their heads to look. "The crucifix over the door, and this Colt 44."

Uncle Thib pulled the gun from under the counter and laid it on the counter with his hand on the handle.

"I think you fellows better get gone before your get is gone for good. And don't ever show your face around these parts again or you'll be alligator bait."

CHAPTER TEN

I had always thought that when you died you would have answers to all of your questions, but that was not what I experienced. Life was more like a scavenger hunt. We were given a lot of questions that we had to go figure out and answer while we were alive. Our family was still struggling with answers, but things had cooled down in our household, especially after Mama called the priest and asked him to come over and talk with Papa. Papa agreed because Mama said he had two choices—either she goes to the police or the priest if the drinking didn't cease. Mama and Papa were working at reconciliation and getting help for Papa's alcoholism, and Papa said that he would try to go on the wagon or at least wean himself. He stayed sober for some time.

We were all looking forward to Saturday night because *joie de vivre* was part of our mindset. It was a special time to dance, laugh, and to pass a good time with our friends. Mama talked with Papa about the challenge of being around liquor, but Papa promised.

"Boy, get yourself in the car. Plan on walking if you're not here in two shakes," Papa said from the front door.

"Sorry, Papa. Sorry. I was the last one in the bathroom."

"Cut the excuse crap and get in the car," he said.

Bobby and Mama were sitting in the car when I climbed into the old Nash Rambler. We chucked along to the fais-dodo with Pooch following the car. Saturday nights and fais-dodos went together like rice and gravy. I smelled *Evening in Paris* perfume from the cobalt blue bottle that sat on Mama's dresser and Papa's Brylcreem hair grease he kept in the bathroom that I thought was toothpaste one sleepy morning. I had even put a little dab of Brylcreem in my hair and carefully combed it into a ducktail. The grease made my hair look dark like Papa's. I had stared in the mirror looking for any sign of German heritage. I still looked like a coonass. I had spent a lot of mirror time getting ready, trying on cool looks and Elvis's lip curl. I even cuffed my pants and rolled the sleeves of my shirt the way the Lake Charles boys wore theirs. The four of us were slicked up and shining like the chrome bumper that I had spent the morning polishing. Unfortunately, the good times were not rolling when we got to the Laissez Les Bons Temps Rouler.

"What's going on here?" Papa said.

Everyone was crowded around Uncle Thib's new Admiral TV.

"That new-fangled contraption is telling you what to think, huh?"

"Gotta special weather report," Uncle Thib said.

He moved the rabbit ears, and someone suggested putting tin foil on them. When the snow and static settled down, a very calm and intense man came on the screen. He adjusted his black, horn-rimmed glasses and spoke in a way that gave everyone goose bumps. A tropical storm had formed in the Gulf of Mexico and was moving over the water straight for us, southwest Louisiana. The newsman warned viewers to continue to watch this storm because the winds could increase to hurricane strength. The screen switched to the familiar face of the weatherman.

"There is no cause for alarm at this time, folks," he said.

The weatherman displayed a map of Texas and Louisiana, showing Beaumont, Lake Charles, Cameron, Creole, Grand Chenier, Pecan Island, and all of Southwest Louisiana in relation to the position of the storm that intensified by the hour.

"For new advisories and information on the changing position and wind speed of the storm, stay tuned to KPLC TV broadcasting live from Lake Charles, Louisiana."

When the station broke for a commercial, everyone in Uncle Thib's bar talked about the storm. Coonie Comeaux stood next to the bar with his wife Clelie. He spoke up and said that they had ridden out many storms and that the high tides had never gotten over the sand dunes. Everyone talked at the same time. They spoke in French, then English, then French and English, sometimes jokingly called Franglish, and always with their hands moving. The room grew silent with thought except for Éli who hadn't a care in the world except the plucking sound of his violin strings.

So, on a Saturday night in June with the news of a possibly dangerous storm getting ready to bash us, Éli sat on a wooden stool and leaned over to listen carefully to the sound of that old violin. He listened. When he listened to his own happy thoughts, he could make your feet move before you knew they were moving. When he listened to his heart, he could bring out the tenderness of the coldest man. His violin changed people. Éli didn't understand the concept of time. He lived from one visual image or musical image to the next similar to our memories. He lived every moment. But then again, maybe he did understand time. Maybe he understood what was really important. His music helped us remember that, and it also helped us to forget our worries.

Uncle Thib cleared his throat and spoke out over the crowd.

"Let's slow down that noise on the TV and pass a good time. *Laissez les bons temps rouler.*"

The band broke out into *A Mosquito Ate My Sweetheart*, which was such a stupid title that everyone started laughing. Couples moved out on the dance floor.

"I've got to tell you, cher, that you ain't never seen dancing until you've seen Cajuns Two-Stepping," Clelie Comeaux remarked to Uncle Thib.

All of the kids moved out onto the porch and drank soda. They played "Kick-the-Can" until they were so tired that they ended back up on the front porch, noses pressed against the windows and the screen door. I was too slicked up for that foolishness. Besides, I liked girls. I looked around until I saw Snukie. I couldn't take my eyes off of her. Her hair was not in the usual pigtails but long and silky against her back. It swayed back and forth when she walked. She was so beautiful it made me shy. I had known Snukie all of my life, but that night I looked at her with new eyes. I walked over to her, trying to be really cool.

"I ain't never seen you with your hair like that before. It makes you look older," I said.

Snukie blushed but was quick with a comeback.

"I ain't never seen you looking like Elvis Presley before neither," she said. We laughed.

"That was a great shot you made to keep that ole gator from getting after us—for a girl that is."

Snukie scorched me with her green eyes. I stuttered, looking at my feet, trying to figure out what to say, and maybe—just maybe, it would make up for that stupid insult.

"I mean, it was as good as anyone of us boys could have done. Let's dance," I said as fast as I could, and I led her out on the dance floor that had already filled up with couples.

Dancing gave me a little more courage knowing that everyone was too busy having fun than to look at me. Besides most of us Cajuns danced when we learned to walk. It was important because if you didn't dance, you would be by yourself and being alone was not good. Dancing also broke the ice. Snukie and I relaxed, and cut a rug several times, laughing just because.

Snukie and I stood on the edge of the dance floor when the band struck the chords of *Jolie Blonde*. The women sighed. They and their men moved out on the dance floor as if the very air was helium that lifted their feet off the floor. I looked over my shoulder at Bobby and the other kids who peeked through the screen door. I could hear them making kissing noises. I waved them away with my hand behind my back. I soon forgot about the kids snickering when Papa dragged Mama onto the dance floor just as the song ended.

"No, Walt," Mama said. "The music is ending."

"Ah, come on, Honey. It'll get going again," Papa said.

I knew that Mama was still mad at Papa for his drunken rage and shooting his gun at the boat with me in it, but Mama knew Papa was trying really hard to stay sober because his family was important to him. I worried that Papa would make a scene. Mama must have been worried, too because she cocked her eye at him to see if he had too much to drink, but the evening was still fairly new so that wasn't the case; besides, Uncle Thib was still in on our conspiracy to give Papa the watered-down hooch after two straight ones. Papa was really trying to cut back. Everyone left the floor except Mama and Papa. I could tell that Mama was embarrassed, but she and Papa just stood there in the middle of the empty dance floor. A hush fell over the crowd. Everyone stared. Before the band began again, Éli lifted his violin to his chin and played a melody that I had never heard before. I knew Éli played from his own intuition. I don't think I have ever heard a melody that expressed the hurts, loneliness, and love that married folks must experience. It spoke to me of promises that can't be filled and air castles that can dissipate into thin air, but the one thing that remains is love. Everyone, including myself, became spellbound when Papa took Mama by the hand as if she were a princess and he a prince. I didn't know if it was the liquor that killed the pain in Papa's leg, the music, the full moon, or the magic of Éli's violin, but he did not limp.

The moon pulled the tides of their hearts and sucked their breaths away when Papa looked into Mama's face while they waltzed. She kept her eyes down like Grace Kelly did in a movie that I had seen at the New Moon Drive-In Theater in Lake Charles. Mama was beautiful in her black dress with the white Peter Pan collar framing her face. Her dress clung tightly against her small waist and the skirt lifted in swirls as she and Papa turned and turned. Her cheeks flushed. He whirled her all around that dance floor and never took his eyes off of her. She finally lifted her eyes and stared into his. They waltzed away all the hurt and anger between them. Their feet and their hearts melded into one and they moved to a rhythm far deeper than the music. Snukie slipped her hand into mine. We pressed our fingertips together so lightly that I didn't know where mine ended and hers began, then we entwined them. The other couples watched Mama and Papa in respectful silence. They always talked about the evening Mary Effie and Man LaCour danced in the dim lights of Uncle Thib's bar, under the evening stars and into a galaxy of a universe that understood love.

When the music stopped, the party was over, and Papa rounded everyone up to leave. We went out on the front porch where Pooch was waiting for me. Mama asked Bobby and me if we would like to stay at Nanan's tonight and stroll Baby Faye back tomorrow morning because Nanan wanted to go to early Mass. Bobby had run around so much outside, playing chase with the other kids and shooting rocks into the Gulf with his slingshot, that I didn't think Mama wanted to ride home in the car with him. In other words, he smelled like a pig. That's what I thought then, but I know better now that I think back. It was like the time when I was little when Papa came home from working two weeks offshore. He lifted Mama up and swung her around and kissed her. He then took handfuls of coins and tossed them out in the grass. He said, "There's ten dollars worth of coins. If you find them all, you and Bobby can split the money. You have to find every one of them now." The door closed and I heard it lock, but I was too anxious to pick the coins out of the grass to think about it.

Bobby and I walked next door to Nanan's with Pooch by my side. We always kept extra clothes at Nanan's, so it was no problem. Besides, we really liked Nanan's homemade biscuits and hot chocolate for breakfast.

After Bobby and I cleaned up, we fell in bed barely getting our prayers prayed before we fell asleep. Nanan always let Pooch come in the house because she understood the bond Pooch and I had. Pooch curled up next to me and went to sleep. In the middle of the night, I woke up with a start. I listened.

"What's that noise," I said sitting up in bed with my eyes wide open. Pooch was growling low.

"Bobby, wake up. Listen."

"What?" Bobby said sitting up in bed.

We listened to an anguished cry coming from the direction of the bar. We ran to the screen porch and looked out.

"What is Éli doing on the roof? It's way too early. Why is he wailing so much?" I said.

"There's a man in front of the bar and another trying to get on the roof," Bobby said.

"Look, that looks like the truck those guys were driving."

"Yeah, the guys that came into Uncle Thib's bar and was asking about Éli's violin," Bobby said.

"It is," I said. "They tried to take the violin from Uncle Thib yesterday."

We looked at each other and said at the same time.

"They're trying to steal Éli's violin!"

"Here's the plan," I said. "You sneak out behind those bushes and pelt them with your sling shot. I'll run around to the back of the bar and get Éli's attention. Okay let's go. Pooch, come with me and no bark, no bark."

We snuck out of the house. Bobby began pelting them with stones, and I ran around the back of Uncle Thib's bar.

"Éli, Éli," I called.

Éli stopped yelling and looked down at me.

"Slide the violin down the roof, and I will catch it," I said.

Éli looked at the man trying to get on the roof and looked back at me. He did as he was told and pushed the violin case down the pitch of the roof toward me, a rare Stradivarius sliding, sliding, almost in slow motion and off the roof. I caught it and breathed a sigh of relief.

"Okay, Pooch, bark and go wake Uncle Thib," Pooch went to Uncle Thib's porch and started barking. I ran as hard as I could to my house carrying the violin. I barreled up the steps and woke up Papa.

"What the hell is going on?" Papa said.

"Papa," I said out of breath, "there are some men at Uncle Thib's bar. They're trying to steal Éli's violin. Éli is on top of the roof. He slid the violin to me, and I have to hide it."

Papa jumped up and put his pants and boots on and grabbed his twelve-gauge. Mama got up and put the violin in the blanket chest under some quilts.

"Walt be careful," she said as he went out the door.

I hopped in the car with Papa, and we headed to the bar. Papa's headlights beamed on the man out front. The other was getting down from the roof. Uncle Thib was on the front porch with his rifle, too. Papa stopped the car and got out and fired the shotgun into the air. The men took off running for the truck, jumped in and peeled out as fast as they could.

Uncle Thib and Papa met in front of the bar.

"I guess that scared the bejesus out of them," Uncle Thib said.

I hope so," Papa said.

"Éli," Uncle Thib said. "It's okay. Come on down."

When Éli came down, I told him that I had his violin in a safe place so that those men would not find it. Uncle Thib told him to use that old fiddle for a while just to be safe. Nanan was standing on the porch with a crying Baby Faye. Papa put his gun back in the car and went back for Baby Faye.

He lifted her and kissed her cheek and put her on his shoulder and patted her back. Bobby and I collected our stuff and we all, including Pooch, rode back to the house in case those men came snooping around again. If they did, I knew that they would come with guns.

CHAPTER ELEVEN

Sunday morning's weather didn't know that a hurricane gathered and gained wind speed out in the Gulf. The sun lazed in through the window, making me sleepier than ever. Bobby rolled over and stretched. I could hear Mama in the kitchen banging pots around, getting Sunday dinner started before Mass.

"Get up, lazy bones. Laziness is the workshop of the devil," Mama said at the bedroom door and returned to the kitchen.

Bobby and I groaned. Sleeping late in the LaCour household was on the same level as a sin. However, I believed that there should be some time to think and meditate. I opened my mouth to tell Mama that thinking could be the work of God but thought better of it and swallowed the words. I never begged to differ with her because when it came to church stuff, there was no arguing. That was one battle I would lose. In a few minutes, Mama came back to the door.

"Laziness is the same as clipping an angel's wings so they can't fly," she said. "Besides, your wings won't grow if you don't do good for someone else."

I groaned, "We're not in kindergarten."

"Get your butts out of the bed this instant!" Mama said while she pulled the sheets off of us. We bolted out of our beds.

"If you can't get up and go to church, you aren't going anywhere else for the rest of the day," she said and stormed out of the room.

I surely wanted to go to Uncle Thib's tonight and watch his new Admiral TV. Watching TV was kind of a religious experience, I mused. You had to have faith and trust that *The Ed Sullivan Show* would come on every Sunday evening. I knew Mama wouldn't see it like that though.

Papa stayed in the house with Baby Faye while Mama, Bobby, and I climbed into the Rambler to go to Mass. I hopped in before Mama and gripped the steering wheel.

"Please Mama, let me drive."

She stood in the open door with one foot on the running board and holding her black patina purse.

"I know I can do it. I can drive Mr. Doguet's tractor all over his field. Please?"

"Well, okay, but you gotta be careful, cher. You don't want to run us in the ditch like Uncle Baby did coming home from the Mardi Gras, or Papa will kill the both of us," she said and waltzed around the other side, probably remembering the good time that she had last night. She climbed in the passenger side.

I turned the engine over and put my left foot on the clutch and the right one on the brake and eased it into first gear. I gave it gas and lifted my foot off the clutch a little too fast. It backfired and conked out.

"It's a little different from the tractor," I said.

In the corner of my eye, I saw Mama glance at the porch to see if Papa had come to the door. I tried again, and this time the engine came to life. Other than swerving too sharply around a few potholes, we made it to Our Lady Star of the Sea church without wrecking. Potted Meat and Snukie stood on the church steps when we drove up. Their expressions congealed for a brief moment when they saw me at the wheel. The church bell tolled an upbeat rhythm. I secretly imagined that the bell rang a driver's debut as a rite of passage for me. It announced to my small world the arrival of a very good driver.

I swaggered into the church with Bobby and knelt down at our usual pew, while Mama went to light a candle. She clasped her hands in intense prayer. I wondered if she was praying about the storm in the Gulf or the storm named Papa in our house. Papa had a headache this morning and wasn't in a mood to be messed with, so he probably needed extra prayers; although, he did not get drunk last night. Mama unclasped her hands, raised herself up and came back to sit with us. She believed in prayer. She said it was kind of like Éli's violin, but much better—it had the power to change people and that was the toughest miracle of all.

I stared at the candles for almost the whole mass. Those bodies of flame lived on the same oxygen that we lived on. They leaned way over when Betty Jean Bourque and her Papa and Mama passed by and then they popped back up just as strong. When Mr. Aguilard fanned himself from across the aisle, a few minutes later that candle flame felt it and hulaed around on its wick.

"'Take courage, it is I. Do not be afraid,'" the priest droned on. I yawned and squirmed because nothing seemed relevant. In my peripheral vision, I saw Mama cut her eyes toward me. I stopped in mid-wiggle. I watched the candle again and thought about how hard it was to get a fire started, but when a flame did catch with a little dry pine straw, it could run through a field of salt grass in nothing flat. There was something sacred about those candle creatures. They were flexible and strong, yet fragile and weak. I wondered if Papa's whiskey breath would make it flame up or die down. Maybe that would make a good science project for the next school year. However, many of my theories were shot to hell in a hand basket like my religious specu-lation about faith and trust. That speculation was shot down the television tubes when we got to Uncle Thib's that evening. *The Ed Sullivan Show* was cancelled for a special weather report.

"The tropical storm has been upgraded to a hurricane, packing nine-ty-five mile an hour winds, and it hasn't changed its course. It is still going in a direct line toward the Cameron Parish coast," the weatherman said. "There is no cause for alarm at this time because hurricanes predictably veer off to the northeast. As far as the research that we have gathered, there has never been a hurricane that did not veer off its original course." The National Hurricane Center has named this hurricane, which is the first of the season, *Audrey*."

All the old folks who had gathered at Uncle Thib's bar still thought it was a lot of caca.

"My house survived the last few tropical storms, and I ain't going to leave her now. She'll stand up just fine," Mr. Babineaux said.

He took off his hat. His face was tanned from working in the sun on roofing and carpentry jobs, but his baldhead was white. His jaw was set with conviction. The younger folks twisted their lips in real serious thought and were not as easily convinced by the old folk's talk.

"They said it ain't going to make land fall until next weekend. We have some more time to watch it, and if it looks like it will be heading our way, me and mine are getting outta here," Potted Meat's dad said.

"I remember that 1940 storm that hit in August," Mr. Doguet said. "The tides were only about 4 feet but them rains caused *beaucoup* flooding and a lot of cattle got stranded. Lost many a head. Me, I can't wait till the last minute to hear from those weather fellows. I'm gonna move my herd on up the road toward Beauregard Parish, but I'm gonna need some help if any of you cowboys can see fit to give me a hand. I gotta few saddle horses if you don't have one of your own. I'd like to shoot for Tuesday morning."

"I'll be there with my chaps and spurs," Uncle Baby said, and few other Cajun cowboys volunteered.

"I can help," I said.

"Now, son," Mama began.

"He'll be a big help. Besides, many of those folks that live way out there don't have TVs or telephones. Boy can go by those places and warn them about the hurricane," Uncle Baby said.

It was settled. I was going on my first roundup. It wouldn't be like a roundup for branding, but for corralling the cattle to load them on a truck.

I was feeling full of myself. Potted Meat and I laughed at all the corny jokes about why hurricanes are named after women: because they were *her* icanes and not *him* icanes.

"Corn, corn, and double corn," Snukie said.

She didn't think it was funny at all because she gave me the cold shoulder. That's when I figured it was fitting that hurricanes be named after women.

"I think it should have been named Snukie," I said.

After the laughter died down, and Snukie tossed her hair and flounced off, I wondered why I had said that and realized that I didn't want Potted Meat to know that I liked his little sister. I wanted to run after Snukie to apologize, but I was afraid of the teasing I would get. I walked out of the bar by myself to wait for Mama and Papa. I was tired of all the talk and tired of the dilemmas. I stood on the porch with the bright lights bearing down on me, wishing for only starlight and decided to walk to the car. I sat on the bumper and felt the breeze in my face. I stared up into the night sky—then out at the dark, heaving Gulf. Fear squeezed my heart.

CHAPTER TWELVE

What was Gene Forrester thinking when he shook the branch that sent Finny falling to the ground and breaking his leg, his career, his life, and then in triumph, Gene jumped from the tree into the river below? What was this sense of freedom Gene felt? I took the clothespin off the page of John Knowles' short story *Phineas* that I had rigged up on the back of a chair so my hands would be free to shell peas. I preferred to read books that I could feel the hardcover. Books were the steering wheel, something solid that I could grip. Reading was the ride that took me into different worlds—the worlds of upper crust New England boarding schools of Finny and Gene that were so far away from the Cajun culture. When I first read the book, I didn't understand it, but when I was underwater drowning, my mind understood my fascination. I was nonchalant because I was no longer the center of the world; I understood myself. During my life, I pretended to be a "goodie-two-shoes," but in reality, I was a rebel. I had thought that Finny was the rebel, but no, it was "goodie-two-shoes" himself—Gene Forrester. Gene was tired of living up to someone else's expectations. He was tired of Finny's control. It was wartime, and this was Gene's war, so he eliminated the enemy.

I sighed and glanced around. The morning looked like it would be a scorcher because it was already hot out on the porch. I had hung a wet towel over the front porch window and put a fan behind it to blow through, so I could cool off a little. As much as I liked quiet, shelling peas was a boring chore, but I had it down: pop the top, pull the string, run your thumbnail under the peas, and toss the hull, again and again. It stained my fingers, the color of newspaper print, even though the color in the pea's name was purple, and it stuffed my thumbnail with pea pulp that bit into the quick.

Pooch snoozed at my feet and gradually became covered with pea hulls—a purple and black mountain peak of progress. Papa had left for the day, and I relaxed since I had read late into the night. Last night I had to turn the light out fast because Papa woke himself up snoring and bungled his way to the bathroom. He would be mad if he knew that I had been reading. The window fan whirred. Pooch sat up and shook the pea hulls off and slinked off the porch. Sitting in a cane bottom chair, I leaned forward on the front two legs and turned the page. I was in the tree with Finny and Gene: one daring, the other scared. Where did I fit in? Time stood still when I was suspended in the story. I didn't hear Papa walk up until he was on the steps. One quick kick at the chair legs, and I pitched headlong into my book. I fell face down on the porch in a rain of peas—the pan crashing down the steps.

"Pick 'em up," Papa said. "Don't let me catch you reading when you're supposed to be working. *L'oeuvre du paresseux*,"—work of the lazy.

"You pick them up," I shouted. I couldn't believe I was hearing my own voice. It was a reaction to being caught off guard.

Papa turned around with steam in his eyes. He came toward me and swung a left at me, but I was too quick for him and ducked.

"You sassy-mouthed little brat. You're not gonna talk to me like that."

"You're the one that knocked the peas over. I think that's your problem," I yelled.

He came at me again, and I slung the pan like a flying saucer and took off down the road but detoured to hide behind the garage and watch.

Papa slammed the front door and came back out with a hunk of cornbread and was gone as fast as he came like a storm that kicks up in the Gulf. I went back and picked up as many peas as I could find and finished shelling the last of them. I did it for Mama. Papa was a jerk. I even liked the thought that maybe the German soldier was my dad. I took the pan into the kitchen and rinsed the peas under the faucet, drained the pot and laid it on the counter. Out of the kitchen window, I watched Mama outside hanging clothes and diapers out to dry, her dark hair floating in the breeze. Bobby, who was supposed to be helping her, walked on his hands, a trick that Cracklin had taught him. What was so comical was that he had red and yellow zinnias in between his toes. He not only entertained Baby Faye but Mama as well. Bobby could get out of work faster than anyone I knew, and Mama would thank him for it. Baby Faye was propped up in her swing that Bobby and I had made from an old milk crate and hung it from the clothesline pole. She kicked and boxed her arms at Bobby's silliness. Satisfied that they would be occupied for a while, I took my book, went into the bedroom and crawled under the bed. I pushed the tin breadbox out of the way and settled in among the dusty fluffs of ghost turds. Reading under the bed made me sleepy, and I was soon out. Suddenly, I heard Mama's voice calling me. I had forgotten where I was and bumped my head on the slats when I scrambled to get out from under the bed.

"Walt," she called again.

I pulled myself out from under the bed and barreled into the kitchen like I had been awake all the time. Ghost turds fell from my hair. Mama gave me a second look but didn't say anything.

"Walt, will you take Nanan's wishbook back to her? Bobby borrowed it from her," she said.

"Yes Ma'am," I said.

It's funny how you don't realize the importance of a simple request at the time of asking. Life was made up of simple moments that lead to something bigger. Mama gave me a huge chance to make up with Snukie that I hadn't planned on. At the time, I just wanted to get out of the house. I pedaled my bike toward Nanan and Uncle Thib's house. I had clothes-pinned some of my baseball cards, mostly Al Worthington cards, to the spokes. It was supposed to make your bike sound like a motorcycle, but the wind picked up a bit, and I couldn't hear the flutter of the cards. Some of the cards came off and sailed across the field into Potted Meat's yard. I jumped off my bike and let it fall in the dirt. I chased the baseball cards across the field, grabbing at the ones that were caught in the tall grass. Pooch tagged along at my heels as usual. I stumbled around in the field kicking clumps of Johnson grass in search of my cards. When I looked up, it was like stepping from the shadows of a forest into a clearing lit up with slanted light. The sun slid down the gilded edge of a book, like Uncle Baby's copy of *Romeo and Juliet*.

Snukie stood at the clothesline in her backyard surrounded by colorful laundry and unpinned each piece and put it in a wicker basket. I came to a screeching halt to talk to her.

"Need some help?" I asked. I had surprised her because she got all flustered, especially when the wind wrapped a sheet around her. She grabbed the sheet and looked at me sheepishly. Her usual plaits were unwoven—a wild tangle whipped around her face.

"Sure," she said.

"My baseball cards flew off the spokes of my bike, and I lost my favorite Ted Williams card," I said.

"I'm sorry. If I find it, I will save it for you."

The sheets and clothes flapped away the silence. We stood facing each other with the sheet between us. Somehow, it made it easier for me to talk to her. The wind died down. I stared and picked at the frayed edges of the sheet.

"Look, Snukie, I'm sorry," I said, "that the hurricane should have been named after you. I was acting like a smart-aleck in front of the guys."

I looked down at my bare feet. I could see Snukie's bare feet from underneath the sheet. She stood still and stopped taking the clothespins off the line. The wind breezed through the sheets again. My heart was pounding so hard that I thought she could hear it over the noise of the flapping.

"I guess I, uh, just didn't want the guys to know that I liked you. You know how they would tease me."

There I said it. It was hard and easy and scary and exciting all at once. I caught my breath.

"What did you say?" she said.

"I said that I didn't want the guys to know that I liked you. They would tease me, you know," I said a little louder.

Snukie took the clothespin off the sheet and let one end drop between us. She stared at me. Her cheeks flushed pink and her eyes were greener than I had ever noticed before. She grinned a little mysterious smile and lifted up my baseball card.

"I found your Ted Williams card," she said and took off running across the yard.

I took off after her with Pooch at my heels, loving the chase. I tackled her under the mimosa tree and tried to wrestle the card from behind her back. We rolled around in the mimosa blossoms until I finally yanked the card from her hand. We stretched out on our backs laughing and trying to catch our breaths. At the same time as if on cue, we rolled onto our sides facing each other. The smiles shrunk from our faces, and we stared into each other's eyes. For a brief moment, I felt the magnetic pull of gravity. She was the earth, and I was falling toward her, falling into the green earth of her eyes. I picked a mimosa blossom from her hair.

"Snukie," her mom called, "get the clothes in before it rains."

We scrambled up self-consciously and headed back to the clothesline. Mrs. Miller stood in the doorway and held the screen door open with her body while she cleaned her glasses. Her silhouette was shapely; although, she was a little top heavy compared to her narrow waist and rounded hips. Snukie looked like her mother in the face with her high cheekbones and green eyes.

"Okay, Mom," Snukie called back. "My mom is blind as a bat without her glasses," she said.

Snukie unpinned the blue jeans and t-shirts from the clothesline, folded them, and put them in the basket. I helped too until I realized, heavens to Betsy, that I was taking down Snukie's underwear. In my discomfort, I dropped her bra. Pooch, thinking it was a game, grabbed it in his mouth and took off. Snukie threw the clothes she had in her hands into the basket, and we both ran after Pooch.

"Pooch," I called. "Come here boy."

I caught up with him and grabbed the end of the bra that dangled from his mouth, and we began a tug-of-war with it. Pooch wouldn't let go.

"Let go, Pooch," I said. I finally had to pry Pooch's mouth open to get the durn thing out. I was so embarrassed that I cast my eyes down and handed it back to Snukie. It was stretched and drenched with dog drool. I took a quick peek at her face; Her cheeks burned a bright red. She was as embarrassed as I was.

"That's my mom's," she said, and she whisked it out of my hands. Snukie turned and ran back to the clothesline.

"I'll see you later," I called. I turned toward the road and busted into laugher all the way back to my bike. Her mom's? I questioned. Her mom's *grand tétons* in that bra? I gestured about the size of Mrs. Miller's melons with my hands. I shook my head and got on my bike and chuckled all the way to Nanan's.

Éli trudged up the clamshell road. His gait was cautious because he carried his violin case in one hand and a basket in the other and he kept looking from one to the other. He wore his black jacket even though it was blistering hot. He was on a mission. Anytime he went anywhere, he wore his jacket. There was no changing his mind, and I had come to accept him just as he was. I had returned his violin to him so he could practice. Éli carried his violin to give back to me for safekeeping. I watched him slowly make his way to our gate. I wondered how Nanan and Parrain would get Éli in the cab of the truck in case they had to boogie out of there because of the hurricane which was still heading straight for Cameron. Éli could be very hard to deal with, especially when he threw his tantrums, but they might get him to ride in the bed of the truck.

Éli put the basket of eggs down on the ground so slow and easy and shook the gate handle until it opened. He let go of the gate to pick up the basket, and it closed on him. He did the same thing again. He would never put his violin on the ground, so he stood there puzzled. He was unaware that I was sitting on the porch and watching him. He knocked on the gate like he would knock on a door. I finally got up and held the gate for him. He got excited, stammered, and shifted from foot to foot. His mouth couldn't form the words fast enough to keep up with his brain.

"Boy Oh Boy," he said.

He had heard Uncle Baby call me that and it stuck. My new nickname was "Boy Oh Boy."

"Hi, Éli."

"I got eggs. Mama Nan say I got eggs."

"Come on in. Mama will like them."

He followed me up the steps holding the basket so gently. He put them on the table and blew out a big sigh.

"Thank you, Éli," Mama said while taking her hands out of the dishwater and drying them on her apron. "How about some Kool Aid, cher? It's so hot out there."

Éli's face lit up, and Mama poured him a glass. He drank it down with total concentration, looked up, and grinned with a Kool Aid mustache.

"Play something for us," Mama said.

Éli opened his case and tightened the bow. He put his violin to his chin and plucked the strings like a chicken clucking. Then he sawed a skittering, frightful piece.

"Chickens gone," he said.

"The chickens got out of their cage?" I said.

"Chickens fly away. Scared."

He sat down in the kitchen chair but jumped up immediately when Papa opened the screen door and came in. When Éli got nervous, he swayed back and forth. His feet stuttered and his mouth stammered.

"Mm Mister Mm Man."

"How ya doin, Fiddle Boy?" Play us a weather report. You know, is it gonna rain or what?" Papa said.

Éli began a low growling note that ended up like thunder. Papa got mad.

"That's hogwash," Papa said, flinging his hands in a get-out-of-here motion and accidentally knocked the violin out of Éli's hand.

The ancient Stradivarius violin flew in the air in slow motion, rising to its height and tumbling down, down, and there I was diving for it, arms stretched, hands reaching for it, and I landed on my stomach on the hard floor. I was Mickey Mantle making the game saving catch for the New York Yankees against the Brooklyn Dodgers to win the World Series. The violin fell into my hands. The crowd roared. I got up from the floor with the violin in hand. Éli held his face and rocked and screamed. I forgot and touched him on the shoulder. He screamed louder. Another thing about Éli was that he didn't like to be touched.

"Shut him up," Papa said.

"It's okay, Éli," I said. "I caught it. It's not broken. Look. It's okay."

Éli stopped screaming and took his violin.

"Boy, get him the hell out of here," Papa said. "What a retard," he said and started to leave the room when Mama spoke up.

"Now Walt, be kind. Thank God IQ is not a requirement to get into heaven, or a bunch of us would be in trouble."

"Come on, Éli. Let's walk on the beach," I said.

He followed me out the door and stepped slowly down the steps with both feet on each step. We walked through the field toward the beach where there was always a breeze. I looked out at all of that water and felt very small—very small. Éli clapped his hands at the seagulls that gathered on the beach, and in his child-like delight, he tried to catch one.

"What would you do if you caught one, Éli?"

"Listen," he said.

I picked up a conch shell and wiped the sand off.

"Listen to this, Éli."

I put it to my ear to show him what I wanted him to do and handed it to him. Éli put it to his ear and his eyes jumped and widened.

"Says water comes. Big water comes."

His answer haunted me. I thought about Éli's comment while we walked to Uncle Thib's bar. The bar called us to come in and sit for a while, drop your cares at the door, sit on your sorrow, and pass a good time. The bar was a place of belonging and friendship not only for the locals, but for the men working the oil patch who were a long way from home. If the walls could speak, they would tell the sorrow of old Dudley Frugé whose wife left him for another man while Dudley worked the "two-weeks on" shift on the oilrig. It would tell of the lost careers from injuries in the oilfield—like Papa's. It would tell of all the broken hearts disguised by macho bravado, and it would speak of Éli's home.

Éli sighed and sat down on the top step. He forgot about what he had said about the water. He opened the case and lifted the violin out and pointed to the *f* holes—the scrolled opening on the front of the violin. He tightened his bow and drew it across the strings. He held the back of the violin next to my cheek and drew the bow across the strings again. I felt the vibration. Éli laid the violin down and placed my hands over the *f* holes. He drew the bow across the strings, and it made a dead, scratching sound. Éli looked at me.

"I get it. The body of the violin has to be open so that the music can vibrate," I said.

"Maybe," Éli said and motions toward his heart.

"Heart open, music happens," I said. Éli shook his head 'yes.'

I nodded, but I didn't get his point then. I wasn't sure if he was being philosophical or just plain stupid. He positioned the violin under his chin and played his own composition which was whatever he felt at that moment. It was soft, dreamy music that made me want to cry for no reason. When he finished playing, he sat and stared into the horizon. A butterfly flew toward us and rested on the end of the bow. Éli sat so still as if he understood the fragility and the briefness of life, music, and the butterfly. We watched the butterfly lift off to flutter into the blue sky. When we could no longer see the butterfly, I turned to him.

"I'm going to take your violin back home, just to be safe, okay?" I said.

Éli nodded. I was afraid those men might come back to steal the violin because the hurricane was still headed our way. We stood and went into the bar. When my eyes adjusted to the darkness, I noticed the "Lake Charles American Press" lying on the bar where Uncle Thib had been reading. The headlines reared up from the page in bold print, HURRICANE AUDREY AIMS FULL FURY AT LAKE CHARLES AND COAST. WINDS ARE PREDICTED TO HIT FRIDAY ON PRESENT COURSE. Another article headlined LAKE CHARLES OFFICIALS, CIVIL DEFENSE BRACE FOR STORM. LARRY STEPHENSON, DIRECTOR OF CALCASIEU PARISH CIVIL DEFENSE, PLACES MOBILE UNITS ON STANDBY. Knowing that Lake Charles was just north of Cameron, I knew we would take the brunt of the storm. I took Éli's prediction of a storm with big water with a grain of salt when Bobby was around, but secretly I was afraid.

CHAPTER THIRTEEN

I thought it was ironic when I saw myself galloping Belle, a sleek black mare, her nose stretching through the early morning mist that hadn't yet burned off. I was on a mission to warn old man Theriot about Hurricane Audrey. It was ironic because in my dream, I was the one drowning in the tidal surge. I was riding swiftly on a dirt road, puffs of dust kicked up, and I was in perfect rhythm, loving the feeling of floating. Belle's hoofs clicked softly on the grass down the center of a rutted road. I had a sense of mission, and I understood Éli's mission to warn people about the weather.

Uncle Baby had picked me up early, and we had headed for Mr. Doguet's place to help him round up the cattle. Mama had wrapped some sandwiches in waxed paper and put it in a paper sack for our lunch. I was excited about being on my first roundup and an added bonus was that I wasn't around the house so Papa couldn't pick on me. The cowboys were unloading their horses, getting their tack and saddling up when we pulled in. They had on their chaps and spurs, and a few stood at the corral gate waiting to shove off, their bottom lips puffed out from a wad of chewing tobacco. I had tried chewing tobacco before, but I got so dizzy and sick that it cured my curiosity. I had on my boots, Levi's, a bandana around my neck and of course, my straw cowboy hat. I felt every bit of a cowboy. Those saltgrass cowboys knew all the brands and who the cattle belonged to because much of the cattle roamed on free range. Most people who lived in the country wrapped barbwire around their mailboxes and any young trees that they didn't want trampled. For the most part, Mr. Doguet's cattle were within barbed wire fences. The horses were in the corral, and Uncle Baby and I headed straight away to saddle them up. I saddled Belle because I had ridden her before, and she knew me. Uncle Baby saddled a dun-colored horse named Slick. Slick was a little testier, but Uncle Baby could handle him. When we were ready to move out, Mr. Doguet told me to ride to the old Theriot place and tell them about the hurricane.

"I'm for sure they don't have one of those telephones, and I know darn well that they ain't got a TV. They just read the sky like the old timers used to do," Mr. Doguet said.

"Okay," I said. "Where will you be when I get back?"

"We'll most probably still be in the North pasture."

I took off, feeling important that I was on a mission to save someone's life. Kind of like Paul Revere when he told everyone that the British were coming. I reined Belle in when we entered the dim light of a dense copse of oak trees. The canopy of the trees made a tunnel that I followed through to the opening. The light splattered the road while my eyes adjusted to the dark. Two squirrels chased each other up a tree and barked at me for the disturbance. Old man Theriot's place was a shack of a house, its shingles lifted up and peeled back. Knotted tree limbs held up the porch and vertical slats held together the history of that house. Behind the house, an old barn listed to the right, its tin roof rusted to a coppery brown. An old plow stood off to the side choked with weeds, as if the earth was going to claim anything that was stationary. I could see old man Theriot's traps leaning against the barn. Muskrat and nutria pelts were nailed stretched out and drying on the barn walls. On the other side of the barn was a worn path to the outhouse.

When I entered the clearing of the house, the first set of dogs came toward me barking. The dogs circled us, and Belle danced around and kicked at them when they nipped at her hoofs and tail. A big old hound dog that had been stretched out on the front porch stood up and bellowed a deep, hoarse bark and wouldn't let me get any closer. I hollered for Mr. Theriot.

I tossed half of my sandwich way off past the porch and the dogs took off fighting over it. An old lady as round as the wringer washing machine that stood on the front porch came to the door. Her gray hair was slicked back, tight behind her ears, and tied in a knot at the nape of her neck. She gestured for me to wait one moment, probably because her English wasn't that good. She went back in and got the old man. Mr. Theriot came out on the porch pulling at his suspenders. His skin was crusty as dried pine bark and his ears were the size of five-inch clamshells attached to each side of his head.

"What's all this racket," he said.

"Mr. Theriot, there's a hurricane heading our way. Mr. Doguet told me to come tell y'all to head for higher ground and take care of your animals. They say it's gonna be a bad one."

"Me, I already knowed we were going to be in for bad weather. I heard the deer and animals tromping through here during the night. Even the turtles, they all been moving to higher ground. The birds been flying low too."

Mrs. Theriot said something in French and pointed to the cat on the windowsill.

"My old lady says that her cat has been washing behind her ears. She does that every time it rains."

It's gonna be worse than you think. Its name is "Audrey" and it's supposed to make landfall on Friday. You better get outta here," I said. "The weatherman says it's heading straight for us. Hundred mile an hour winds or better."

"I'll study on it, son. I'm kind of like a captain with his ship, you know. You see over there," Mr. Theriot said pointing to an area with an old iron fence.

Five cross-shaped grave markers were lined up like sentinels guarding the graves.

"Those are my people and their ghosts walk all around here. I ain't gonna leave 'em."

"Don't mean any disrespect to your people, but Mr. Theriot, you might be joining them if you don't get out of here. Ghost or no ghost, you take the Mrs. and y'all head on to Lake Charles to one of them shelters," I yelled and turned Belle back toward Mr. Doguet's fields. I rode the dark horse out of the copse of trees and looked back to see Mr. Theriot watching me until I was out of sight like I was a phantom that had come and gone.

CHAPTER FOURTEEN

I remembered the morning before the storm hit. Papa had beaten me for the umpteenth time. It wasn't the usual beating, but a pitch of cold iron, heavy with oppression, heavy with a life of unfulfilled expectations. I knew he really didn't want to kill me, but he wanted my spirit to conform and grow in the hothouse of his expectations. Nature and the world around me filled me with respect. I was rabid for learning. Curiosity ran crazy in my mind, getting me into more trouble than I dared to tell. I felt older than the years of my body. Maybe he was threatened by my mind, or he didn't like the fact that I was kind of puny. Maybe that was it—Papa didn't like small even though I surpassed the growth of the pole beans and rivaled the corn stalks for my age. Maybe, he wanted to throw me back the way he tossed the small fish back into the Gulf of Mexico when they got caught in his nets. I tried hard to convince myself of the many reasons that I concocted for Papa's meanness toward me, only ending the onslaught of thoughts by facing the blunt truth. Papa knew.

That morning thunder rumbled me awake from a dream where I rode a westbound train. The wind from a small window whipped my face, wakening my senses to the freshness of dry air and the smell of mesquite trees. The scenery fleeted across my eyes, the sky dipping in the valleys between mountains. I was on a train hurtling toward the freedom to be me. I opened my eyes to a gray day, and I looked around my cubbyhole. When the wind gusted, the bedroom curtains flapped like they wanted to take off and fly with the fine mist that came through the window screen. I got up and fought the curtain in my face until I lowered the window. I smelled the salt in the air. The wind blew in from the Gulf. I strained my eyes to determine the weather, but the Gulf and sky were melded in in the dark, predawn colors. I respected deep water, because when the forces were right, the Gulf could rise from its boundaries and baptize your world and sweep it clean.

I got back in bed and glanced at Bobby who slept snail-like against the wall. Bobby liked the steady, strength of the wall against his back, an anchor for his nighttime insecurities. That wasn't for me. I never wanted to be boxed in a corner, confined, or without an alternative plan—always needing an escape route. I wanted the freedom to fall out of the bed if I felt like it, and fall out of the bed I did when the scent of dark roast coffee lured me to put one foot in front of the other. I trudged into the kitchen in my underwear, still drugged by that dream of going west and being a hero. Mama wore her frayed house robe, her dark hair still in pin curls, and Papa was in his muscleman tee shirt. They sat at the old cypress table with a red oilcloth covering and listened to the radio. Papa clenched his unshaven jaw and held his cup of coffee with both hands. Oil from working on engines and motors of every kind etched a dark line under his fingernails. Mama's face was scrunched, and her bottom lip was a red gash from biting it. The air was filled with tension, but I wasn't the cause of it. Thank God. Papa hadn't said anything mean to me. For that matter, he hadn't even realized that I had come into the room, and I was glad for that. I preferred to be invisible—just like Papa wanted I supposed, so I dilly-dallied around the room pretending that no one could see me. I filled a cup with half coffee and half cream, a couple spoonfuls of sugar and I took a sip of just right. I lowered myself into a kitchen chair and focused my attention on waves of static interspersed by a baritone voice from the radio.

"Early this morning the Lake Charles Weather Bureau announced that Southwest Louisiana from the Sabine River to the west end of Vermillion Bay is under a hurricane watch; however, the New Orleans Weather Bureau has posted hurricane warnings for the entire Louisiana coast. The hurricane is reported to be moving northward at about seven to ten miles per hour with winds of 100 miles per hour heading directly for Cameron, but a slow turn toward the northeast is expected. It should hit landfall in the early hours of Friday morning. Those in low lying areas should move to higher ground."

"Mary Effie, I think we should plan to get out of here tonight or at the very latest on Thursday morning. I'll borrow Thib's truck and pick up some lumber to board up the windows," Papa said.

"Maybe you should gas the car up first. Everybody will be filling up. Don't want the station to run out before we've tanked up, or we will be stuck for sure."

"Yeah. You're right about that."

"I'll start packing." I could tell Mama's mind was racing. "What about the dog?" she said.

I knew I couldn't voice my opinion because I would have my face rearranged by Papa's flying backhand. My mind screamed, the dog! The dog is a golden retriever and he has a name! His name is POOCH! He's as much a part of me as my heart. You can't leave him!

"I don't know if the people at the shelter will let us bring a dog in," Papa said.

I held my breath and thought of running down the highway toward Lake Charles with Pooch, or standing up to Papa and saying, 'If he stays, I stay.'

"Well," Papa continued, "if worse comes to worse, he can stay in the car."

The tightness in my chest eased, and I exhaled. Papa paused and rubbed the frown lines on his forehead. He turned his attention to me, which was always a scary proposition.

"Boy, I've been out in the garage looking for my pulleys and hammer. Have you seen them? I want to pull the motor out of the old truck and suspend it from the ceiling so that in case there is any flooding, it won't get ruined. I think I can fix it if I can get the parts."

Papa gestured pulling the motor up with his hands. He lived in the world of moving hands when he worked or when he spoke—hands calloused from hauling shrimp nets. You talk about suspended! My breath was suspended when I thought of the hammer and pulleys getting wet where we left them. Bobby forgot to put them away. I took a sniveling breath.

"I think they're under the oak tree," I said.

"Outside? Outside getting wet! You didn't save my tools?" Papa said. "Do you think money grows on trees, and we can afford to buy new ones? Go find them."

He stood and in two big strides crossed the linoleum floor to the washroom. He opened the backdoor. Cramming his old, straw hat on his head, he loped down the back steps with me following several paces behind him in nothing but my underwear. I was too scared to take the time to put on my clothes because where Papa was concerned there was no time but his time.

The huge, live oak tree wore a mantilla of moss and muscadine vines— the perfect hideout for our fort. Papa marched a hundred paces across the yard with me trotting behind him. He stopped abruptly when we got to the tree. Papa was stunned.

"The stupidest thing I ever saw. A fish out of water. How in," he began.

He turned to me with the rain dripping off the brim of his hat.

"Where did you get that boat?"

I rounded my shoulders and huddled. Some wild west hero I was! The rain dripped off my head. My voice quavered, and I relived the last time Papa had seen the fort and shot a hole in it during one of his drunken tirades. My mind scrambled for an acceptable answer.

"We found it in the marsh. It was all muddied up, and you shot a hole in it in case you forgot. I figured that it had washed up in the last storm. Didn't think it was good for anything. Thought it would make a great fort.

I knew Papa had been too drunk to remember when he shot at me. Papa eyed his pulleys and hammer lying in the mud under the tree. His face was a study of rising rage, cresting to the breaking point.

"Ain't this a fine howdy do. You left my tools out in this weather so you could put a boat in a tree? Are you crazy? You don't have any idea of what things cost, and you don't know your boundaries. What's mine is mine and you keep your grimy paws off my stuff!"

He stormed over to the tools and glared at me.

"You good-for-nothing little brat. You don't have a lick of sense. The next time you leave my tools out will be the last time. I'll, I'll," his voice rose in frustration.

He picked up the heavy iron pulley, and in a rage, threw it at me. I turned my back just in time, and it hit me under my left shoulder blade with a serious thud, impacting me so powerfully that it knocked me off my feet. It knocked the breath right out of me. When the awareness registered in my brain, pain ripped through my body. I lay face down in the mud for what seemed an eternity until my lungs decided to inflate again, and I inhaled a mouthful of mud and dank, leaf mold. I rolled over on my back. I heard Papa's footsteps approach and stop next to me. He stooped down.

"Are you okay, son? Lost my temper; didn't mean to hit you."

I opened my eyes and nodded that I was okay, but I really wasn't. He put his hand out to help me up, but I stared at his extended hand and rolled back over face down in the mud. Papa picked up the two pulleys and the hammer from the mud, and without a second thought, he turned and headed in the direction of the garage.

My devoted Pooch, the one that cared about me more than anyone in the world, crawled to me and snuggled, licking my face, resting his head on the back of my neck, trying to console me with his whimpers and desperately wanting me to show some sign that I was not badly hurt. The rain cooled my skin and coursed over the welt that I felt rise on my back. I stayed there for a while stretched out, racked with sobs. When I was twelve, I don't remember if I really understood what I was crying about, but now as an adult, I understand. I didn't cry because of the stabbing pain in my back, nor did I cry because my feelings were hurt. I cried for all the sons that didn't measure up. I cried for the plight of all orphans and fatherless children whether their fathers were present or not. I cried for all the judgments meted out on defenseless people that said they were worthless. I cried great tears into the earth that I embraced. I emptied the tears of my soul. I closed my eyes and heard the lonely strains of Éli's violin wishing the morning sun well, grateful for the rising.

CHAPTER FIFTEEN

Writing my memoir was purgative. At last I could tell the truth in spite of someone thinking I was crazy. Some events were blurred, but the memories of drowning and the beautiful lady who called me to come up were crisp and clear. I remember floating over my body that was stretched out face down in the water. When I felt myself beginning to lose consciousness, I remembered another time that I lay stretched out with my face in the mud. It felt like an eternity. I was amazed that I had been so determined to get the boat in the tree. My downfall was being blinded by my stubbornness to my agenda. Pain was the payback.

Bobby had forgotten to put the hammer and pulleys back in the garage, and I was paying the price. I couldn't blame Bobby because I had forgotten to ask him about it. Pooch whimpered. I could hear Papa hammering in the garage. With every clang of the hammer, pain hammered my back. The pain rose to my head, screaming and pulsating. I wondered if my ribs were broken. I turned over in the cool mud and stared up into the sky. Pooch cradled his head under my chin, and I lay still, watching the terns fly north with their tail feathers split from the wind, a sure sign that a storm was brewing. I wanted to fly away with them, rising and floating on the wind current, and break free from this caged life. I knew Papa was leaving for Uncle Thib's when I heard the Rambler's starter grind before the motor turned over.

I stumbled back toward the house. I felt so bad that it didn't faze me that several tub loads of crawfish were crawling across the road, heading for higher ground. What easy pickings for a crawfish boil, but pain spoke louder than the pleasure of food. Those creatures were smarter than people gave them credit for. They knew something big hulked on the other side of the horizon. I couldn't think about the storm or anything but the pain in my back. I imagined that it was swelling to the size of a purple eggplant. When I got to the house, I groped up the back steps, through the back door to the kitchen and fell across the blood-red oilcloth covered table. Utensils clattered to the floor. Mama screamed. She immediately put ice in a towel and put it on my back.

Later that afternoon, I fell asleep to the sounds of the radio barking warnings of the hurricane. It had not changed its course which wasn't normal for hurricanes. It was still expected to hit land on Friday, but the announcer said not to be alarmed yet, but prepare to get out and to keep a wary eye on it. Most of all, the sound I heard before I fell asleep was Mama chewing Papa out in French. I couldn't understand everything she said, but I knew she was talking about me and that Papa could have killed me. My body begged for sleep, but my mind wouldn't let it. Finally, my body won. I faded off to the sounds of gusting rain like someone pelting the window with seeds. I dreamed that voracious, eggplant vines grew by the minute covering the house and sprouted into purple, bruise colored gourds that covered the roof. In my dream, Papa was caught up in the vines. They wrapped around his throat and strangled him. His head turned a dark purple. I thrashed through the vines trying to get to him. I kept screaming "Papa" until I woke up to the sound of hammering. The hammering pain in my back quieted down to a dull ache.

I got out of bed and crept to the window. Papa nailed plywood boards to the outside of the windows while Bobby handed the nails to him. It was so dark outside that I was confused as to what day and what time it was. I shuffled into the kitchen where Mama was bent over cleaning out the refrigerator. She stood up and checked on the gumbo warming on the stove. The hands of the clock on the wall pointed to 11:30.

"Why are you making gumbo this late at night?" I asked.

She turned around and smiled. She glanced at the clock.

"Well you finally woke up sleepy head. It's 11:30 on Wednesday morning. How do you feel?"

Never in my life, except when I was a baby, did I sleep past 7:00 a.m.

"I'm sore but I'm okay."

From the kitchen window, past the windowsill lined with Mama's bottles collected from beach combing, I saw that it was still drizzling.

"I guess the sun forgot to rise this morning," I said. Then I remembered.

"Papa is going to kill me for sleeping late."

"No, he's not. He's the one who let you sleep. He said you needed to sleep in order to get better. He and Bobby are boarding up the windows. We are loading up the car and plan on leaving this evening or first thing tomorrow morning."

She turned back to the pot and ladled gumbo into my bowl, spilling it on the top of the stove. I noticed that her hands trembled, and I realized for the first time how scared she was. The screen door slammed when Papa walked in wearing his overalls and wiping his hands on a handkerchief.

"Boy, how's your back?" he said like hitting me with a pulley was an everyday occurrence.

"Okay."

I glanced at him with an effort to be pleasant, but I still felt miffed. Papa went to the sink and lathered his hands.

"Walter, do you think we ought to leave tonight?" Mama said. "The Millers are leaving in a few minutes—around noon. Their car is packed to the gills. She said that they have kin folk in Lake Charles that they are staying with."

Papa was wolfing down a cup of gumbo.

"We can't leave until I fix that flat tire," Papa said in between bites. "I must have picked up a nail when I followed Thib to the lumber yard. Bobby, you gotta give me a hand with that tire."

Later that afternoon, the barking of the radio died down to static and finally went completely out. I wished it would all end with the death of the radio. We lost electricity that evening and ate supper by the spooky light of weeping candles.

Papa was the head of the household and Mama kow-towed to him, even when her intuition told her otherwise. Mama asked Papa again if he thought we should leave now.

"You know when we get to the shelter, we will be sleeping on army cots," he said. I'm tired; I think a good night's rest in my own bed would help."

"I suppose it would be better for Baby Faye," she said.

"Bobby and Boy, I want you to lay your shoes and clothes out. We're leaving at first light," Papa said.

Bobby and I carried a candle to our bedroom and groped around finding our things. We laid everything out just like Papa said, and then crawled into our beds. I stared at the ceiling and the movement of the shadows the candle made. Bobby asked in the tiniest voice that came from somewhere far away.

"Are you scared?"

I thought for a sliver of a moment that felt like an eternity. Should I be strong, or should I be honest? Which was best for Bobby? I decided that being honest was better than lying. It was better than staring at your hands like Gammy with the Dress and Auntie La La and believing that you weren't old.

In a low voice that came from a well deep inside of me, I answered, "Yeah."

Bobby choked on a sob that turned into a whimper.

"I wish we could have left today."

"Me too. It's okay to cry, but we will be out of here before the hurricane hits."

I prayed that I would be right. I wiped my eyes and stared at the aged water stains on the ceiling. I began praying the rosary out loud and counted each decade on my fingers. Bobby joined in, and we kept our eyes on the picture of the Virgin Mary, Queen of the Angels with her dark hair peeking out from under her veil, holding baby Jesus in her arms. It had hung on the wall opposite the foot of our beds for as long as I could remember, but I had become blinded by its familiarity. I thought it was strange that I questioned my beliefs when everything was fine, but the minute I got into trouble, I started praying like crazy.

"Forgive me, Lord. Help my unbelief," I whispered before I fell asleep.

CHAPTER SIXTEEN

I t was early Thursday, before the sun, before the birds, before the hunger. I woke up to the sound of water sloshing under the house. I opened my eyes in the dark room and wondered what time it was. A strip of gray light shone through a crack between the boards that covered the window. I remembered my fear and the storm. I strained to listen.

"Bobby, wake up."

I got out of bed and nudged him.

"Bobby."

"What?" he said struggling to open his eyes.

"Listen!"

Bobby sat up in bed.

"Sounds like water," he said, and we both scrambled out of bed and peeked through the crack of the window.

"What's Pooch doing on top of the car?" he said.

I squinted through the opening. Bobby was right; Pooch was perched on top of the car. We ran into the front room and opened the door. I stepped out on the porch and couldn't believe my eyes. Muddy water lapped the top step of the house. I realized that yesterday, the wind wasn't any gustier than an afternoon shower which gave us a false sense of security.

All of us had thought that we had more time, but we had not counted on the water rising so high and so quickly. It was the thief in the night that crept in and stole our escape route. It was too late to leave by car. I wished I hadn't put the boat in the tree. I berated myself. My heart wrenched at my stupid decisions.

"Papa! Mama!" Bobby screamed. "Pooch is on the car, and it's floating down the street!"

It was heading straight for the oak trees where it would surely crash. Oh, Mon Dieu, help poor Pooch. I heard Papa coming up behind me. Papa stepped out on the porch and looked around. There was water everywhere.

"Holy smoke! Look at all this water," Papa said.

Mama, carrying Baby Faye, followed Papa out of the door. She screamed when she saw the water. Baby Faye wailed, so Mama went back inside to hush her and stood at the door.

"Mon Dieu, Mon Dieu. What are we going to do, Walter?" she said over and over.

The wind died down momentarily, and each of us stood in silence.

"Listen," Papa said.

From a distance, we heard Éli's violin. He was playing the first piece he had ever played for us on the porch of Uncle Thib's bar. It was the swan song that I had figured was for his mother. From the other end of the porch, I saw Éli dressed in his black jacket, standing on the roof of Uncle Thib's bar trying to change the weather. We listened in stunned silence until the wind gusted and beat the vines against the house. Éli's music was lost to our ears.

"Listen to that crazy son-of-a-gun," Papa said. "He doesn't have a lick of sense. Not even enough to come in from the rain—a hurricane at that. I hope Thib can get him off the roof."

"He won't listen to Uncle Thib," I said. "I can get him down."

"The wind is picking up. Unless you have a bull horn, I don't know how your voice could reach him," Papa said. We all fell silent thinking of what to do next.

"We could try to walk to the courthouse. I could get the rope from the garage and tie it around everyone's waist," Papa said.

My heart sank at the thought of my bad choices.

"Papa," I said quietly. "The rope is in the oak tree."

Mama came back out on the porch, and we all stared in disbelief. Papa's silence was worse than any beating he had ever given me. We were not supposed to die like this. I felt the drowning sensation of knowing that we were stranded in high water, and the hurricane had yet to come ashore. Water was everywhere. You couldn't tell where the beginning of the Gulf was, or where the land ended. The houses and buildings were the only landmarks that gave you a sense of direction. The water lapped at my feet as if it were a creature that would not be satiated until I was devoured. I had never been in a hurricane and didn't know what to expect, but I knew we were in big trouble. We were doomed.

"We've got to try to make it to the courthouse before the hurricane hits land because it's only going to get worse," Papa said. "Boy, help your Mama with Baby Faye. Bobby, get on my back."

We were still in our nightclothes, but we listened to Papa. We had to leave now. It was our only chance. I stepped down the porch steps and into the water. When I stepped off the last step, the water rose to my waist, sending a chill up my spine. We waded straight down from the porch toward the road where the water came up to my chest. It was hard to tell where the deep water of the ditch was. I knew how the blind felt with their groping steps. Baby Faye wailed the cry of the inconsolable, crying the way we all wanted to cry, but it would not have changed anything. Mama screamed when a water moccasin swam by. It was scared too. We managed to walk a hundred yards or so down the road when a strong current knocked me down. I pawed through the water and finally regained my footing. The pain in my back pulsated, but I ignored it. I stepped toward Mama to help her get her balance. Her long nightgown bound her legs and made it difficult for her to walk. We braced ourselves against each other and the current. We looked wildly about and surveyed the situation. Papa and Bobby were ahead of us. In spite of his bum leg, Papa was resisting the current. I saw the courthouse in the distance, but Mama and I knew that we would never make it. Farther up the road, I saw some men, I couldn't tell who they were, making a human chain and catching people that were swept away by the current.

"Papa," I screamed. "We can't make it." Papa turned back toward us.

"I have an idea," he said. "Go back to the house."

We waded back to the house where the current wasn't as strong. Papa and I got to the front porch, and he bolted through the door.

"Bobby and Boy strip the sheets off the beds," he said.

Papa began tearing twenty-four-inch-wide strips of sheet, twisted and tied them together to make a long rope. He took a wide piece and tied Baby Faye to Mama. Another strip he tied to Bobby's wrist and the other end to his own. He tied the cloth rope around his waist and then to Mama and me. I brought up the rear when we stepped off the porch into the water. The water was too deep for Bobby, so he got on Papa's back. We forged our way back to the road and step by step toward the safety of the concrete courthouse. We were making progress and hope began to rise in my mind. The sheets, tied like a rope, helped to steady us, but when one went down it had a domino effect. We all went down. We got up and tried again. Step by step, slowly but surely; then Mama slipped and fell in the water. I tried to stay upright but couldn't manage with the extra weight of Mama pulling me down. I came scrambling up spitting out dirty saltwater. Papa and Bobby fell down too. Thankfully the strip of sheet that bound Papa's wrist to Bobby's saved him from being swept away. Papa managed to get back up. We all regained our balance and managed to stand huddled together looking like drowned rats. Mama had a clutch hold on Baby Faye, who was also wet. Water dripped off Faye's hair and down over her red, balled-up face. Her screams were lost in the rush of water and wind.

I looked back toward Uncle Thib's bar. Éli still stood on top of the roof, and from the looks of things, he had no intentions of coming down. His black coat flapped in the wind. His violin was under his chin and his bow arm moved up and down. Uncle Baby stood in a boat under the flagpole with his hands cupped around his mouth. He called to Éli to come down, but Éli would not turn around. Although, I couldn't hear him, I could see Uncle Baby calling to him. Uncle Baby pulled out a pistol and fired it into the gray sky to get Éli's attention. He didn't flinch. He continued to play his violin. The flag snapped in the wind. Uncle Baby set to work lowering the flag. He unhooked it and slung it around his neck while he brought the rope down. He tied a life preserver to the rope and slung it on the roof at Éli's feet. Éli was oblivious. He had sealed his fate. The wind blew the life preserver off the roof, and Uncle Baby reeled it in. When Uncle Baby turned around, Mama and Papa and all of us waved our arms and screamed like madmen.

"Édmond!" Papa yelled into the wind.

"Uncle Baby!" Bobby and I chorused.

Uncle Baby saw us and waved. He pulled the choke on the motor and turned the bow toward us. The metal boat parted the murky water. Our hopes surfaced from our drowning thoughts. Help was on the way. We cheered, laughed, and cried. A wave crashed over the boat and stalled the motor. We stood and watched in dismay. Uncle Baby pulled the choke several times but to no avail. He grabbed the oars and struggled to move through the water inch by inch toward us. We walked step by step toward him, until the current spun the boat around. Uncle Baby threw the life preserver attached to the rope to Papa, but it fell short. He reeled it in and tossed it into a tree to anchor the boat. It held. He stabilized the boat and began to pull it toward the tree and closer to us. I held my breath and bit my nails.

The current knocked a young bull off its feet and its legs flailed in the water. The current pushed it dangerously close to the boat. The bull righted itself and tried to put its front feet into the boat which would have surely flipped it. Uncle Baby whipped his pistol out of the holster and shot it in the head. The bull sank into the water, its head spurting blood. Uncle Baby lost his grip on the rope and the boat careened out of control. It knocked him off his feet, and he fell backwards into the boat. The strong flow of the current carried Uncle Baby, the boat, and our hopes of being rescued further away from us. My hopes of being saved sank like the bull with blood spurting from its head.

We started walking again, but the current was too strong.

"Walter," Mama screamed to Papa. "I can't make it."

Papa saw us struggling against the current.

"Take Bobby to the courthouse and come back for us," she said. Papa walked back toward them, his face carrying the weight of resignation.

"We have to stick together," Papa said. "Besides, the way the water is rising, I would never be able to get back."

He led us back to the house. Once we were inside, we went to our bedrooms to change clothes. I looked at Bobby struggling with the buttons on his shirt. Water dripped down his nose and onto his hands while he fumbled. My hands shook, too. I managed to finish dressing and then helped Bobby. He looked up at me with fear in his eyes. We didn't speak. There were no words big enough. I looked at my own trembling hands in a slow, detached way as if they didn't belong to me. Our hands were red from holding on to the sheet and wrinkled from being in the water too long. I didn't recognize my own hands. When Bobby and I went back into the kitchen, Papa had pulled the stove away from the wall and turned the gas off. Mama was unusually calm. She put several candles on the table.

"Sit down," she said as she put her hand in the circle of her Rosary and looped it back and forth until it was tight against her wrist with the Crucifix resting in her palm.

"Usually in a hurricane, gale force winds come ashore first. I think we are beginning to see that happen now," Papa said.

Papa drew a picture of the hurricane on the inside cover of the telephone book because he couldn't find any paper.

"The hurricane force winds come next. When the eye comes ashore, the winds will stop, and it will appear to be calm. Don't let this fool you because the back part of the hurricane will come over after the eye with even stronger winds. Depending on how fast the hurricane is coming toward us, and where the eye comes ashore will determine how long you may have. It may be calm for about ten, fifteen or even twenty minutes, or even an hour when the eye passes over, so stay put and don't go out. When we finish eating, we'll climb into the attic. I'm going to open all of the windows so the house will flood. I hope that it will sink and not rise off the pilings and float like a boat, or we may end up in the Gulf."

Mama took the milk out of the freezer where she had put it when the electricity went off last night. The freezer had not completely defrosted, so the milk was still cold. She poured each of them a glass and set out the rest of the cornbread. She opened a jar of apple sauce for Baby Faye. Stillness seeped through the room. We weren't hungry, but Papa said that we would need the nourishment because he didn't know when we would get our next meal. It felt like a long time at the table to us, but it actually only took about five minutes. The important thing was that we were all together giving each other strength, and Papa encouraged us to be brave and to listen and obey him. Papa kept saying that we were going to be okay. We often stopped chewing to listen. Our ears strained to hear clues of what was happening outside. The pitch of the wind grew even louder as it moaned around the corners of the house. The house creaked and strained against its own bolts and nails. We heard noises of tin being ripped off and branches hitting the house. We held hands around the circle of candlelight, and Mama prayed for our safety and deliverance from the hurricane. I was glad that she could still pray because I could not. I tried but I couldn't focus. I couldn't think.

The screaming wind created a chaos that took my thoughts away. We prayed the *Lord's Prayer*. Even Papa held hands and prayed.

Before we had finished eating, we heard the water hitting against the side of the house. With each wave, water slid through the cracks under the doors and across the floor. More and more water came in. The house shuddered and rocked. It felt as if it was trying to lift off the brick pilings. Papa decided to get all of us into the attic before he tried to open the windows. Then he remembered that he had nailed boards to the windows, and it would take longer for the house to sink. I realized that the house would float for a while. We stood up and staggered to the washroom where Papa had pulled the table underneath the attic opening and climbed on it to reach the ceiling. He banged on the attic trap door with a hammer and then slid the board to the side. Mama clutched Baby Faye who was dark red from screaming. Bobby started crying, but Papa told him to be strong and to be a man. When the waves hit the house, we braced ourselves against the table to keep it from sliding. The water was over our shoes by now and continued to rise with each wave that hit. Papa rested the hammer inside the attic and turned to Bobby. He lifted him up to the opening, and Bobby scrambled in.

"Take your sister, son," Papa said while he took Baby Faye in his arms and handed her to him. "Boy, you are next."

I climbed on the table while Mama steadied it. I jumped as Papa lifted me up, and I pulled myself into the attic.

"Help pull your Mama up," Papa said. Mama handed Faye's baby bottle and the flashlight to me, and I handed them to Bobby. I straddled the attic opening and grabbed Mama under her arms when Papa lifted her up. I wasn't even aware of my shoulder blade hurting anymore until I sat down. Papa got his shotgun and shells from the rack in the washroom and handed them to me.

"Careful, son."

I wondered why he would need his shotgun and figured that it was a treasured possession for a hunter. I thought of how Uncle Baby had shot that bull in the head and was glad that Papa thought to get it. A wave crashed through the back door and water rushed in. The wind blew the candles out. The table jerked out from underneath Papa and crashed into the stove. Mama screamed, and Faye began to cry again. Papa held on to the attic opening with his elbows and forearms and pulled himself up. The attic was dark except for the circle of light from the flashlight that strained against the darkness and then gradually grew weaker. Bobby and I found a box to sit on before Papa turned the flashlight off to save the battery.

Mama groped toward the leather-strapped trunk and sat down on a trunk full of memories and the diary that I had read. She took Baby Faye into her arms and held her close. Mama's eyes were fearful, but she remained calm. I remembered the picture of Mama and Papa on their wedding day. It just didn't seem right to begin a life together with such high hopes and end up floating in the attic of your house.

Baby Faye had finally quieted in Mama's arms and drank her bottle. When I leaned my head near her, I could hear little oinking noises as she tugged furiously on the nipple. Occasionally, I would hear a faint strain of *Ave Maria* when Mama leaned forward to hum in Baby Faye's ear. Papa directed the beam of the flashlight through the opening into the washroom and the kitchen. I could see the marks on the doorframe where Mama measured us and wrote our ages and heights on the wall. The water was past the mark for 3 feet and rising with each wave that hit. That would mean that the water must be at least 6 to 7 feet deep outside. I sat stunned and thought of the house that had protected me from so many storms and winters— the house that I walked to after school— the house that remembered when I was born and grew two feet, three, four and five feet tall— the house with its door framed testament of splitting cells of bodies that were made up of mostly water— the house that Bobby and I had painted last summer. When the mark for 5 feet on the frame of the utility room door went under water, I quit looking.

Baby Faye fell asleep on Mama's shoulder, exhausted, her black curls sticking to her face and neck. Bobby sat next to me and held his knees to his chest. We sat quietly for a while, listening. I could see the wheels of Papa's mind turning, planning his next course of action. Papa took the hammer and beat the boards of the attic ceiling, but he had a hard time making a hole. Bobby sneezed from the dust. Papa took his shotgun and cocked it.

"Mary Effie, stuff your ears with something and hold the baby's ears," he said. "We don't want to be trapped in here if the house breaks apart."

Papa tore the hem from his shirt and stuffed it in his ears.

"Okay. Here we go. Boy and Bobby, hold your ears. One, two, three, he counted."

The shotgun boomed and blasted a big, gaping hole in the roof. The sound of the blast was immediately swallowed up in the sound of the storm, but our ears pulsated from the boom. It filled my head with chaos. Splinters and rain fell on us. Papa pried the boards with the hammer and broke off the long sharp fragments. The wind screamed around us and continued to pepper us with rain from the opening. Enough gray light shone through that we could see each other's faces. Papa stuck his head through the hole and gave a report on what he saw.

"There are trees, telephone poles, and lumber floating as far as I can see. Mr. Babineaux's house is floating off to the left of us," he said.

"What about the Miller's house?" I yelled trying to be heard over the wind.

"I don't even see it," Papa yelled back into the attic and then sat back down.

He wiped the rain from his face. When I started crying, Papa stopped the tears in their tracks.

"Boy, this is not the time for tears. We have to keep our minds strong and steady, so we can think clearly; besides, the Miller's left yesterday."

I exhaled a big sigh and was grateful for that reminder. The wind screamed like a dying woman. I cringed and felt myself folding up. With the pressure of each surge against the joists, the house moved forward, and then it was sucked backwards again until it jerked and hit something big—something solid. The water that had risen to the ceiling of the kitchen and sloshed into the attic It anchored the house, and we no longer felt like we were moving as fast. Minutes later we lurched forward again, and Papa looked out of the hole.

"We have to get onto the roof," he yelled. "The Comeaux's house just hit us. It's broken up, and ours will probably be next."

They climbed onto the roof and crouched against the wind. The blast of wind in my face made me gasp. We crawled, groping over the pitched roof of the main house and stepped down to the flat roof of the washroom. The roofing shingles shredded our hands and knees and the saltwater added insult to injury. However, fear made us ignore the pain. We huddled against the side of the house and tried to shield ourselves from the driving rain that felt as if we were being blasted with bits of glass. Mama held Baby Faye close to her to protect her from the sting. The destruction was unbelievable. The tops of trees snapped like toothpicks. Some of the trees were completely uprooted and floated near our house. The wind and rain prevented us from seeing too far. I saw Mrs. Comeaux float by on a mattress, clinging clumsily. I could still see the darkened canopy of the big oak tree with our pirate's fort. It had survived so far. Freezers and refrigerators bobbed up and down with the lightness of marshmallows. Cattle and horses swam with wild thrashing and flashing of hooves. Many of the cows and calves that had fattened all spring floated by, apparently drowned. The storm unearthed the dead. Caskets from the local cemetery drifted by. I thought it was resurrection day. I thought it was the end of the world—*La fin du monde.*

A wall of water, higher than the pitch of the roof, which from the ground past the rooftop would be at least twenty feet tall, headed straight for us. It looked like a tall grey building that hurdled toward the shore. The house surged forward as we tightened our hold onto each other and the side of the house. The wave crashed over us and broke the flat section of the roof that we were on from the main house with a loud crack. I saw a gush of water blow through the hole that Papa had made in the roof like the blowhole of a whale, and the house exploded in a rain of roofing shingles, splinters, and boards. I felt the washroom pried from its joints and break up beneath us. We floated on the roof like a raft. After the surge, our raft took off over the marsh. Then we were pulled by a suction that carried us back toward the Gulf. There was a rhythm to the surges as if we were in the inhalation and exhalation of something alive and methodical, something oblivious to destruction.

The second time the wall of water came toward us, Baby Faye was wrenched out of Mama's arms. Mama had forgotten to tie Faye to her again when she took the strip of sheet off in the attic. I glanced over my shoulder and saw Bobby slide off the roof backwards. Mama's mouth was open in a scream, and she lunged toward Faye. Her arms lashed the water and air, but Faye was too far away.

"Walter," she screamed. "Faye!"

I was going to jump in to save Bobby, but Mama grabbed me to keep from being washed off. I held on to her and saw Papa jump into the water to save Faye. I knew it was hopeless because she had been flung too far from where Papa was. I saw her body tossed up like a doll and then swallowed by the waves. Her baby bottle was tossed with another heave of the water. I looked around for Bobby and saw him swimming to reach a dead cow. He made it and held on to the horns. He was way too far away for me to reach him.

Mama turned her head and screamed, "Bobby!"

I watched him being swept away as he held on to the cow, and I prayed that it would not be the last time that I saw my brother. A strange phenomenon of time occurred in a second. I moved in slow motion. Clock time and what I experienced in that time were not equal. The second felt like an eternity. Everything appeared to be in slow motion.

Papa bobbed up and down in the turbulence looking for Faye. He gave up and dog-paddled back toward the roof. He stretched out his hand for me to help pull him up. I knelt paralyzed—frozen in time and fear. I saw the hand that had backhanded me so hard, it had nearly broken my nose; I saw the hand that had thrown the pulley at me and beaten me throughout my life. I looked at it as if it were a still photo. I wondered how I could think such things. There was so much confusion and chaos. I looked away, paused, and then turned back and stretched out my hand for Papa, but it was too late. I saw Papa gasp as a wave went over him and pushed him away from me. I screamed. The slow motion I had experienced sped up to real time.

"Papa!"

In an instant, I jumped into the churning water as if I could save him. I went under and came back up and looked around for him. I saw him bob up like a cork a little further away. He turned his head to look around, and a telephone pole hit him in the back. He was pushed upward, out of the water, his mouth opening like the air had been knocked out of him or in a silent scream of pain. His body lifted up out of the water once again, then he went under. I was sucked under again. When I surfaced, my arms flailed at anything that floated by. A window from a house washed toward me, and I grabbed hold of it. I held on to it with both arms and rested my head on the glass, which surprisingly had not broken. The wind pushed it back and forth. I saw Papa's body and I paddled toward it. I grabbed the sleeve of his shirt and tried to hold on to him. I rested my head on the window waiting for the next surge. When I opened my eyes, I saw Papa's dead face pressed up beneath the windowpanes. I gasped at his wide-eyed death stare.

Another wave hit and washed Papa's body away along with the window that I was holding onto.

I went under and felt the silence and calmness of being in the interior of my own being where I felt very much at home and welcomed. I felt a solid, changelessness deep beneath all the chaos. I floated face down and I knew I was drowning, but somehow, I didn't seem to care. My life seemed to flash before my eyes, and I understood so much. I wasn't afraid, even though my lungs felt like they were bursting. Then, I heard a woman's voice like the soft sound of doves. Was the voice Mama's? Was it the Blessed Mother? Was I dead? I didn't know. I couldn't distinguish what it said and then I heard someone calling my name.

"Walt, Walt, come up."

I was Jonah in the belly of a huge whale. Each rib was the rung of a ladder that I tried to climb. Suddenly, I was spewed out in chaos and confusion. My body was thrust up breaking the skin of the water, and I gasped a huge, glorious breath of air. My lungs inflated and begged for more. I began breathing hard. I wasn't aware then that I had broken the skin of death and was born into a life of regret. I opened my eyes and saw a lady standing among the dark, wet limbs of the oak tree. Her long, black hair blew in the wind. I thought I had seen her before and wondered briefly who she was. She was so calm. I went under again but scrambled and kicked as hard as I could to get back to the top just to see her. When my head broke the water, I looked around, and there she was, waving for me to come toward her, encouraging me to swim, giving me hope. I kicked hard against the water. My arms struggled to propel me forward. Another wave rushed over me and pushed me toward the tree. I looked again and all around for the lady with the long, black hair, but she was gone. She must have been swept away after that last wave, I thought.

I saw what was left of our fort, but the boat was still in the tree. I couldn't believe my eyes. Pooch was in the boat! He had survived! I thought he had been swept away for sure. Pooch sat in the boat until he saw me. He grabbed the frayed end of the rope swing in his mouth and took a flying leap into the angry water and swam toward me. Adrenalin shot through my body, and I swam as hard as I could against the pull of the tide. I knew the next wave would slam me and Pooch into the oak tree. I felt my body rise higher and higher with the incoming wave. I grabbed onto the rope and pulled myself toward the boat. Pooch swam along side of me. When I reached the boat, I pulled myself over the side, and then struggled to pull a pawing, scrambling Pooch over the edge just in time. A wave crashed over us and shook the metal boat, but the chain and the rope held it in place. I prayed that the oak tree would not be uprooted. When the wave receded, the water inside the boat drained out of the bullet hole. Pooch and I huddled down in the bottom of the boat as it lurched and lunged against the slack of the chain that held it to the tree. The screech of the wind inside the metal boat made me long for the quiet and calm that I had experienced underwater. I thought of the beautiful lady with the dark hair that had motioned to me. I thought of the picture in my bedroom of the Virgin Mary, but I shook off those drowsy thoughts and tried to stay focused. I prayed that the boat would not break up. I had one arm around Pooch, and I pressed my ear against his wet fur. I put my finger in the other ear and felt my head, shoulders, and knees draw toward my heart as if to build a fortress around the only part of my body that felt a small measure of peace.

Suddenly, the winds stopped, and the surges were not as forceful. I remembered what Papa had said about the lull when the eye passes over. I stayed crouched in the boat for some time until I thought it was safe. I sat up blinking; although, there was so much cloud cover that I couldn't see very far. I was limp with exhaustion and felt so alone. It felt like Pooch and I were the only living creatures left on earth. I shut my eyes and curled back up inside the boat. I heard the increased intensity of the wind, but it came from a different direction. The chain rattled against the metal boat.

Again, the boat lurched, and water rushed over us. Papa was right. The second part of the hurricane was stronger than the first. I looked over the edge of the boat and saw a huge barge rolling and being tossed on the water. It looked like it was heading straight for the tree. The barge would surely uproot the tree. My mind was so confused that I didn't know what to do. I was as helpless as Baby Faye. There was no exit, no way to avoid something as big as a barge. The barge listed to the right. I saw the wall of water lift it up like a matchbox. It came hurdling toward us. I ducked inside the boat, expecting to be crushed. I felt a huge blast of water swamp us. When the water receded, I looked up and saw the wall of water push the barge through the trees with a deafening crash. It had narrowly missed us. I was limp with exhaustion. I curled back down inside the boat trembling.

I could no longer focus. My mind chattered with images: the barge tossed in the waves, rolling toward me; Éli, a dark figure on the roof standing against the wind; Pooch, shaking the frayed rope; Baby Faye's body tossed like a doll; Faye's bottle heaved; water rising over our growth records; Papa's hand; the red table slamming the white stove; the strange lady; Papa's vacant stare; Bobby's eyes; Pooch jumping into the water with the rope in his mouth—defiant; me—huddled inward, fetal-like—giving in and giving up—sissy. Enough, enough, enough! I stood in defiance. I clenched my fists and braced myself.

"No!" I screamed.

I yelled a noise as if a volcano of a wound exploded in me. The sound of my voice exploded from my gut like that I had never made before. Éli was an idiot but he defied death. Pooch was an animal and he defied death, and I too would defy death.

"I will survive!" I yelled into the wind.

I stood up and the rain blew sideways and pelted me. The water surged over me, but it did not topple me. I sat down in the boat exhausted and in a stupor. It was the first time that I realized that the wind had blown the shirt right off of my back because I was shivering violently. I couldn't remember what else occurred. Finally, I realized that the wind was no longer blowing.

CHAPTER SEVENTEEN

The wind died. The relief was welcomed. The surges finally stopped. I was thirsty. My tongue stuck to the roof of my mouth. I moved my jaws. My mouth was pasty. I looked up into the tree and opened wide, but the rain tasted salty and only made me thirstier. I hadn't noticed the smells when the wind blew, but now I smelled a mixture of raw earth, saltwater, sewerage, dead animals, and oil. I knew that when the sun came out, it would get worse. I really didn't care about the odor; I was alive or at least alive for now. I looked around and saw a refrigerator floating toward the tree. I took a large branch that had fallen over the boat and reached for the refrigerator. I nearly jumped out of the boat when a snake slithered on the limb. I shook it off. The snake fell in the water and swam off. I managed to hook the refrigerator with the branch and pulled it close enough to reach out and grab it by the handle. Luckily, it floated with the door up. I opened it and gasped at the putrid smell. I hung on to the handle and covered my nose with my other hand and took a deep breath. Pooch shook his head, even though dogs tolerate bad odors better than humans. I rummaged around in the tumbled contents of the refrigerator and found two RC colas and a Falstaff beer. What a find! It was better than any treasure, but how was I going to open them? I tried prying it off on the edge of the boat by hitting the cap, but it kept slipping, so I looked around for something else. I noticed a nail on the branch where the chain was attached. A big moccasin was on that branch, and I was afraid to go near it. I sat down and watched the snake in hopes that it would leave on its own accord. As seconds turned into minutes and minutes turned into an hour, I struggled with the dilemma.

I grew thirstier and my head began to ache. I should try to get the snake off the branch before nightfall or it might drop into the boat, I reasoned. I watched the snake, trying to get my nerve up because it didn't appear to be going anywhere anytime soon. I decided to take the branch that I used to retrieve the refrigerator and push the snake away from the boat. Hopefully, it would fall into the water.

"Okay, Pooch. Get ready." Pooch's eyes were riveted on the snake. I pushed the snake off the limb, but its tail clung to the limb and its three-foot length hung over the boat.

"Holy Cow. Look out, Pooch!"

I pushed again, and it fell into the boat. Pooch nearly knocked me out of the boat trying to get to it. In a flurry of yellow dog fur, Pooch bit the snake behind the head and shook it, just like he used to do with the end of the rope swing. He let go and the snake sat there stunned with its cottonmouth open and fangs exposed. I picked it up by the tail and threw it overboard. I checked Pooch out to see if he had been bitten.

"Thank God, Pooch. You're okay. That was a close call."

I sat down feeling weak and realized that dying of thirst meant taking desperate measures. The nail was handy at getting the cap off the bottle. At last, I took a long swig and felt the burn of the carbonation go all the way down my throat, and soon I felt the sweet liquid revive me. Pooch had been drinking the rainwater before it drained out of the boat, but when I poured some cola in my hand for Pooch, he lapped it up. We drank both bottles. Later that evening, I drank the Falstaff. I had sipped the foam off Papa's beer, but I really hadn't had one all to myself. It really wasn't that good, kind of bitter, but it was wet.

When darkness fell, the stars vaulted out of the sky. The hurricane had passed. I half expected the big dipper to tip over and quench my thirst. I was delirious. I thought of the ancients and their drawings of the stars. I thought of Columbus, De Soto, and other explorers of the New World that used the stars as a guide to map the position of their existence in time and space. I thought of baby birds, the indigo bunting, in particular, that learned the position of the stars from their nests and could fly great distances at night without fear of losing their way. God's universe filled me with awe, and I felt very small and humbled in the grand scheme of things. I thought scientists had enough knowledge to stop the cruelties of nature, but that was not so. When everything fails, people pray like crazy and run like hell. I heard the cries of stranded nutria and the desperate shrieks of other animals. I felt like crying along with them, but I was too dehydrated to spare any of my tears. I wanted to retreat into the dark womb of sleep and maybe in the morning things would be better.

Pooch and I cowered together in the bottom of the boat. I put my arm around him and buried my nose in his fur and breathed his wet-dog smell. At that moment, Pooch was all I had left of my former life. Finally, I fell into a deep, coma-like sleep. Hours later, Pooch licked my face until I stirred, and I realized that my mind had been praying or rather chattering the Hail Mary. Cramped muscles, aches, and cuts that I didn't even know that I had, began their litany of complaints. I rolled over on my back and opened my eyes to the eggshell color of dawn. I stared while my mind scrambled to take in what had happened. I lifted a branch that had landed on the boat and shoved it over the edge. I heard it splash into the water below. I sat up and looked over the edge of the boat and realized that the water had receded to about 6 feet deep. It lapped the 2 x 4 structure that was nailed to the tree. The 1 x 6s that made the floor of the platform to our fort were gone. My mind and my heart were not prepared for the destruction I saw when I raised my head and looked around. Maybe that was why Gammy with the Dress and Auntie La La had never looked up. They wanted to stay in their curled world because they were afraid of what they might have seen.

Cameron was underwater. The ocean had claimed the land. Debris floated everywhere: cars, lumber, sofas, dressers, mattresses, and watermelons, possibly from Mr. Doguet's field. Dead cattle, horses, and, and—people—bloated beyond recognition, floating grotesquely, doll-like. Grief swelled in my chest and threatened to explode. I gripped the side of the boat unable to move, unable to take my eyes off the wreckage. My eyes and emotions became numb from the sights. I stared at each body that floated by and wondered if it was Mama or Bobby. I knew Baby Faye was gone. I knew Papa was gone. I groaned over my thoughts and my timing. Regret was a split-second of missed timing. Regret was the hesitation, the lost time, the poor decision. Regret was the weight of the world on my chest. I tried to pray that God would protect Mama and Bobby and help us all to find each other again, but I was too emotionally and physically exhausted to think. My mind continued to chatter the Hail Mary from the far reaches of my memory which astounded me because I was not consciously praying. It was almost as if someone was praying through me. My chest felt tight. It seemed that my tears began deep in my chest and were carried by waves of sorrow that rose through my neck and out of my eyes. My heart squeezed. After a bout of tears, I just stared. I looked farther into the distance and saw the courthouse standing and the old ante-bellum home that was one of the original homes in Cameron. There were other houses jumbled together. I didn't see any part of our old house. I saw a shrimp boat that had lodged inside of a house and wondered if Papa's shrimp boat had remained afloat or was it laid on its side in a watery grave like Papa. I saw the barge that nearly hit us further up and stuck in the mud. I willed my eyes away, closed them and held onto Pooch and felt his warmth.

Pink light floated across my face, and I opened my eyes again. The sun rose in a pallet of gold and magenta and poured its colors onto the sky and all the destruction below. I stared at the strange beauty of the dark silhouettes of the trees bent as if to hold the weight of the sky, but it was really the trappings of our lives that it held. Junk hung from the branches: a plaid shirt, barbed wire, sheet metal, and lumber. A rubber tire hung on a top branch like a crown. The trees and the debris were black against the colors of the horizon. It was another one of those pivotal points in my life. I decided that I had to find beauty in the broken to become whole again. I did not speak or think these words exactly, but it was just something that I knew. I laid my head against Pooch, closed my eyes, and listened to his heartbeat. We had survived the storm.

When I had gathered enough strength to sit up again, I looked around the boat wondering how I was going to get down. If I shimmied down the rope, how would I get Pooch down? I knew I couldn't climb down the tree because it was covered with water moccasins. I eyed a snake nearest our boat. It lay coiled on the limb, a lump of solid, waterlogged rope as long as a baseball bat and as big around as the head of the bat—its serious eyes wide with watchful survival instinct. Pooch and I and the snake stared each other down. I wasn't that afraid; I tried to convince myself. The snake had probably struck so many objects that it didn't have any more venom. Besides, Pooch could grab it around by the back of its head, shake and snap it quickly, cleanly just like he did with the other one. But this one was much bigger. I didn't want to risk it. Pooch had been bitten so many times that venom didn't have much affect anymore. He would be listless and have some swelling for a couple of days, and then, he would be back to his old, Pooch self. This one was different. Pooch had never been bitten by one this big. I decided to stay clear of it.

A big raccoon had taken up residence on the 2 x 4s that were left from the platform. The raccoon growled at us when Pooch barked at it. I hushed Pooch because I knew he was no match for a scared coon. Pooch and I, the snakes and the coon respected each other's space because each of us was scared of the other. Each of us tried to maintain a balance: on the limb, the platform, the boat and an interior balance of blood chemicals for breath and movement. Was it possible to co-exist with danger? Yes, we were doing just that only because we were fearful for our survival too, and because we had something bigger to fear than each other. Hatred was a topic for another day.

I flipped through a catalog of solutions in my brain to determine what to do. If I got the boat untied from the tree, would it float? I looked around for something to stuff in the hole so that it wouldn't sink. There was nothing except the underwear under my jeans. Now that I had a plan to solve the problem of getting the boat to float, how was I going to get the boat out of the tree? I could unwind the chain, but the rope was another story. It was water-logged. I tried to untie it, but the constant jerking from the wind had only tightened it more. I looked around for something that would cut it. A piece of tin floated nearby, but it was covered with snakes. From the height of the tree, I saw the destruction that looked like a war zone. I lay back in the boat. My stomach growled and startled Pooch. Hunger is a startling thing. I decided to yell.

"Hello! Help! Is anybody out there?" I yelled with all of my might.

I strained to listen. Other than the lapping of the water, everything was quiet. I decided to wait until the water receded enough to walk to the courthouse. Surely, someone would come and rescue us. A short time later, I heard a helicopter and stood yelling and waving my arms, but I doubted that they saw me in the tree. I doubted that anyone could have heard me because my voice was failing. It was more like a croak.

Disappointment filled me, and I fell asleep again and dreamed of Papa's hand reaching for me. I dreamed of Mama's small, frail hands. I dreamed of Baby Faye's bottle tossed on the waves. I dreamed of Baby Faye lying in the marsh somewhere like a muddied doll that I once saw on the road to Lake Charles. I saw Bobby's huge eyes as he held on to the horns of a dead cow. I saw the long, black hair of the strange lady. I saw the wall of water as if it was a big gray building moving toward me. I wasn't sure if I was dreaming or thinking. Just crazy, nonsensical thoughts pushed my brain to the breaking point. I didn't know how many hours I had sat there, but the raw sound of an outboard motor broke the battering to my brain. I knew that my survival depended on my voice above the chaos. I could see the boat in the distance and screamed and yelled, again as much as my sore throat would allow. Pooch seemed to understand that we were stranded and barked his head off. I stood up in the boat and waved. I heard the motor cut off, and I renewed my screaming. Heads turned in our direction. Pooch barked, and I continued yelling.

"Over here." I saw someone wave, and the motor revved up again. It headed in our direction. I laughed, then cried, and hugged Pooch who continued to bark. The men drove up in a trailing wake of dirty water. They wore hard hats with the initials CD for Civil Defense stamped on them. They also had handkerchiefs around their necks that they used to cover their noses.

"Hi, son," the man said. "Are you okay?"

"I'm okay," I managed to say through croaky sobs.

"We're going to get you down from there in a jiffy. Give us a minute to get the boat in the right position."

He maneuvered the boat under the rope swing.

"Okay, son, he said, "can you grab the rope and slide down?"

"What about my dog?" I asked.

"I don't think we have room for a dog," the man said.

He took off his hardhat and scratched his head.

"We've got to save room for other people," he said. I burst into tears.

"My dog saved my life. I can't leave him. You go on and get other people. I'll stay here until the water goes down, and then Pooch and I will walk to the courthouse," I said.

"Nothing doing, son," the other man said. "I think we can find room for your dog. I'm going to throw a rope and a blanket up to you. Make a sling with the blanket and tie it under your dog's front legs and use the rope to lower him down," he said.

The man tossed the rope and the blanket up to me, and I rigged it up to Pooch. The problem was holding onto the rope and lifting Pooch over the side of the boat; finally, I threw the other end of the rope over a branch and tied it around my waist. Pooch seemed to understand what was going on when I lifted him over the side of the boat. He cooperated as much as a dog could, and I lowered him down into the waiting arms of the men below. I untied the rope and shimmied down the rope swing and into the safety of the boat. I started crying again, and the big man that said he could find room for Pooch gave me a hug.

"You're going to be okay, son," he said. "You're going to be okay," he said again as he patted my back. "What's your name, son?"

"Walter LaCour Jr. Everybody calls me Boy."

"My name is Tom, and this here is Charlie. You're shivering. I think you need a blanket and something warm to drink." Tom wrapped the blanket around my shoulders.

"I need water first," I said. I took the cup with trembling hands and drank the lifesaving water. I downed another cup. I gave Pooch a drink of water from my cup and continued to fill it up until he had had enough. I drank some coffee from a thermos and felt revived. I could see tears in Tom's eyes as he quickly turned his attention back to the motor and revved it up.

Tom piloted the boat around all kinds of debris. I strained to look for my family. Maybe Mama was still floating on the roof. Maybe they have already been rescued and are safe somewhere, probably in Lake Charles or at the courthouse. Maybe they are looking for me. Maybe Bobby made it to the courthouse. Uncle Baby's boat was probably wedged into a tree or a house. Uncle Baby was strong, and I prayed that he was all right.

"There's a body," I said and pointed in the direction of a floating telephone pole.

They pulled up to it, and I burst into tears for the third time when they lifted Cracklin's swollen body into the boat.

"You knew him?" Charlie asked. I nodded.

"His name is Maurice Bilbo. He was my best friend."

They covered Cracklin's body, and I stared at his feet sticking out from under the blanket, the feet that used to run through the marsh with me, the feet that climbed up into our pirate's fort, the feet that lay still before me.

I squeezed his cold, wet foot and said, "It's okay, Ti Maurice, It's okay." I was trying to tell him that it was okay to die.

I thought of Cracklin's mama and papa, sisters and brothers—the twins Donna and Don, Rose, and little Callie. I wondered if they had survived. I had been enamored with Cracklin's family. Love lived there. Ti Maurice and I had moved so adeptly in and out of the black and white world that it became a comfortable gray. Much of our world was gray—the dawn, twilight, moss, and most of the time the Gulf of Mexico. Cracklin had known his place in society more than I did. I remembered when we traveled to Lake Charles for a shopping trip in the back of Uncle Thib's truck. In the Newberry store over the water fountain and restrooms, a white sign hung imprinted with black letters stating for *colored*. The other fountain and restroom stated for *whites*. It was the first time that I realized that I was different too. When I ordered fried chicken, I asked for dark meat, and the waitress laughed and said, 'I'm sorry son, we don't serve dog meat.' I was treated differently because I spoke with a Cajun accent. Ti Maurice taught me to focus on our similarities. 'We both have eyes and ears, don't we? Our blood is red, ain't it?' Ti Maurice would say. He and I harmonized to the tune of black and white keys, and we were happier for it.

I remembered going to Cracklin's for supper. After supper the whole family gathered outside—some in chairs, some on the steps, and some dangling their bare feet off the edge of the porch. What a sight and sound it made with the porch roof sagging under the weight of the purple wisteria. Mr. Bilbo picked up the harmonica and banged it against his thigh. He lipped it a little to make it wet so his lips would slide over it easily, blew a few sad notes, and then, he began a knee-slapping tune. Cracklin's mama and all the sisters sang and harmonized *Down by the Riverside, Joshua Fought the Battle of Jericho, Swing Low Sweet Chariot*, and a lot of other old-time hymns and spirituals, singing like their hearts would fly out of their throats. The clapping and praising charged the air. The fire crackled starbursts in the night sky. The music slowed like driftwood smoke and one by one, they stretched, yawned, and entered the house to find their colorful, quilted pallets while Pooch and I slid off the porch and headed for home to sneak in the front door, the backdoor, or a window so that we wouldn't disturb Papa. If Papa ever asked where I had been, I lied. Cracklin and his family were good, hardworking people and I loved them, in spite of Papa's prejudice.

"I'll remember you all of my life," I whispered under my breath.

"Let's bring her in," Tom said.

Tom and Charlie exchanged a knowing look. They recognized the shock and despair of what I had been through, especially with the added burden of seeing my friend's lifeless, limp body stretched out before me. A small twig of oak leaves clung to the nap of the blanket that Tom wrapped around my shoulders. I took it off and laid it on top of the blanket covering Cracklin and prayed an Our Father and a Hail Mary. Tom turned the rescue boat north. He slowly maneuvered it around an uprooted tree and a pile of junk that had collected against it when they saw a man lying across a refrigerator. At first, we thought he was dead because he was so swollen, but when we got up to him, he lifted his head up.

"I fell in some barb wire," the man managed to say.

He was so weak that it took the three of us to lift him. When we got him into the boat, we noticed that the marks were not from barbwire but from snakebites. Charlie, Tom, and I looked at each other. We knew. No one told him. He was an elderly man—gray fringe, bald on top, gray hair on his chest, and the remnants of a work shirt clung to his shoulders. His big, white belly was covered with cuts and fang marks. Tom asked him his name, but he wouldn't or couldn't talk anymore. He just moaned. Charlie put a blanket around him and tried to help him sip some water. He became very still. Water dribbled out of his mouth, but I saw his Adam's apple move up and down as he swallowed. He was still alive. He must have been in shock or dying because he stared like he didn't know where he was. Charlie tried to get him to drink more water, but he refused. Tom helped him stretch out. We watched his legs swell up to twice their size.

Tom raced the boat around the debris as fast as he could to a tugboat that was transporting people to the Port of Lake Charles. When Tom docked the boat, he yelled for help and the Civil Defense men hurried to get the man out and give him first aid. I said my goodbyes and thanks to Tom and Charlie with a tearful hug. Pooch and I climbed out of the boat and onto the tug. The Civil Defense men attempted to give first aid to the man with the snakebites, but he had already died. They covered him with a blanket. I scanned the tattered survivors on the tug, but none were my family or circle of friends. I sat by Cracklin and watched the mountains of wreckage and ruin, shards and brash along the Calcasieu Ship Channel. The tug glided by, like a funeral procession through the waterway to Lake Charles. When we arrived at the Port, buses and ambulances were lined up to take the victims to the hospitals or to one of the refugee centers. I, with Pooch at my heels, got out of the boat and watched as they lifted Ti Maurice out of the boat on a stretcher. The heaviness and stillness of death hit me in the stomach, and I doubled over as they carried my friend inside Shed #5 where they kept the dead bodies lined up waiting to be identified.

A lady with the Red Cross came up to me and offered a ham sandwich and a cup of water. Her eyes were kind and thoughtful. Her outstretched hand offering food helped me to overcome the phobia of seeing an outstretched hand and failing to reach out.

"Come with me, son. I'll take care of you," she said.

Pooch and I sat down by her station wagon where she and her friend gave out sandwiches from the back. It was filled with boxes of sandwiches wrapped in waxed paper, jugs of water, and ice chests filled with soda.

"People from all over Lake Charles made these sandwiches," she said.

I gave Pooch the rest of my sandwich, and I got another. Pooch's long tongue lapped the water from a paper cup. I ate another sandwich and forced myself to stay awake. With sleep weighing my eyelids down, I watched the incoming boats pull up. I looked at every refugee's face as they got off the boat. They were quiet. Deathly quiet. Their facial muscles were limp; their movements were slow. I supposed that they were like me, so exhausted that I could not speak. I looked at every dead body that they brought in. I recognized several people from Cameron, but none of them were my family. I asked some of the survivors if they had seen my family, and they shook their heads. I started to cry again from sheer emotional exhaustion. The Red Cross lady said it was time to get on the bus that would take me to one of the local schools, either Fourth Ward, Lake Charles High School, or the McNeese State College arena, where they would give me some dry clothes, food, and a place to sleep. She droned on so that it nearly put me to sleep.

"I can't leave until I find my Mama and my brother and the rest of my family," I said.

"They may already be at one of the schools. You can ask about them. They keep a list of people that come in," she said.

With renewed hope, I agreed. Pooch and I climbed aboard a school bus that took us to Lake Charles High School. When we got to the gym, I registered with the lady at the door. I gave her my name and she typed it, adding my name to the list. She scrolled the paper up and down checking through the names to see if Mama, Papa, Bobby, Nanan, or Parrain's were on the list. I was shocked because I gave her Papa's name as if I expected him to have survived. I knew differently, but I just couldn't admit it. She shook her head slowly. Wisps of gray hair fell around her face. She avoided looking me in the eyes; however, she managed a quick look, being careful to protect herself from my sorrow. She looked at Pooch and opened her mouth to object, but something stopped her. She must have seen the despair on my face. I was prepared to sleep outside with Pooch if they had not allowed him in.

When I finished my registration, a too-cheerful lady from the Salvation Army showed me a box of clothes. She helped me find a pair of jeans that looked about my size. She kept talking about one shirt being more stylish than another and which color did I prefer? She chattered incessantly like the words were too hot to handle. I didn't care if the color was red, purple, or chartreuse. My eyes saw only shades of sorrow, shades of bad choices. She dug through a box of shoes and found a pair of tennis shoes about my size. They were too big, but I thought I would give them a try.

Another lady with a Red Cross armband led me to an empty army cot, and she showed me where the locker room was so I could take a shower. I was so exhausted that I sat on the floor of the shower and let the warm water run over my body. Pooch sat in the shower with me. He would not leave my side. I shampooed him, too. I surely didn't want anyone kicking him out because he stunk. He was all I had left. After I showered and changed clothes, I stretched out on the cot and went to sleep with Pooch at the end curled around my feet. I had to be touching Pooch, or I couldn't sleep. I finally understood Bobby's need to be touching the wall next to his bed because it gave him the security to fall into unconsciousness. Sleeping is a risk we take. My last thought was that I was going to sleep a few hours; then, I would find Mama, Bobby, Parrain, and Nanan. I knew that Baby Faye did not survive, but something in me kept hoping that she would be found alive. I knew that Papa had drowned, too—no thanks to my temporary mental lapse, no thanks to my paralysis by fear, no thanks to the hesitation that grew like a tumor in my brain. If only, if only, if only, I thought. The thoughts wore me out, and I fell asleep.

CHAPTER EIGHTEEN

The days immediately following the storm were days of desperation. All I could think about then was finding my family. I felt like my very skeleton was going to come apart and my joints unhinge. The worst part was waking up from a fresh sleep and remembering. Still, the remembering hurts, but the familiarity of that hurt seems to numb as time goes by. I remembered waking up from sleep when I was in the Lake Charles High School gym. Screams of a couple being reunited shattered my sleep. I bolted up wondering where I was and how I had gotten there. I remembered and fell back on the cot. A couple in their thirties hugged and cried. The man had a white gauze patch on his forehead—clean and neat—trying to bring order to the chaos of injury. It didn't look like she had any injuries, except for some scratches, but the emotional injury showed in her body. The skin under her blood-shot eyes draped like dark blue bunting and made her look hollow.

"I was swept out from under the house when it collapsed," she said. "I ended up floating on a mattress."

"I was standing near the back door when a wave hit me and washed me outside. I grabbed hold of that scrawny gum tree out back—spent the night hanging on," he said.

"Paw Paw didn't make it—the crusty, old coot. Refused to leave his rocker downstairs. Wouldn't get in the attic," she said.

She leaned her head on his slumped shoulder. They were elated to have each other. Loneliness filled my being to the bursting point. It felt like I was on a boat going down a fast-moving river never knowing what peril was around the bend, heading for a waterfall where I would drop off the planet. I longed for Mama and Bobby. How I wanted to see Bobby's huge eyes: mischievous eyes that faded in my memory to eyes that were afraid to disappoint Papa, eyes that were afraid of death, eyes that I feared knew death too soon. Would I be glad to see Papa, heavy-handed Papa? Would I be happy to smell his whiskey breath and fish stink again? Yes, yes, I wanted that messed up life with all its smells, with all the anger, and disappointment. I wanted to try again. I had spent far too much time thinking about what was wrong with Papa, rather than what was right. I wanted to tell him that I was sorry for being a bad son. I wanted that chance again. I begged God for that chance again. I didn't care if he was my real father or not. He was the only father that I knew.

I dropped my eyes from the couple because it was their sweet moment of happiness. Their silence made me raise my eyes to them again. They were tired of grief. She sat on the cot, staring, her hair sticking to her swollen, tear-stained cheeks. The man leaned forward, rested his scratched and bruised arms on his legs and dropped his head. Everyone experienced loss and the *what ifs*. I realized that I wasn't the only one.

I thought of Mama and Papa and decided to go to everyone in that gym and ask if they had seen or heard of Walter and Mary Effie LaCour or my brother Bobby LaCour from Cameron. From cot to cot I went, disappointment mounting. Some of the ones from Cameron knew Mama and Papa, but they didn't know what had happened to them. Most of the people in the gym had arrived before the hurricane hit. They were from Cameron, Creole, Grand Chenier, Pecan Island, the Johnson Bayou area, and from God knows where. I told them about being trapped in the rising water and floating on the roof. Their eyes filled with sorrow, and they hung their heads low and stared at their hands as if to speak to them to do something. But they didn't know what to do. The last couple I talked with just shook their heads.

"I'm sorry son—for you and your family—I hope you find them," the man said.

I went back to my cot, sat down and stared at my hands. Sleep came to me, and I was thankful that I didn't have to think anymore.

When I woke up, Pooch and I went to the front door. I looked out of the gym door and saw a caravan of cars pull up in the parking lot where refugees staggered out and made their way up the steps to the gym. I looked carefully at each one of them praying that one of them would be a member of my family or someone that I knew. They lined up to register so orderly and so silently. Everyone handled tragedy differently—the almost unendurable, silent sadness that engulfs your being—the unseeing focus on your shoes, the lifting of your eyes to meet another's, holding the gaze for a moment, eyes glistening, and the awkward look back down at your shoes. I watched other people manage their grief because I had never had to handle such sadness before.

I swallowed the cry of sorrow in my throat, and I gathered my courage to ask the lady at the desk if she would check the list again. I didn't know what had happened or how many people had come in since I had been sleeping. Maybe, Mama and Bobby were right here in this gym, and I didn't know it. I just had to know. The unknown seared me. I approached the lady with the gray, wispy hair. Pooch sat down by my feet. The wrinkles on the lady's face looked heavier and deeper. Her eyes had a slow, going-through-the-motion tiredness.

"Please, Ma'am, would you check the list for my Mama and Papa?" I asked and looked up hopefully at her. She did not see me, or she was very good at ignoring people. I asked again.

"Excuse me. My name is Walter LaCour, Jr. Would you be so kind as to check your list to see if any of my family are on it?"

She did not respond.

"Ma'am excuse me. Ma'am, please," I said. I gently tugged on the sleeve of her navy, polka-dotted Swiss blouse. Other people were talking to her, but she didn't hear me. She treated me like I was invisible.

"Maybe, I'm a ghost. Maybe, I didn't survive," I whispered. "How did I get here?"

I looked down at myself. I looked at the too large white shirt that some-one had donated. *Maybe, I'm really dead, and she doesn't see me,* I thought. The weight of the emotion that surrounded the incoming people must have made her deaf. Maybe, she locked her heart away so that she could do her job. I needed her attention now. I thought of Éli and how detached he was. He only needed his violin. I imagined the violin case floating on the waves; I saw the steam rising from the strings as the first water touched it. I looked at the woman again, and I felt as invisible and thin as air. I remembered drowning. Maybe, I really did not survive. I panicked. I stepped on a chair and onto the wide deck of the lady's desk. I felt nothing. My bare feet should have felt the cool, slick finish of the varnished wood, but they didn't. Dead was no feeling. *Then I must be dead!* I thought. I was in the vice grip of panic. It squeezed me and I couldn't breathe. My voice erupted over the crowd of refugees as well as Lake Charles residents who were there to offer housing.

"Can you hear me, or am I dead?" I shouted. All eyes turned to me. The wispy-haired lady at the desk was shocked out of her tiredness. She stared up at me with her mouth open. The crowd got quiet. I knew I wasn't dead.

"Does anyone know anything about my papa and mama, Walter and Mary Effie LaCour and my brother Bobby LaCour? We are from Cameron," I said.

The crowd shifted, mumbled a little and shook their heads.

A lady wearing tattered pedal pushers said, "We've seen a lot of folks, but we didn't know their names."

"Have you seen or heard of Alcide Thibodeaux?" I asked. "He's my Parrain." My words trailed off and were absorbed in the silence of their response. Sobs weighed my voice down. I couldn't speak. No words could replace a sob. I had cried so much since Audrey hit that I began to believe that Papa was right. I was nothing but a big baby, a little sissy. A tall man with reddish hair, graying at the temples and long freckled arms came up to me.

"I'm Dr. Andrews," he said. "You can come stay in our home, and I will help you find your family. They may be at one of the hospitals."

He lifted me off the table in his freckled arms and hugged me. I hung limp, my face against his chest trying to control my sobs. I thought Dr. Andrews was Papa holding me when I was a little boy. The wispy-haired desk lady, whose face wore another etching from the shock, typed Dr. Andrews's name, address and phone number next to my name, just in case my family came looking for me. I introduced Dr. Andrews to Pooch, and he patted his head and his soft golden ears. Pooch grinned in mutual admiration.

"Pooch jumped in the water with the rope swing in his mouth and swam to me. He saved my life," I said.

"Pooch the rescue dog, you will be an honored guest in our home," Dr. Andrews said as he continued to pat his head. Pooch lifted his paw in a handshake and Dr. Andrews shook it. Pooch grinned with his tongue hanging out and he panted in excitement. We left through the heavy gym doors with Dr. Andrews. The sun was shining on the fallen tree limbs darkened by the heavy rains. The woody flesh of the snapped treetops jutted toward the sky. Roofing shingles and standing puddles of water glittered in the sun in a bizarre beauty. Lake Charles was not spared from the hurricane. Although, it had not experienced the tidal waves that Cameron had, it received the damage of a brutal wind and flooding from the rain. I had not noticed any of this when I first arrived. When we walked through the parking lot to Dr. Andrews's Plymouth, I heard a circle of people talking about a lady stranded on a roof.

"She was curled up like a baby when they found her. She had a rosary tight, tight in her hand and she didn't move a muscle no, 'cause the roof was covered with snakes, mostly water moccasins, and they were crawling all over her, but she had not been bitten, no siree," a man holding a Civil Defense hardhat said. "It was a down right miracle for sure," he continued.

"How did they get her down?" someone in the circle asked.

"Well, the roof was wedged up against the bridge and one of them big army trucks, *ducks* they call them, made it through the highway to the bridge. They didn't want to get too close, so they wouldn't rile them snakes up. They hooked a hose to the exhaust pipe of the truck and told her to hold her breath and close her eyes. They blew that exhaust on the snakes and they crawled off the roof."

I remembered Mama wrapping her rosary around her hand in the circle of yellow candlelight in our kitchen. I stopped immediately.

"Pardon me," I said, "do you know her name? My Mama had a rosary wrapped around her wrist." The man shook his head.

"She came in on my boat, but she wouldn't talk to us. She was dehydrated, they said, and they put her in an ambulance. I don't know which hospital they took her to."

"What did she look like?" I asked. "What color was her rosary? Do you remember?" The words tumbled out of my mouth in my excitement.

"It's hard to tell," the man began. "Dark hair, dark eyes. Pretty much like most of the population in Cameron Parish. The rosary. Let me see," he said stroking the stubbles on his chin. It was black, but you never know, it could have been so waterlogged that it looked black. It was amazing that the durn thing didn't break," the Civil Defense man said.

I looked up at Dr. Andrews.

"My Mama had a black rosary wrapped around her wrist."

"A lot of people could have been holding black rosaries," Dr. Andrews said in a quiet voice meant to cushion any possible disappointment. "I'll tell you what we can do. We can check at St. Pat's, Memorial, and West Cal-Cam hospitals, and if they are not there, we will go by the McNeese College arena and check there. The majority of the refugees are sent to McNeese. We are not giving up, son," he continued.

We walked with a hopeful step to Dr. Andrews's car.

"We are closest to Memorial Hospital. We can try there first, but I think we should stop by my office and take a look at the cut on your ankle. We don't want it to get infected. It won't take long. It's on the way to the hospital," Dr. Andrews said.

"Okay," I said, even though I hardly noticed the pain anymore. "It's not too bad anymore. I don't remember getting cut. Didn't notice it until after the storm and some saltwater got into it."

The lull of the engine relaxed me while Dr. Andrews drove down block after block toward Memorial Hospital where I prayed that I would find Mama and Bobby lying in comfortable beds. There were limbs in the road that Doc maneuvered around and a lot of shingles that had been blown off. Some of the streets were still flooded. When we turned down Oak Park Boulevard, Dr. Andrews said that the hospital was just up the street and his office was near it. Weaving in and out of the branches made me realize that there would always be obstacles. I had to know the goal and the solutions would come. My goal was to reunite my family.

I sat on a table in an examining room at Dr. Andrews's office. On the white walls hung a row of neatly framed diplomas and a picture of a fat doctor listening to the heart of a young boy. A yellow dog sat at the boy's feet. It reminded me of Pooch.

"Do you think you could check Pooch out?" I asked.

"I thought of that myself. My neighbor is a veterinarian, and I'll ask him to examine Pooch when we get home."

"Thank you, Doc," I said, elated.

The room smelled sterile. Whiffs of alcohol stung my nostrils. Doc cleaned my cuts and scratches. I listened to my own heart with the stethoscope while Dr. Andrews closed the cut on my ankle with strips of tape and bandaged it. Doc said that I would need a tetanus shot. When I saw the needle, my stomach turned queasy. I remembered the flash of Mama's needle, the needle that binds. I realized why that image kept coming back into my thoughts. Mama held the fabric of our family together. She always had. It was Mama who tried to heal all the hurts that Papa's alcoholism had created for our family. I would find Mama.

Doc said that the injection would not hurt as much as the cut on my ankle. He was right. To my dismay, he said that I also needed an injection of penicillin for the infection. After what I had been through, a needle was nothing. I didn't look away this time, but watched the thin hypodermic needle pierce my skin. Doc helped me down, and we resumed our mission to find Mama.

When we got to Memorial Hospital, Doc said that he would go in to inquire about her, and he asked me for her full name as well as Papa's and Bobby's.

"I worked through the night at Memorial. I didn't treat any LaCours, but that's not to say that they may not be in there now. I just got off work when my wife called and told me of the need to take in refugees. That's why I'm here."

Doc pulled into the parking lot at Memorial Hospital.

"Stay off of your foot for a little longer. Scrubbing and disinfecting made it bleed a little more," he said. "I'll come back to get you if they are here."

"Thank you, sir," I managed to say.

Doc returned shortly. I watched every move as he walked to the car carrying his black doctor's bag. I knew my family was not in there.

"Sorry, son. No one listed by the LaCour name and no unidentified male or female patients in their age ranges, either. We're not giving up," Dr. Andrews said. "We have two more hospitals to check out."

I knew Doc was thinking about the funeral homes, but he didn't say it. I couldn't bring it up either. Again, we drove mostly in silence. I was not much on conversation or answering questions. Dr. Andrews respected my silence. When we turned on South Ryan St. and rumbled down the brick road to the front of St. Patrick's Hospital, I knew that I had to go in.

"I would like to go in this time, if you don't mind. My ankle is okay and all," I said.

"Of course," Doc said and nodded. There was a cemetery on the left in a stand of almost stripped trees, but a few branches still had leaves, emerald leaves. Hope rose in me because it was the first time that I had noticed color since the sunrise. A fallen tree lay across the cemetery, roots sprawled, detached. I walked and breathed and moved as if I were inside a concrete culvert.

I felt as though I was a long way away from myself. My voice sounded different to my own ears. I sat in the passenger seat and gripped the handle of the car door. I had never been in a hospital before. All I knew was that it strengthened the living and eased the dying. I released my grip and felt the blood return to my hand. I was tired, so tired. My hopes had been dashed so many times before, and this time would probably be no exception. If Mama and Bobby were in there, were they dying? I was afraid to face the possibilities of where they were and in what condition. I was so afraid. Dr. Andrews turned the motor off and took the key from the ignition. He looked over at me and seemed to understand.

"If they are not here, we will continue to look for them. We are not going to give up. The only way to know is to take that first step," he said.

I realized that once again, fear had paralyzed me. I looked at my limp hand and willed it to pull the handle. It did so with determination, and I stepped out of the car. Pooch stuck his head out of the window and barked.

"Stay here, Pooch," I said. "I will be right back."

Dr. Andrews opened the doors of St. Patrick's Hospital and moved freely with the ease of familiarity. A nurse with her white cap perched on her head like the fan of a dove's tail greeted him, and he asked her about patients with the name of LaCour. She looked at me with sad eyes. Once again, I was the object of pity. I must have been very pitiful looking, but I didn't care. The nurse said she did not have a record of any LaCours being admitted. My heart fell to my feet, and I felt as though my bones would crumble and bury it. Dr. Andrews asked if there were any unidentified patients. She nodded yes and looked at her book for the room number. There was a woman in room 323, and an elderly man in ICU. We climbed the stairs to the third floor, a long road to heaven. Yes, heaven, I hoped.

"Often when people experience emotional trauma they go into shock. They become very disoriented, not knowing the day or the date or even their own name. If this woman is your mother, she may not recognize you," Dr. Andrews said.

"That's okay," I heard myself say. "If she doesn't know that she is my mother, I will know that she is. It will be okay."

I stared down the long hall. The doors passed us like the slow days of the month—March 19, March 20, 321, 322 and there in bold letters 323. The number and the door loomed before me. Dr. Andrews knocked gently and entered. I followed immediately, refusing to let myself hesitate.

The room was dim, except for a streak of light spilling from a crack in the drapes. When my eyes adjusted, I saw a dark-haired, disheveled woman curled in a fetal position with her back turned to us. A bag on a pole with a long tube led to a pale wrist lying still on the bed. She was too small to be Mama. My heart sank to the bottom of my being. It wasn't Mama. Would

I ever be happy again? Dr. Andrews bent over and lifted her pale wrist and felt her pulse. It was then that I noticed her hands—the small hands with the little oval fingernails that looked like small, wet seashells. It looked like Mama's hand! She stirred.

"I'm Dr. Andrews. "How do you feel?"

The woman turned slowly and raised her head to look up at him. Her eyes were filled with a heavy fog. I gasped. She looked over toward me. I held my breath for an eternity, so it seemed. The fog of recognition began to lift. She rose up on her elbows.

In a weak, voice she said my name, "Walt?"

"Mama!" I screamed. "Yes, it's me. It's me. It's Walt." I ran to her bed and kissed her face over and over and over. Tears streamed from Mama's eyes. I looked up and saw Dr. Andrews dab his eyes.

"I thought I would never see you alive again," Mama whispered.

Her face had the imprint of the crucifix on her cheek where she had fallen asleep on her rosary. I lifted the rosary off the pillow and put it in her hand. I was so overwhelmed with happiness that I laid my head on her pillow and cried. I wondered if my next reunion would be tears of joy or sorrow.

CHAPTER NINETEEN

My heart paced in my chest like the sea paced the shore. I was helpless to stop the restlessness. I knew that I had to shake this sadness because Mama needed me. I slept on the floor next to Mama's bed where I floated in and out of consciousness. I got up every time she cried out in her sleep calling for Papa, Bobby, and Baby Faye. When she called my name, I told her that I was standing right next to her, and that it was going to be okay.

"Shh, shh. Go to sleep, so you can get well. We will look for them," I said.

"Snakes are crawling on me. I can't move; I can't breathe. Oh God, Oh God, get them off."

"They're gone, Mama. You're safe and you were not bitten. It's going to be okay."

I left the room and went to the nurse's station and asked if she could have something to help her sleep.

"She thinks snakes are still crawling on her."

I went back to the room and waited on the nurse. She came in shortly and gave Mama a sleeping pill. Twenty minutes later Mama fell into a deep sleep. At last she was quiet and at peace. I too had trouble sleeping. When the initial state of exhaustion was satisfied with all the sleep I had at the gym, restlessness set in. Real sleep had a way of eluding me. When I felt myself falling asleep, my body jumped, my hands reached out and grabbed at things that weren't there. I tried and tried and finally, I gave in to consciousness, rolled over, and stared at the ceiling. I thought of Snukie and wondered how she and her family were. I knew they were in Lake Charles when the storm hit, so they must be okay, but I still wanted to hear from them.

Snippets of my childhood played in my mind. I remembered Bobby as a baby. His dark eyes had reminded me of a snowman with huge pieces of coal for its eyes similar to a drawing I had seen in a picture book. When Bobby was older, we rolled around the living room floor until one of us hit too hard, and Mama would tell me to be careful that he's just a baby.

I tried to remember the good times with Papa, before he became mean. The early morning duck hunts we went on, wading to the blinds, setting out the decoys, watching the sunrise, and looking for the ducks. I remember the first time I went hunting with Papa. I was so trigger happy that I shot at something in the dark. We heard the flutter of the ducks as they took off. When the sun came up and we could see to shoot, there were no ducks. Papa had not even slugged me then. The thing I remembered the most was that last trembling hug when Papa pulled me from the water when Pooch went overboard. That trembling hug replays like a loop in my brain.

I must have fallen asleep because when the door opened, a slice of light from the hallway shone in my face. I opened my eyes and from the pallet on the floor, I stared under Mama's bed at the nurse's white shoes and stockings. She carried a breakfast tray for Mama. Gee, I must have really fallen asleep because I missed the early morning vital signs check. The nurse came back in with another tray for me. I was very appreciative, even though I knew she felt sorry for me. I was too proud for pity. Later, Dr. Andrews came by when he finished his rounds. He thought Mama was well enough to be discharged, so the nurse put her in a wheelchair and rolled her out the front doors. Once we were outside in the bright sunshine, Mama's spirits began to lift. Her dark eyelashes fluttered as her eyes adjusted to the light. She appeared to see the world with renewed clarity.

Dr. Andrews drove down Ryan Street toward his home off of Prien Lake Road. He lived in a rambling, ranch style home with a large picture window. The yard of St. Augustine grass had recently been mowed and neatly manicured. The yard workers were loading the wood from a downed, giant cherry tree, the last reminder of Audrey. Dr. Andrews parked his car under the porte cochere and took them through a side door into the house where Pooch greeted them with a happy wag of his tail and a big grin. Mrs. Andrews greeted me warmly and introduced me to their daughter Suzy who looked like she was a year or so older than me. For the first time, I felt self-conscious in my oversized shirt and jeans. I stared at my bare feet and wished that they would curl up and run right up the legs of my pants. I remembered that I had left my tennis shoes under the cot at the Lake Charles High School gym. They were too big for me anyway. Suzy was friendly, and I felt more comfortable when I heard her laugh at Pooch's tricks. It was the first time that I heard someone laugh since Audrey hit. Laughter made you feel light. Laughter was good.

KPLC TV ran the footage of the aftermath of Audrey. We knew it was bad because we lived through it, but we didn't know the damage had been so widespread. Nearly five hundred lives were lost so far, and many were unaccounted for. Those numbers must have made Mrs. Andrews uncomfortable, and she changed the subject by offering coffee. Mrs. Andrews, or Carol as the Doc called her, was about Mama's age. She was slender like Mama, but she was fair with blue eyes and had long, slender fingers that could run scales up and down the piano.

I saw Mama look at Suzy's framed baby picture on the piano, touching the frame lightly. She sat down on the sofa and sipped her coffee. Her eyes brooded. I felt that I had to protect Mama. I didn't know what I would do if I lost her. She and Pooch were all I had left in the world. Mama's attention riveted to the TV when the announcer held up a sign on the screen with a telephone number to call for information on survivors. She scrambled for a pen on the coffee table and wrote the number on her hand. The announcer stated that the authorities requested that the next of kin should go to the

Port of Lake Charles and check with the authorities at Shed #5 to identify the bodies of the deceased. The icehouse was an alternate location where the deceased were taken, and they also posted the telephone number. Mama wrote the number on the paper that Mrs. Andrews had given her. The public was also reminded to check the local funeral homes and again they listed the funeral homes along with the telephone numbers. I looked down at my hands and said a silent prayer that we would find Bobby. Please God help me find my brother. Mama asked Mrs. Andrews if she could use her phone.

"Of course," she said.

Mama dialed the number to Shed #5. I saw her fingers tremble over each dial hole of the rotary phone. I watched the tension in her face, the flicker of her eyes. I heard her ask for Papa and Bobby.

"No?" she said, elation in her voice. "Walter LaCour Sr. is thirty-eight years old and Bobby LaCour is ten years old. You have several unidentified men and many young boys?" Mama said, disappointment creeping into her voice. Then, mama asked if any baby girls had been found. "Yes?" she said, her voice slowing. "Thank you, I'll go by the Port. By the way, are there any baby girls at the icehouse? No babies at all? Okay, thank you."

She started to hang up with the heaviness of knowing that there were some infant girls and young boys that had been found.

"Oh, by the way, I have another quick question for you. Do you have an Alcide or Althea Thibodeaux on the list?" she said. Mama's screams raised goose bumps on my arms. She wrote the number on her hand and again, gushed her thanks and hung up.

"What is it mama," I said.

"Your Nanan and Parrain are staying at the Fry home." She said. "The man said that they had come by a few days ago looking for Uncle Baby but didn't find him."

Mama dialed the number and crumbled on the floor when she talked with Parrain, her brother. I sat down next to her and put my ear to the phone. She cried.

"Walt Jr. and I are fine," she said.

"We're okay, too. Still in shock," Alcide said. "We made it to the court-house and rode it out there until we were rescued and taken to Lake Charles. Someone said that Baby is staying with a friend here in Lake Charles. I haven't spoken with him, but they said that he is okay."

"We haven't found Walter, Bobby, or Faye, yet," Mama said in a small voice. There was a slight pause before Parrain spoke.

"Guess who I have here who wants to talk to you?" Alcide said. Mama held her breath.

A small voice came on the line.

"Mama?" Bobby said. Mama screamed and burst into tears. Tears came into my eyes too. It was a welcomed relief.

"Bobby, cher bébé, are you okay?"

"I'm okay," he said. "Are you?"

"Yes, cher, I'm fine," she said.

"I held on to the horns of a dead cow and rode it back and forth over the waves—almost like the rodeo," he said. "But it wasn't fun. Some soldiers picked me up, and I rode a tugboat to Lake Charles. Nanan and Uncle Thib were on the tug too."

"Merci, Mon Bon Dieu," Mama said making the sign of the cross. "Someone wants to talk to you," and she handed the phone to me.

"Bobby, it's me, Boy." We laughed and laughed—a good, long laugh. We were crazy with happiness. If it had not been for all the sadness, we would have never known how happy we could be.

Later that afternoon, Mr. and Mrs. Fry drove Parrain, Nanan, Bobby and, to our surprise, Uncle Baby to Dr. Andrews's home where we were reunited in sweet sadness. Mama ran along the side of the Fry's Pontiac

Catalina, and as soon as Bobby opened the door, she swooped on him with kisses. I got to Bobby next, and we wrestled on the ground. Pooch joined in and couldn't stop jumping on Bobby. We all hugged and kissed each other. Uncle Baby got out of the car and I could see the bulk of bandages under his shirt around his shoulder. Nanan said that Uncle Baby was a hero because he carried several people to safety.

"Aw that ain't nothing," Uncle Baby said. "You got to believe in something bigger than yourself. You gotta take action like you believe in yourself. If that makes any sense to you."

"Kinda like if you had a pencil and no paper or a spoon and no soup," I said.

Uncle Baby looked at me, his eyes twinkling.

"You got that right, Boy. You got to have the both of them or you're pretty useless, and I'm useless without God."

Uncle Baby bowed his head in humility. He was the real thing, and I was proud that he was my uncle. We gathered in a circle with our arms around each other's shoulders. We prayed the Our Father and Hail Mary. Each of us tearfully said what we were thankful for. Mama was thankful for finding me and Bobby and she prayed that that we would be reunited with Papa and Baby Faye. We rode the highs and lows of the waves of emotion. We gave thanks for a safe deliverance from the hurricane and for the lives of family and friends. We were especially thankful for our new friends and all who lent a helping hand. Uncle Thib gave thanks for the few, short years that we had known Éli whose gifted presence was miraculous. May God rest his soul.

I never knew Uncle Thib could be anything but funny. Tragedy brought out an eloquence that most assuredly surprised him too. Nanan later told us that she and Uncle Thib had tried their best to get Éli to come down off the roof and go to the courthouse with them. Uncle Baby tried too. Éli's stubbornness and his talent were parallel rails of a train track, and he was bent on traveling down those rails in a run-away train. For someone who was afraid of spiders, bugs, and the human touch, he was fearless in the face of real danger. It's almost like Éli knew that he was an unusual phenomenon, and he was facing another unusual phenomenon—the very turbulent action of the molecules of water that the wind whipped into a hurricane, defying all the historical odds and the ability of scientists and meteorologists to predict storms. Audrey went on a straight course for Cameron and never veered from that course. Éli had that kind of focus, but he was about goodness not destruction.

The morning light crept up the walls of Dr. Andrews's guest room until the room was filled with warm, yellow light. The bed that Bobby and I slept in felt like it floated on an ocean that was dry and safe. Comfortably stretched out in the bed, I thought of how the mind was a strange creature, a great orator that convinced me that a truth was a lie and a lie was a truth. It was so confusing that I wanted to take my head off and shake it like a piggy bank until the coins of memory dropped out, and I could spend it on something stupid. Depressed? Angry? Definitely. I didn't care about bowling shirts or cuffed pants. I didn't care about cool talk. I didn't care anymore. I had walked on eggshells for most of my life, especially around Papa. Always, 'yes sir, no sir, I'll think like you sir. I'll be who you want me to be, sir', and never listening to my own intuition. That's what you call crap in crystal. Yes, the mind is a strange creature. It convinced me that Papa was still alive, and that all I had remembered was nothing but a nightmare.

Mama was the same way. She believed that Papa and Baby Faye were still alive. She had called every funeral home looking for Baby Faye, but to no avail.

"Papa is looking for us," she had said last night as she tucked us into bed. "We must find him. Baby Faye is alive, too," she continued. "I just know it. Someone is taking care of her because her body has never been found."

Poor Mama. Her heart had convinced her mind that Baby Faye was alive. Every time she heard an account of a baby being found alive, floating on a dead cow or on a log, she was convinced that it was Baby Faye. Each time she found out otherwise, her spirit fell off a cliff and never hit ground.

Bobby stirred. Although his face appeared so peaceful when he slept, Bobby jumped a hundred times during the night, and cried out. I know I did the same thing because I woke myself up yelling 'help,' and was completely bewildered as to where I was. I forgot about those plaguing thoughts when Bobby sat up in bed.

"I smell biscuits baking," he said.

"Me too."

I rolled out of the boat-bed into the ocean of yellow. I breathed yellow and hoped that it would fill me and make me forget, make me happy. Pooch woke up, stretched and shook the sleep from his eyes. He pawed his nose and looked up at Bobby and me with a cockeyed grin that said, "I'm glad I'm here." Dr. Andrews did not mind Pooch sleeping in the bed with us. He understood Pooch and me after he heard how Pooch saved my life. He also knew how healing an animal could be for its owner who has been through trauma. He encouraged Bobby and me to keep a journal. Dr. Andrews was the kindest person I had ever met. He was one memory coin that was a keeper.

After I let Pooch outside to do his business, Bobby and I scooted into Mrs. Andrews's big kitchen. It was a homey kitchen that even had a fireplace with copper platters and plates decorating the mantel. Mama and Mrs. Andrews were up to their elbows in flour. They chatted like long-lost friends about cooking and Cajun recipes and the like. Food always makes a good talk because everyone likes to eat. Hunger said to me that I was alive. Hunger was good when you knew where the next meal was coming from. Although there was a sisterhood between Mama and Mrs. Andrews, I knew Mama stood on the brink of collapsing. She was fragile. We must find Papa and Baby Faye.

I remembered so vividly drowning, but the second-most-remembered event was going to shed #5. I remembered it like it was yesterday. After breakfast, Dr. Andrews drove us down Lake Street toward the Port. We drove by crews that worked on telephone poles and downed power lines. We maneuvered around trucks filled with remnants of houses, roofs, and trees. Everyone was busy about the job of cleaning up as quickly as they could, so they could forget about Hurricane Audrey. I wished forgetting would be as easy as sawing limbs and throwing them on the back of a truck. We drove into the parking lot at the Port of Lake Charles where we saw Nanan and Parrain waiting for us. A truck had just backed up to Shed #5 and a couple of men with bandanas around their necks unloaded bare pine boxes. I smelled the scent of freshly cut pine when we walked by, and I thought to myself that the smell of Christmas would never be the same. I heard the carpenter say that they had shifts working day and night. Over three hundred more coffins were needed.

My legs felt like concrete columns. I willed them to move toward the building, the temporary housing of the dead— the victims of Hurricane Audrey. Hurricane Audrey was a killer storm, a devastating circle of energy that wiped out Cameron Parish and went on up the coast all the way to the state of New York where it exhausted itself and died, too. It left in its wake the trappings of unfinished lives. I feared that my mind would never heal from the images of dead people and animals. I also would never forget the household things—refrigerators, mattresses, clothes, washers, and dryers bobbing in the endless ocean. And books, I thought for the first time. Grandmère's books! My heart squeezed.

Before we went in, Dr. Andrews asked if Maurice Bilbo's body had been claimed. I had told Doc about riding in the rescue boat with the body of one of my best friends. Doc didn't want me to go through that trauma again. The supervisor at Shed #5 told Doc that a family member had claimed the body, and it was taken to Combre Funeral Home. I was relieved that someone in Cracklin's family survived, and that they would give him a proper burial. People went in to view the bodies with rags soaked in a little ammonia over their noses. I understood why the coffin carpenters had bandanas around their necks. Dr. Andrews gave us some Vicks salve to put in our noses before we entered. We used the ammonia rags as well. I followed Mama, Parrain, and Nanan inside. Bobby had stayed with Mrs. Andrews. Mama wanted me to stay as well, but I was determined, and she changed her mind.

Once we were inside, I realized how important the ammonia-soaked rags and the Vicks salve were. It was bad enough to see dead people but much worse to smell them. Except for Cracklin, the only other dead person I had ever seen was Gammy with the Dress. She was a pretty, dead person, though. I could still see her lying in a satin lined casket. She wore a white lace blouse with a cameo brooch at the neck, and she looked like she had fallen asleep with her glasses on. These dead people looked like they didn't belong to themselves or to the human race. Many were bloated, lips swollen, mouths opened revealing black tongues, eyes staring, and arms and legs twisted at strange angles. Some still had grass and mud in their mouths. Their bodies were so bloated that the seams in their jeans had ripped. The pine boxes were lined up neatly, and as each body was cataloged, it was sprayed with formaldehyde and put in the box.

Mama and I looked closely at a number of babies. Hurricane Audrey took its toll on the most vulnerable: the infants and children. We looked carefully at all of the female babies, but Baby Faye was not among them.

Mama exhaled a sigh of relief. She was convinced that Baby Faye was alive. Mama twisted the ammonia rag in her hands and occasionally held it to her nose. Her eyes scanned for Papa. I heard Mama whispering a prayer that we would not find Papa there. I shuttered when I saw Mr. Babineaux's body—a surprised by death expression on his face. Poor Mr. Babineaux, he had been a carpenter when he was younger and a good one at that. He prided himself in the construction of his house. "It's solid—made of cypress," he had said. I remembered him bragging that night at Uncle Thib's bar that his house could withstand any tropical storm or hurricane. He was old and thought he had seen everything that life had to dish out. No one had been in a hurricane like Audrey. He was right about his house, though. It floated off the piers, but it did not break up. No one ever knew how it ended up floating in Calcasieu Lake. No one expected the high water and waves that caused most of the damage. No one expected that so many people would be killed, especially, by drowning. Mr. Babineaux's wrong choice sealed his fate.

Mama moved on ahead. We all heard a sob or was it a choke that came from Mama's throat? Did the ammonia rag get to her? No. My worst fear was realized, a fear I already knew but would not face. Mama had found Papa wrapped in an American flag. She knelt down on the ground at Papa's feet and wept. I was stunned to see him so calm in death. His furrowed brow that added to his mean expression in life was as smooth as a baby's. At last, he was in a place where he was at peace. He didn't have to drink anymore to ease the pain and disappointment of a life that he believed to be unlucky. He had never learned to be grateful for what he had. He chose to be angry for what he didn't have. Mama tugged on his wedding band to remove it, but it wouldn't budge. She put some of the Vicks salve on his bloated finger and pulled it off. She slipped it on her thumb. Mama was well acquainted with grief, but apparently, she never got used to it. She collapsed on the floor next to Papa.

"Oh Walter," she said. "I always thought I would be with you when the end came. You were supposed to be old and gray. You were supposed to be in our iron bed, propped up on our pillows, nice and comfortable. A priest was supposed to give you the last rites and I was to hold your hand and whisper 'I love you. Go with God my love until I see you again.' You were to take one last peaceful sigh and your spirit would separate from your body. You weren't supposed to die like this!"

Mama's voice began to rise in pitch.

"Oh God, what am I going to do. I have our three children to care for. Walt, tell me what to do."

She broke down in sobs, and Parrain helped her up and put his arm around her shoulders.

"Sh, Sh," he said. "Mary Effie, listen to me. I'm your big brother and I will take care of you and the boys. My home is yours. We will figure all of this out. Don't worry."

Parrain helped her walk to the car. Dr. Andrews spoke to a man who was in charge that stood nearby trying to avert his eyes. He wrote Papa's name on a tag that would be tied to his toe or his wrist when they left. I asked about the flag. The undertaker said that he didn't know, except that a man by the name of Édmond LaCour brought the body in, but he didn't stay long enough to leave Papa's name. Why didn't Uncle Baby tell us? I guess he figured we would find out the next day when we went to the port. I guess he wanted to spare us one more day of knowing.

I stood there and stared at Papa's body. I didn't cry at first. Papa would not have wanted me to. I stooped down beside him. Anger scalded me; it rushed my mind. I took Papa's shoulders and shook them.

"You stupid, dumb, drunk," I said. "Why did you die on us? Why? Why didn't I save you?" I broke down in tears and kept saying, "I'm sorry, I'm sorry."

I would always feel that Papa was disappointed in me. Dr. Andrews put his arm around me and led me outside where I took a deep breath of fresh air.

"It's okay to be angry, son," he said. "Anger is a good thing because you let it all out."

"I want to kick every barrel, throw every stone, break every window, and kick every tire. I want to crush something, twist something, and scream my brains out," I screamed. Dr. Andrews hugged me.

"I know, son. I know. Hurricanes have no motivation; things just happened. Humans have motivation and make things happen. What do you think you could make happen?" Dr. Andrews said. I was standing on a threshold between good and evil. Out of the fog of what seemed like another lifetime, I remembered saying something to Mama.

"I just want to live a rightly life," I said. I knew that I meant I wanted to live a life of grace and that coin was a keeper.

CHAPTER TWENTY

Hourless and minuteless days followed. Days painted with broad strokes of a brush dipped in colorless, painful paint. My family and I, along with many other families of the dead, stood at the edge of mass graves one hundred and fifty feet long by eight feet wide dug by bulldozers. Draglines lowered pine boxes, suspended briefly between earth and sky, into a six-foot-deep gash of soil. Men standing in the grave guided the boxes and lined them side by side. I stood solidly on the ground looking into the grave when I had the sensation of being bounced on a limb that I clung to and of falling— falling from the tree. I looked at the pine coffins and noticed the way the sun made them brighter as if the sun was a shroud that draped over each one. I took a deep breath of air and the blood began to rise to my head. I heard the aching groans of the dragline, the soft drone of the priest's prayers, the slight shuffling of the crowd, otherwise quiet, and the sounds of sadness that fell on my senseless ears. Nothing moved me except the finality of the thud of a gargantuan lump of dirt pushed by a dozer to cover the graves. I remembered the dim flashlight in the attic straining against the darkness. Does the darkness win in the end? People were born into pain and they died in pain—they had to make the most of the in-between. I stood at the foot of Papa's grave in the best clothes the Salvation Army could offer me. I felt regret that permanently stained my soul. It was something that could never be washed off or burned from my memory.

I felt a hand slip into mine. I turned around and faced my beloved Snukie. She had found me. I hugged her and had difficulty looking at her because my own tears were on the verge of a major overflow.

"I thought I would never find you again," she said tears streaming down her face. "Mama saw the announcement for the services in the paper. I'm so sorry."

I couldn't speak, but my arm around her said everything.

Our heartbroken family walked away from the gravesite into the South Louisiana heat, to Dr. Andrews's car that waited to take us to the cemetery where Cracklin was being buried. When we reached the burial site, I saw Cracklin's Mama and Daddy and went up to Mrs. Bilbo and hugged her. Their family lost Cracklin, Rose, and little Callie. We stood arm and arm and sang in French and in English.

La Grace du Ciel est descendue
Me sauver de l'enfer
J'etais perdue, je suis retrovée
Aveugle, et je vois clair.

Amazing Grace how sweet the sound
That saved a wretch like me. I once was lost but now I'm found
was blind, but now I see. 'Twas grace that taught my heart to fear
and grace my fear relieved. How precious did that grace appear
the hour I first believed.

Recovery was slow, and Uncle Baby went around rallying the troops. His actions during World War II proclaimed him to be a war hero. His actions during Hurricane Audrey raised him to a mythical level in the eyes of Cameron residents. When his boat careened out of control, he rode the waves back and forth. He threw a rope out to a several people and pulled them in. They hung on to his boat until he could pull them over the side. When the eye of the storm came over, and there was a lull in the chaos, he spotted a body tangled in fishing nets. When he got the body into the boat, he realized that it was Papa's. Uncle Baby's boat ended up crashing through a window of a house. He stayed there staring at his brother's dead body until the wind stopped and the water receded. After the worst of the storm, he carried people on his shoulder to the courthouse, which was made into a temporary hospital. Finally, Uncle Baby went back to his boat and wrapped his brother in the American flag that he had taken down in front of Uncle Thib's bar, threw him over his shoulder and boarded the tugboat that took him to Lake Charles. Not until he left Papa's body at the temporary morgue that he sought help for his own injuries. He saved many lives that day, and he did it all with a broken clavicle and a separated shoulder.

Uncle Baby went about organizing a townhall meeting to bring folks together to let go of the past and discuss the future. He called and recruited several people to participate. He was determined to unite the community. Uncle Baby wasn't the only hero during Audrey. He called the beloved Dr. Duhon, who also risked his life to walk in waist-deep water to the hospital to care for the injured. Dr. Duhon evacuated the hospital when he realized that it was not safe, and he transported patients to the courthouse where he treated all who came in with snakebites, broken limbs, head injuries, and a whole gamut of wounds and ailments. He learned later that members of his own family had not survived.

Uncle Baby talked to a priest.

"Do you think it is too soon to have a service, Father?" Uncle Baby asked.

"No, son, I think a ceremony for all those who died and whose bodies have not been recovered is an appropriate closure for their families."

Uncle Baby called the Mayor and councilmen and asked,

"Do you think people will come?"

They didn't know. People were fed up with hurricanes and the dangers of living by a body of water that was subject to the weather that had no mercy. Uncle Baby, Bobby, and I, along with Uncle Thib and others, worked with the National Guard and soldiers from Fort Polk to clear the debris around the courthouse and the streets so that people could come back and make their decision to stay or not. The newspapers were contacted as well as the radio and television stations so the word would get out to come to the townhall meeting and memorial service.

The evening of the meeting came. It was a clear day with a robust sun inching its way down the western sky. All the officials, dressed in their Sunday clothes, were standing in front of that stately courthouse that had protected so many people. Everything was ready: a banner was in place, the donated folding chairs were set out, and a makeshift podium set up, but the question in everyone's mind was, 'Is the spirit of the people strong enough to motivate them to return?' It had crossed my mind, and I wondered how the people would react. Uncle Baby was slicked up in a white shirt and tie. He thumped the microphone and spoke into it to test it. The microphone was fine, but Uncle Baby was nervous. Beads of sweat formed on his forehead and he kept patting it with his handkerchief. He looked at his watch again and again. It was 5:45 p.m. on a Saturday near the end of July and the meeting was to begin at 6.00 p.m. The mayor and councilmen, a couple of newspaper reporters, a camera man from the Lake Charles TV station, Uncle Baby, and our family were the only ones there. I along with Mama, Bobby, Nanan, and Parrain sat in the empty sea of folding chairs. Nanan took her straw hat off and fanned herself. Most of the residents were still in Lake Charles and had not returned to begin rebuilding yet. Uncle Baby looked at his watch again. His shoulders slumped as 6:00 o'clock approached. At 6:30 he gave up.

"Well, Mr. Mayor. It ain't gonna happen. I think that hurricane destroyed the community spirit. I guess we will have to call it a day," Uncle Baby said.

"It sure is a shame. I thought the people of Cameron had a little more gumption than this," he said.

Uncle Baby started to descend the steps when we heard rumbling trucks coming toward us. Army deuce-and-a-half trucks came in carrying the residents. Uncle Baby looked at the Mayor and councilmen, and we were all brought to tears. The trucks parked and the Cameron residents, black and white, came out in full force. The people got out of the trucks carrying flowers and followed the priest who carried a crucifix lifted high. Uncle Baby, the Mayor, and all of us looked at each other and joined in and sang with bravado; we sang with grief; we sang with our souls, our voices becoming one voice and one heart singing.

There is a balm in Gilead to make the wounded whole.

There is a balm in Gilead to heal the sin-sick soul.

Sometimes, I feel discouraged and think my work is in vain.

But then the Holy Spirit revives my soul again.

There is a balm in Gilead to make the wounded whole.

There is a balm in Gilead to heal the sin-sick soul.

If you cannot preach like Peter, if you cannot pray like Paul,

You can tell the love of Jesus and say, "He died for all."

There is a Balm in Gilead to make the wounded whole.

There is a balm in Gilead to heal the sin-sick soul.

Everyone followed the priest and gathered around the water's edge for the memorial service where the priest prayed for the deceased and their families. We stared sadly at the very water that was the cause of so many deaths. We lifted our eyes to the heavens and hoped that our loved ones were watching our futile efforts to reconcile their deaths. We kissed the flowers and tossed them into the golden water as the sun lowered on the horizon. Mama, Bobby, and I threw flowers for Baby Faye and Papa. Uncle Thib and Nanan put flowers in the old student violin that was left in the bar and found in the rubble after the storm. It was waterlogged and broken but they floated it in the water for Éli.

The residents walked back to the meeting site in front of the Courthouse and settled into the chairs. The building was battered, but it was erect and stood among the trees that had survived. The fresh wood where limbs had been broken off and the leaves had been stripped from branches were stark reminders of the power of wind and water. The crowd sat under the barren trees, and a hush fell over them when Uncle Baby stood up.

"Me, I thought y'all weren't going to pass yourselves back here. I thought all was lost and then you come up here singing your hearts out. You know we have had some hard times. You know we have had some sad times and you know that Cajuns don't give up. They don't call us hardheaded coonasses for nothing." Everyone laughed. Uncle Baby continued.

"We don't make a big to do about things, but we keep coming back. We work hard and help each other and ourselves. We are married to this land and like a good marriage, we don't give up. Our grandparents, fathers, mothers, sisters, brothers, and our children are buried here. Our sweethearts are buried here. We laugh and cry and make our living here, and we will stand by our town. We will begin anew. A thousand trees come from one acorn. A thousand miles begins with one step. One step after another begins a new road and a new vision for our town. Our slate has been wiped clean. We have new roads to walk down. We must begin again with a vision for our future. This old courthouse is still standing because it was built right. It stands as a sentinel of our community, the very spirit of Cameron, Louisiana. Let's join hands and bond together, help each other and rebuild this town for our children and grandchildren and in memory of the victims of Hurricane Audrey so that their life's work here in Cameron was not in vain."

Everyone clapped and cheered. Then the Mayor and councilmen gave their speeches. When all the talk ended and questions had been answered, we were energized. We vowed to be stronger than before.

A few days later, Dr. Andrews drove Bobby and me, Uncle Thib, Nanan, and Pooch back to Cameron where we lived in a tent donated by the American Red Cross while we began the bitter task of rebuilding our lives. Mama stayed in town because she was still looking for Baby Faye. When the electricity was finally restored to Cameron, Uncle Thib ran an extension cord from the pole to our tent, and we were able to have light in the evenings. We really didn't have much need of light at night because we were so tired from working all day that we collapsed on our cots at sundown. The canvas tent that had been erected for us was tall enough to stand in, and it had netting over the door to keep the mosquitoes out. Parrain had it positioned so a breeze from the Gulf would keep it cool. We each had a cot, and it proved to be okay. It was like being on an extended camping trip. Nanan had a kerosene camper's grill to cook on. She fried fish and shrimp and made gumbo. Sometimes we roasted hot dogs over a campfire. Parrain rigged up a temporary shelter that he covered with netting and put a picnic table inside where we ate our meals. Pooch was my constant companion, sleeping at the foot of my cot, and if I worked on the roof of Parrain's new house, he would curl up by the ladder and wait for me to come down. If I swam in the Gulf, Pooch swam with me.

The early evenings were special because Bobby and I talked more with Parrain and Nanan than we ever did with Mama and Papa. We didn't have TV or books, but we talked and told stories. Parrain took his role as Godfather seriously. We prayed a rosary every night under the stars. Bobby and I became good at naming the constellations, and occasionally we would see a shooting star. I would think of Mama and wonder if she was getting well. I often wondered if Papa and Baby Faye could see us.

Mama stayed through the summer at Dr. Andrews's where he paid her to cook and clean. She enjoyed Mrs. Andrews's company, and our family desperately needed the money. We had a cot for her when she visited us on weekends. The routine of life began to flow like the slow, lonesome rhythm of Uncle Thib's accordion. Someone gave him a used accordion to everyone's delight. Most of the people of Cameron, Creole, Grand Chenier, and all the surrounding areas came back to build their houses and towns stronger than before. They were married to the land where their kin had died, and they were going to stick it out in good times or bad. Not everyone came back. They had enough of hurricanes and the destruction. Snukie's family was one of them. Mr. Miller got a job at one of the industrial plants in Beaumont, Texas, and they decided to leave. Since they had nothing left to move, Mr. Miller said 'that it was the easiest move he had ever made.' I took it the hardest and suffered another lonesome loss.

Late one afternoon when the sun ripened the fields and marshes to a golden glow, Potted Meat, Snukie, and their parents came to say goodbye, not only to their friends and neighbors who came back to rebuild, but to the very site where their house once stood. They walked around the sunken site looking for anything that was a reminder of their life before Audrey. Snukie's eighty-year-old grandfather, Paw Paw Miller hobbled with his cane to the area that was about fifteen paces from what was once the back door.

"Right here, son," he said to Mr. Miller, Snukie's dad. "I know I buried it between the peas and the carrots."

"Okay, Pop. I hope you buried it deep enough, or it would have washed away," Mr. Miller said.

He pushed his hat off his brow, stabbed the ground with his shovel and dug into the promise of a life savings buried away for a rainy day. I couldn't think of a time more saturated. This was as wet as it got. Paw Paw Miller had lived through the bread lines of the depression and didn't believe in banks, Snukie had told me. Banks had betrayed him. The poor, rail-thin man leaned on his cane in his long-sleeve white shirt and baggy brown pants cinched with a belt that had missed a few loops, anxiously waiting to find out if the earth had betrayed him, too. He mopped his brow with his hanky and adjusted his glasses with his feeble, liver-spotted hands. Everyone peered into the hole and hoped for his sake that his treasure would be found. Mr. Miller's shovel hit something solid.

"I believe we've got something here," he said.

A few more shovels full of dirt and he was on his hands and knees lifting a rusty, metal box. When they wiped the dirt away and pried the lid off, they found four quart-size mason jars filled with rolls of tightly wound one hundred-dollar bills with a rubber band around each roll. Other than a little condensation collected on the inside of the jars that dampened the bills, they were still in good condition.

"Well, if that don't beat all. Mais garde donc ça, Pop. You were right as rain," Mr. Miller said.

He took his hat off and wiped his forehead. Paw Paw nodded his head, pleased and relieved that it had been found. Snukie and I helped Paw Paw to the shade of Uncle Thib's tent. Uncle Thib broke out a bottle of Falstaff from a cooler, and everyone toasted Paw Paw.

"If that ain't as exciting as finding Jean Lafitte's treasure," Uncle Thib said.

"That soil's so rich, no wonder you always had a mess of peas and carrots," Uncle Baby said.

The men drank beer while Bobby and Potted Meat hung around listening to their stories and jokes. I picked up a stick and threw it to Pooch. He chased after it, and I followed him as an excuse to leave the group. Snukie soon followed. We had only a moment alone, so we walked to the mimosa tree that had been in her backyard. It leaned a little, but it had survived.

"I got a tractor stuck in the mud trying to upright this tree," I said to her. "This tree was really important to me."

I knew minutes were born with invisible wings and would light on me so softly that I wouldn't even know they were there until they had gone. I didn't waste any time. I showed Snukie the backside of the mimosa tree where I had carved a heart with the initials WL + SM. Snukie looked up at me and blushed. We put our hands together, and again I felt the sensation of not knowing where my fingertips ended and hers began.

"This is the bridge to our hearts," I said. By entwining our fingers, the bridge was made stronger.

"No matter how many miles or minutes come between us, we will always stay connected," she said.

I kissed my finger and placed it on her lips and held her gaze with my eyes. Her eyes filled with tears, and she blinked to control them. We took small, slow steps back to the road delaying the inevitable goodbye. Pooch walked beside us trying to get me to throw the stick again. Snukie's parents were saying their farewells to Uncle Thib, Mama, Uncle Baby, and some of the other neighbors. All the jovial jokes and chiding that went on suddenly ceased. The silence spoke the pain in our hearts. Snukie's dad leaned against the open car door and held the seat back so Paw Paw Miller could get in.

"Take care of yourself, Mary Effie. I will hold you and yours in my prayers," Mrs. Miller said placing her palms together.

Mama's lips curved slightly in an attempt to smile. She nodded.

"Thanks. I'll do the same for you. Come back soon," Mama said.

A quiet hush fell over Mama, and she looked tired. Snukie got into the back seat of the car, and the last image of her that I saw was her hand pressed to the car window and her face turned toward me with sadness brimming from her eyes. I held my hand in a goodbye wave, knowing that my fingers formed one half of a bridge and knowing that I was fragmented without her. I still felt the warmth and tingle from the tips of her fingers while I watched the car roll away in a trailing veil of dust.

I thought of Snukie every day while I carried lumber to rebuild Uncle Thib and Nanan's house as well as some of the neighbors' houses. I thought of Snukie while I pushed the wheelbarrow, laid foundation, hammered and sawed. I thought of Snukie when I skinned my knees laying roofing shingles. I thought of Snukie through what I thought was an endless, blistering summer. I thought of Snukie to keep from thinking about Papa, Baby Faye, Cracklin, and all the neighbors that we had lost. She was the only sweet hope that I had left in my heart.

Bobby and I turned a healthy bronze that summer. The sun and the manual labor strengthened us. I grew about a foot. I grinned wryly to myself and thought that I probably would have grown taller if my heavy heart had not weighted me down. Bobby grew as well and matured physically. In the quiet before sleep, Bobby brooded. But for the most part, he became an idiotic daredevil. One breezy day, when Bobby and I were laying shingles on the roof of Uncle Thib's house that overlooked the Gulf, Bobby put his hammer down. He tossed the shingle he held, and it slid across the roof.

"I've had enough of this," he said.

Bobby stood up and stretched, twisting to the left and to the right and before I could blink an eye he kicked into a handstand on the pitch of the roof. I tried to pretend that it didn't bother me, but the truth of the matter was that I was scared to death.

"Don't be a fool, Bobby. Have you lost your mind? For Pete's sake, cut it out," I said. Bobby kicked his legs down and stood upright and faced the Gulf. He laughed a long laugh in the face of the sky.

"It's not my time, brother! It's not my time!"

"It may not be your time to die, but you may be spending the rest of your time in a wheelchair," I said. "You want to hurt Mama again?"

"Life is a balance. Éli knew that," Bobby said.

"Éli was an idiot. He died because he wouldn't get off the roof."

I didn't believe that, but I thought it would be a good argument to get Bobby to stop acting like a fool.

"You act like an old man. You never have fun anymore," he said.

"You can have fun, but you don't have to be stupid about it. Let's get down and go inside for a while. I think the sun is getting to you."

I sat on the front porch of Uncle Thib's new house, and it was my time to brood. I felt a responsibility toward Mama and Bobby. I was the man of our small family now, a position that I really didn't want. Finally, the long summer had come to an end, and we finished Uncle Thib and Nanan's house. We were proud of the job we had done. Everything inside and outside was clean and new: the flint colored roofing shingles, the screened porch, and the fresh white paint. Bobby and I hated to paint. We agreed that if we died and woke up with a paintbrush in our hands that we would know that we had surely gone to hell.

Mama found a small house to rent, and Bobby and I moved in with her so that we could go to school in Lake Charles because the schools in Cameron had been destroyed. We went to visit Parrain and Nanan on the weekends. Mama continued to work for the Andrews, and Bobby and I fell into the rhythm of the school calendar. As soon as school was out, we planned to move in with Parrain and Nanan. They were the only family we had left, and all of us worried about Mama. Dr. Andrews said that time would heal her sorrow. It would heal Bobby's and mine as well, even though Bobby pretended that nothing could hurt him. Dr. Andrews encouraged all of us to write in a journal. I took his advice somewhat, but Mama and Bobby did not. Instead of journaling, I wrote stories with characters that went through loss. I thought at the time that it helped me to let it go, but I was still haunted. We had to be patient; these things took time to heal. Mama clammed up and barely spoke to any of us. Three months went by, and there was no improvement. Mama was not well.

One soft evening in late September on a weekend when we were in Cameron, Nanan washed the supper dishes while Mama continued to sit at the table picking at her food. Her hair wasn't combed, and she wore the same shirtwaist dress she had been wearing all week. It looked like she had slept in it. Parrain and I got up and went to the screen porch and sat in the rockers. Bobby sat on the porch swing and brushed Pooch's fur, getting the burrs out. We watched the moon come up over the marsh. When the wind blew, the marsh grass waved and made the silver moonlight ripple.

"She wouldn't eat, again," Parrian said between puffs of his pipe. A haze of smoke floated off. In the silence between sentences, we heard the cries of frogs, crickets, and nutria.

"I know," I said. "She pushed the rice around her plate like she was hunting for the one grain that wasn't done, like she was trying to make sense of something."

Our conversation was cut short when Mama hurried to the door with a startled look.

"That's Baby Faye," she said. "That's my baby!"

Nanan came to the porch curious about the commotion.

"She's out there," Mama said.

Mama wiped her hands on her apron and opened the screen door and stood on the top step listening. We heard a cry that sounded like a baby. Mama ran down the steps. Uncle Thib and I looked at each other like she had lost her mind.

"You better go get her, son," he said.

Mama ran down the road toward the marsh.

"Faye," she screamed. "Faye!"

"Mama!" I called. "Stop!"

I ran after her and caught her. We fell down on the dirt road. I hugged her and felt her waif-like ribs. She struggled to get out of my grasp. I held on to her to keep her from running into the marsh.

"Let me go, let me go, it's Faye," she cried.

"Mama, that's the nutria. They sound like babies crying. It's not Faye. Faye drowned."

"No, no," she kept saying. "That's my baby. My baby is out there."

It was a strange experience for me that evening. Although I was on my knees holding Mama, I saw myself from above, kneeling in the dust, holding Mama like a frail bird not strong enough to fly. She rocked and sobbed in the glow of the silver moonlight. We were surrounded by the sound of human babies crying as the nutria cried their own sorrow into the night air.

I, too, was not well. I had nightmares of Papa's hand reaching for me, always reaching for me, and grabbing me by the throat. I saw his dead face at my window. Many nights I woke up gasping for breath and wondered how nightmares could steal my breath and breathe like they were living parasites that needed my lungs and my brain to be real. Yes, I too was haunted.

CHAPTER TWENTY-ONE

1966

Memory after memory, I recorded. I remembered most events by the way they made me feel. After the hurricane I felt sad, but I was so busy trying to bring normalcy back to my life that I never grieved. High school was a blur. College was a new start for me, and I was determined to make something of myself.

"Your mother called," was scribbled on a note that had been slipped under the door of my room in the Blue Dorm. "Has news. Come home if you can." That was it? There was no further explanation? Was this good news or bad news? I wasn't sure if it was Mama's lack of explanation, or some clown's lack of note taking.

"Damn, I have plans too," I said.

I was going to go to Scalisi's and shoot pool with the guys, but I guess I'll scratch those plans. I walked up and down the empty hall knocking on each door to find out who left the message. Everyone was out or at fraternity meetings to prepare for the onslaught of weekend parties, especially since it was football season. I didn't belong to a fraternity for two reasons: money and money. That wasn't a completely accurate statement. If I had really wanted to do something badly enough, I would have found a way. The truth of the matter was that I didn't like being told what to do, how to dress, and all the meaningless crap that goes along with it. I had to rethink that because I was in advanced ROTC and they certainly commanded you to dress a certain way and behave in a certain way, but they paid me $40 a month. ROTC was more of a strategy of survival. I didn't want to be drafted. When I did go into the military, it would be as an officer. I glanced at the door of the closet where my ROTC uniform hung with its polished brass gleaming. My boots were polished and shone from the work of my own spit and elbow grease. The Vietnam War waged its toll on guys who partied too much and didn't make their grades to stay in school. I had been at war one way or another all of my life. Self-preservation, whether physical or emotional, was a war that I was well acquainted with. I even warred against my own expectations of the way I wanted my life to be. It was difficult accepting my own mediocrity. Would I ever find a separate kind of peace?

I knew I had to lighten up a little, not be so serious and brooding—not that I hadn't had my share of good times. I did all the high school stuff, proms, and the like. I worked after school and weekends at Uncle Thib's bar, except during basketball season, to earn money to buy corsages for Peggy Andrepont and several other dates throughout my high school career. I had preferred to save my money for a truck, but I reconciled that expense as part of the high school scene, more like a rite of passage. Graduation was a necessary conclusion to high school: the ceremonious, formal goodbye to the high school years that shaped our lives and our futures, the formal kicking out of the nest and flapping of our own wings. My youth was ravaged by a hurricane. My father was dead on my account, and I never got to say goodbye. My paralyzed hand wasn't even offered as an anchor, much less raised in a gesture of goodbye.

"Damn me," I said out loud.

I looked at the note again and tried to imagine the motivation behind it. There was no way I could get a hold of Bobby. I knew that Bobby had a date tonight. When did Bobby not have a date? I picked up the receiver of the pay phone at the end of the hall, dug in my pockets, but didn't have the change. I slammed the phone down and went back to my room, kicked the door open and plopped on the bed and glanced around the room like I was seeing it for the first time.

My room was a typical dorm room, nothing special. A 1 x 6 board resting on top of a couple of cinderblocks next to my desk made a shelf that held my books and all of my school stuff—bare-bone basics, yet convenient, on the run living at its best. Everything was temporary, even my eyes seemed to view life as a temporary thing. There was good and bad in that thinking. Sometimes I had to give my attitude a kick in the temporary to get myself motivated. I glanced around my side of the room; my roommate's side attested to my ability to ignore, except when the Dean called last February to tell him to remove the line of chocolate milk cartons from the windowsill.

"C'est la vie," I said out loud.

I grabbed some books, a huge load of laundry and headed for the parking lot. Opening the door to my Chevy truck, I threw my used Biology and Speech books along with the laundry on the front seat, hopped into the driver's seat and revved the engine. My rosary swung from the rear-view mirror. The lilting strains of the McNeese spirit song *Jolie Blonde* floated through the open window when I passed the football field where the McNeese Cowboy Band was practicing for tomorrow night's game with the Ragin' Cajuns of USL. It had only been a couple of weeks since I had started another semester; what could Mama possibly want? I knew Mama needed me; she needed to have her family around, especially since Bobby started at McNeese, too. The scholarship I had won for being valedictorian in my high school class helped Mama save and pay for Bobby's college. We had lived on the poverty level for so long. Mama scraped by, saving and borrowing money from Uncle Thib when she absolutely could not make ends meet. She didn't know how much longer the money would last or where the next tuition would come from, but Mama was determined to keep Bobby and me in school to avoid the draft and the Vietnam hellhole, although Mama would not have put it that way. I was already motivated to do well in school. Trying to stay in school with the threat of Vietnam was like walking a tightrope without a safety net.

After Hurricane Audrey, running and reading were the only balms for my sleepless mind. In the afternoons, weather permitting, I ran down Highway 82 to the high school and back. I had to exhaust myself so I could sleep. When I wasn't running, I buried myself in books. I had read everything from *The Hardy Boys* and *The Catcher in the Rye* to the labels on the cans in Nanan's pantry. In the afternoons when school was out, and I wasn't passing a broom or a mop over the floor, I read the *Lake Charles American Press* at Uncle Thib's rebuilt bar which he had re-named Éli's Laissez Les Bons Temps Rouler. A bar was not exactly a fitting memorial for someone who had died, but it was well intentioned. I understood Uncle Thib. Neither Éli's body nor his violin was ever recovered. Losing Éli made me grateful that I had known him. I also regretted the loss of his violin. I had researched the Stradivarius and discovered that it was worth in the millions of dollars. If we had only had it when we were rebuilding. It would have helped Uncle Thib and certainly would have helped Mama have a house of her own or at the very least paid for Bobby to stay in school with some left over to help our neighbors and others in our community. Uncle Thib had a large framed picture of a Stradivarius violin with *Éli's Violin* inscribed below. He continued the same décor by hanging a cheap, old violin on the wall at the end of the bar near Uncle Baby's stool. He also hung pictures of the destruction of Hurricane Audrey lest anyone had forgotten. Uncle Thib commissioned a local artist to draw a picture of Éli playing his violin on top of the Laissez Les Bon Temps Rouler.

Uncle Thib's bar was where the phenomenon of an idiot savant was appreciated and the crowds always applauded and cheered Éli, but he never played for applause. God knows you couldn't slap him on the back and say 'great job' without him freaking out. He never knew crowds only individuals, and he could name everyone in the room, even though he didn't converse with them very well. He lived every moment with extreme focus especially when he lost himself in his music. When that happened, time had no constraints. Éli had no ego, caring little for the approval of others because he followed an inner voice.

I remembered how Éli tried to show me the scrolled openings on the violin so long ago. Because the violin was open, the sound vibrated inside resulting in music. I didn't get it then. My mind finally understood it, but my heart hesitated. Éli could look at a person and play just the music that the person needed to hear at that moment. Mrs. Comeaux told us after the hurricane that Éli had saved several people. Evidently the water had lifted Éli up and pushed him toward the trees that Uncle Baby had thrown the life preserver into and lost. Éli had grabbed a branch of the tree and held on. He found the life preserver and had calmly unknotted it. He sat on a branch of the tree and was looking to throw the life preserver to whoever was swept by. Clelie Comeaux said that she was thrown from the mattress that she had been riding on and was flailing in the water. Éli threw the life preserver to her, and he reeled her in. He saved a few other people in the same way. In fact, when he saw Pooch swimming by, he yelled, "Boy's dog," and jumped in with the life preserver and caught Pooch. They were swept into the tree where our fort was, and Pooch swam to the boat and had scrambled in. The wave made Éli slam his head into the tree. Then he went under and never came back up. When I heard the story, I broke down and cried. It was the first time that I had cried for Éli. It was the first time that Éli had snapped out of his world and into reality. Maybe Mama was right. Miracles come in strange packages. Maybe, he was a different kind of angel.

During the summer of rebuilding and recovery and encouraged by Uncle Baby, my reading gradually graduated to the classics. Shakespeare was a perennial favorite. Some of my big favorites were the Nobel and Pulitzer Prize winning authors: Faulkner, Steinbeck, and Hemingway. I especially liked Hemingway's *The Old Man and the Sea*, and *For Whom the Bell Tolls*.

One of my favorite characters was Phineas in John Knowles' *A Separate Peace*, although I liked the brooding Gene Forrester as well. Finny was a larger than life character, but I identified more with Gene. I had read the short story the year of the hurricane, and I read the book in high school, trying to understand Gene's guilt and my own. I read to keep my mind from remembering. The only thing my mind and the Gulf had in common was that we were both insomniacs.

I turned my old truck onto Highway 27 toward Cameron, flipped the radio on and sang along to "I'm Leaving It All Up to You."

"That's a former number one hit by Dale and Grace brought to you by KLOU broadcasting from Lake Charles, Louisiana. That's Grace Broussard, a Louisiana native of Cajun descent from Ascension Parish," the D. J. announced.

When I was closer to the Gulf, I stuck my head out of the window and smelled the briny marshes and the Gulf waters in the air. The drone of mile after mile always made me slip into a life review, except when I was in love and that wasn't a happening scene at the moment. Love was expensive in more ways than one. It was 1966 and Bobby and I had grown up a lot since 1957 when Hurricane Audrey uprooted any semblance of stability in our lives. Mama, Bobby, and I came out of that storm with nothing but our lives, since we were only renting the house that we had lived in. We didn't even have a baby picture of ourselves, or sweet Baby Faye. That bothered Mama a lot.

"I can hardly remember what she looks like," Mama would say to me. "I wonder if she looks like me or Papa."

Mama never accepted the fact that Faye had drowned. She still thought that someone had found and raised her and that the next time she went to the Piggly Wiggly Grocery store in Lake Charles, she would see this dark-haired girl at the checkout register that looked like her. She also thought for a long time that Papa had survived the storm, suffered from amnesia and couldn't remember who he was or where he lived. That was a nightmare in itself. I reminded her that we identified Papa's body, and we buried him in a mass grave. During those recovery years, she didn't want to believe it because she didn't have the physical energy and mental stability to face the truth. Even though my father was a flawed character, he was the only papa that I had ever known. I didn't have another one to compare him to. I preferred not to think of him, though. That kind of thinking brought on the 2 a.m. nightmares. I had often wondered about Mama's German lover, Johann, but I never got the courage to ask her about him.

Approaching Cameron, I realized that I didn't even remember passing the turn off for Creole or turning onto Highway 82. I had driven this route so many times that my truck knew the way. I did notice a new hand-painted sign that read, 'I clean duck and gooses too'.

"4:35 on a rocking Friday afternoon," the D. J. said.

I glanced at my watch. Yep, Mama should be clearing off her desk, so Monday morning would be a new start. I grinned at the thought of her learning to type several years ago. Shortly after we settled in Uncle Thib's new house, Mama had somewhat of a nervous breakdown. Uncle Thib came home with a little, black typewriter and a big, old calculator that crunched the numbers like someone eating raw carrots.

"Mary Effie," he said, "I've got a project for you. Me, I'm not good at typing and ciphering dem numbers. No. I need someone to help me with the books for the bar. My fingers are just too fat to hit these keys; besides, as smart as you are, you can learn to type and calculate in no time."

I knew where Uncle Thib was going with this. I knew he really didn't need the help; he just wanted to get Mama interested in something and get her mind off Baby Faye and Papa. I thought Mama was cute biting her tongue as she tried to figure out how to roll a piece of paper into the machine. She pecked out her name using her index fingers. I flipped through the manual.

"Mama you've got to read this manual. It teaches you how to type using all your fingers, so you can type really fast," I said, "kind of like playing the piano." She and I sat down and laboriously learned to type. By the time I entered high school, I could already type. I aced my typing class, which I had to take anyway because it was a requirement. I didn't have near the frustration that some of the other students had. A classmate of mine, old Rodney Robicheaux, got so mad at the typewriter that he picked it up and threw it out of the second-floor classroom window. Several of us boys jumped up to see the black keys skittle across the sidewalk. Our teacher said, "Mr. Robicheaux, I suggest you go pick up the pieces and take them to the principal's office."

Mama became an expert typist and a whiz at calculating without looking. Those two machines were a godsend. She worked in a back room at Uncle Thib's bar keeping track of inventory, expenses, quarterly reports, and the whole gamut of running a business. Uncle Thib was in the black in no time.

Mama was still a beautiful woman, but she had never dated since Papa died. It wasn't because she had never been asked; plenty of men came around to Uncle Thib's bar trying to interest the little bookkeeper with the big, black eyes. She would never look for a man in a bar. If she ever looked for a man again, he would have to be a teetotaler. We were proud of Mama, and she liked the respect. She wanted to be independent and not always feel beholden to Uncle Thib; although, she was grateful to her brother. When she was offered the secretarial job at the courthouse, she took it. Mama's delicate psyche recovered because she had a reason to get up in the mornings.

I rounded the corner in front of Uncle Thib's bar and saw Uncle Baby get out of his truck. His wife Bubbles, who had been sitting slap dab next to him, silly at their age, slid out behind him. Uncle Baby was gray, but still handsome for an older man. At least he still had hair. Uncle Thib had lost most of his. Uncle Baby had married Bubbles, a Korean girl he had met at the

VFW several years ago. He couldn't pronounce her name, so he made one up. Bubbles waited tables for Uncle Thib on weekends; I'm sure she wanted to keep an eye on Uncle Baby because the bar was his second residence. Surprisingly, Uncle Baby was not an alcoholic. He could take it or leave it because every Lent he gave up drinking. He simply liked the camaraderie at the bar, and he enjoyed having an audience for his craziness. I didn't have time to stop, but I honked the horn and waved and leaned out of the window. They waved back.

"Comment ça va, Uncle Baby and Bubbles?" I yelled.

"Ça va bien! Boy Oh Boy," Uncle Baby yelled back.

I turned into the courthouse parking lot and turned the engine off. I was curious to find out what was up with Mama. I glanced in the rearview mirror and combed my brown hair with my fingers. My hair had turned darker than it was when I was a kid. I sort of looked like Papa, but that was a stretch. It was a big stretch, I thought to myself because I had light skin that burned easily. I really looked more like Mama. I quickly blocked that thought and turned my attention to the courthouse. In a couple of months another hurricane season would be charted off the calendar. I mounted the concrete steps of the courthouse and remembered the role that it played in the survival of so many people. It was not only a safe refuge during the hurricane, but during the reconstruction period it became the central location where the citizens gathered to determine their resources and bolster their courage to rebuild with the future in mind. It was the heart and strength of the community.

I walked down the hall and up the stairs of the crusty, old building, past Judge Clarence Chevalier's office to his personal secretary's office, my Mama's. *Mary Effie LaCour* was printed in neat black letters on the clouded glass window of her door. I stuck my head through the open door. Mama faced a gray filing cabinet, scrutinizing documents and flipping through files with a purposeful efficiency. I tapped on the doorframe and walked into her office. She glanced over her shoulder and peered over her reading glasses. She dropped her papers on top of the cabinet.

"Walt," she said, "Cher bébé."

It was funny how Mama still called me bébe, even though I was 6'1" and still growing. After Papa had passed away, everyone started calling me Walt since there was no longer confusion with Papa. I was glad that they had dropped the Boy of my childhood. In fact, everyone stopped calling me Boy because it was such a reminder of Papa. Almost everyone, except I was still Boy Oh Boy to Uncle Baby. However, I was glad to start over with a new, more mature name.

"Mama," I said grabbing her and swinging her around the room. "How's my favorite Mama?"

"Your only Mama," she said laughing and gave me a kiss. "I'm fine, I'm fine. And how is my favorite first born?"

"Your only first born. Ça va bien."

I sat in a chair across from her desk and glanced around the room. Mama had a thing for pictures. She had a picture of all of her family, except Papa and Baby Faye, in frames around the room. Understandably, when a monster storm like Audrey came for a visit, picture taking became a nostalgic obsession. My gaze settled on a bouquet of a dozen red roses. Why hadn't I noticed them earlier? My mind scrambled to think if it was her birthday or a special occasion. None came to mind. There was a lightness of excitement in her face and movements, something that I had not ever remembered seeing before. Mama looked at me carefully.

"I could be better," I said. "What's so important that you called me home on a weekend that the Cowboys are playing at home?"

Mama gasped.

"Oh, I'm sorry, Walt. I guess I'm out of touch; I didn't realize—I guess I have been a little preoccupied lately," she said.

"What's this all about?" I asked pointing to the roses. Mama giggled.

"Well son, that's what I wanted to talk to you about," Mama said glancing away, her face coloring. She turned her eyes back and looked directly at me. "Mr. Clarence asked me to marry him."

"Mr. Clarence? Judge Clarence Chevalier?" I asked. Mama nodded. I reeled with shock. That was about the last topic I had expected to hear from her.

"He's at least twenty years older than you," I said in surprise. "He's an old man."

"I know," she said quietly. "I feel old myself."

"Why, Mama? Is it the money? Is it to keep Bobby in school, so he won't be drafted?" She shook her head.

"Money always helps, but that's not the reason I'm marrying him. You know me better than that, Walt."

"Do you love him?" I asked and leaned forward, elbows on my knees and staring at my clasped hands. It was strange talking to Mama about her relationship with a man.

"It's a different kind of love—respect, concern, and admiration. Mr. Clarence and I are comfortable together. He makes me laugh. We think alike. Your Papa was a handsome man. I chose to love him. I've known the fire in marriage. Mr. Clarence is kind. He appreciates me and tells me so. He respects me as a person. He's the most unselfish person I know. He said he would take care of me, and I told him I would take care of him, and another bonus is that he doesn't drink."

"Does he not drink because he doesn't like it, or maybe because it goes against his principles, or is he a recovering alcoholic?" I asked.

"He just doesn't like it that much. He has seen too much in his business—too many lives destroyed over alcohol," she said.

I nodded my head thoughtfully.

"You're willing to risk losing another husband?"

"Walt, there's no guarantee that I'll outlive him. No one knows the future. Hurricane Audrey taught us that. I can't believe that I'm sitting here asking for my son's approval. All of my life, I've had to ask for some man's approval. I had to ask my Papa for permission to marry your father; then after I married him, I lived a life of mealy-mouthed groveling. I am my own person, and I deserve to make my own decisions. I'm like that oak tree out there. I'm a survivor, and I choose to love Mr. Clarence." I stared down at my clasped hands, totally bemused by Mama's uncharacteristic outburst.

"Do you think *Chevalier* will fit on that door, or will they have to scrape your name off and start over?" I asked.

I had misgivings, but I faked it nicely. I surely didn't want to stand in the way of Mama's happiness. She deserved to have a supportive son.

Before I drove to Nanan's, I could see Pooch on the front porch barking. He recognized the sound of my truck. I didn't realize how much I had missed Pooch until I saw his excitement that I was home. I got out of the truck and ran to him, hugging him, scratching his ears, and telling him how much I loved him. He couldn't move very well, and I could tell he was in pain, but just to see me I knew lifted Pooch's spirits and to see Pooch lifted mine too.

The smell of Nanan's crawfish pies wooed Pooch and me to the kitchen, where I hugged Nanan and gave her a kiss on the cheek.

"I always get a hug and kiss when you're hungry," she said. I laughed.

"So, you figured me out."

"Get yourself cleaned up. You're Mama's Mister Clarence is coming for dinner," she said.

Judge Clarence had spent a lot of time around Nanan and Uncle Thib. He was very comfortable and seemed to fit in our family. At the dinner table that night, Judge Clarence expounded on law as a career. I listened politely and told him that I wasn't sure what I would do. I told Judge Clarence that I was interested in psychology, but I knew that my interest was for purely personal reasons. I still enjoyed reading, but I wasn't sure what I could do with an English Lit. degree, I had told Judge Clarence. At this point, I was just trying to keep my head above water. I finally ended that subject when I stated that I was majoring in S-O-N.

"What's that?" Judge Clarence asked.

"Staying outta 'Nam," I said.

Judge Clarence said, 'that was a very worthy major.' After dinner when Judge Clarence left and Papa and Nanan had gone to bed, Mama and I sat out on the porch and talked. Being away at college made me realize how much I had missed the night air—the cricket's chirps, the frogs' croaks.

"Walt, I want to apologize about the comment I made about your Papa," she said. "My mealy-mouthed groveling was my problem—not his."

She paused that golden moment that I remembered as a kid, allowing the words to sink in.

"I loved your father. He had his own problems as you and I well know. Before we were married, he was tender and kind—very empathetic. He pursued me. He worshiped me and after we married, he continued to be that way until he hurt his leg and started drinking. I didn't know who he was anymore, but I had made a commitment for better or worse. Most people can't live up to sainthood. No one is perfect. We all need forgiveness—to accept forgiveness and to forgive."

Mama sat quietly like she wanted to tell me something. Hesitation hung in the air between us. I thought she was going to tell me about the German guy, but to my surprise she didn't.

"Your father will always be a hero in my eyes," she said and wiped a lone tear from her cheek. "When that tidal wave washed Baby Faye out of my arms, your father jumped in that raging water to save her."

She paused trying to gather her composure.

"Your father couldn't swim!"

Fresh tears welled in her eyes. I was shocked. I remembered an image of Papa dog-paddling back to the boat in the storm.

"I remember he always wore a ski belt when we were on the boat. Why didn't he ever tell us that he couldn't swim? Why didn't you tell us?"

"He was so ashamed and considered it a weakness. You know how macho he was."

I smiled and nodded.

"He made me promise never to tell anyone."

"That's why he couldn't join the Marines with Uncle Baby," I said.

"That's right. Mama paused.

"Your father drowned trying to save our baby, your sister. I will always be grateful for that sacrifice."

Mama brushed the tears off her cheeks again. For the first time since the hurricane, Mama admitted that Baby Faye had drowned in the storm. It was the first time that she acknowledged that Papa had also drowned. My heart was crushed with guilt and shame. I didn't have the heart to tell Mama the truth that I had had the opportunity to save Papa and I didn't. She would hate me for the rest of my life. I would commit suicide before I would ever tell her. Not a bad option, I thought; however, my real feelings about suicide was that it was a slap in the face of God. It was like telling God that there was nothing He could do to help you, that He could never make you happy again. It was a denial of the power of God.

CHAPTER TWENTY-TWO

"I'm not ready to lose you, old man," I said.

Pooch looked up at me with big, adoring eyes. He licked my hand to show how grateful he was to go for a ride.

"I'm the one that should be grateful to have a pooch like you. I reached out and felt the soft silk of his ears. I'm going to take you to the Doc to see if he can give you something to help you move a little better. Okay, buddy?"

Pooch contented himself to sit by me on our trip to the vet's office in Lake Charles, enduring the tension he must have felt in me. Pooch buoyed my spirits. Today was Saturday and the vet closed at noon, I reminded myself. I eased my foot down on the gas pedal and the old truck hummed along mile after mile. Mama certainly surprised me with her announcement of her pending marriage to Judge Clarence. I had thought they were just friends, but I supposed that sons would always have a problem viewing their mothers in a romantic light. I remembered how shocked I was when I read her diary. I certainly had a problem with her German lover. She always insisted that I was born early, even though she never knew I had read her diary. I wasn't convinced. Things had been tough for Mama, and I simply wanted her to be happy and at peace. Her life had finally settled into a rhythm of predictability. Gone was the drama of mood swings, temper flares, and drinking binges that she had endured with Papa. Poor Papa. He was so unaware of how much stress he put on other people. The world was his glove, and he was going to wear it. Even after his death, he still controlled me. I thought time would be my friend and I could let those memories go, but that wasn't the case. Mama's admission that Papa couldn't swim knocked my socks off. I had tried writing which was supposed to expunge me of the haunting memories. The only problem was that I wrote around the issue. I could not face my guilt much less write about it. Some things were so secret that I would not have written it on a grain of rice, much less a diary that someone could read. I already learned a lesson about reading diaries. I never asked Mama about the German soldier she was in love with. I didn't want to add to her sorrow. It just didn't matter anymore, so I thought.

Pooch whimpered in pain when I rounded a curve causing him to shift his position.

"It's okay, old boy; we are almost there," I said scrunching the soft fur of his neck. "You're still my best friend." I thought of the history Pooch and I had which was stronger than the water-logged rope swing that he held in his mouth and swam to me during the hurricane. The loyalty and selfless actions of this dog brought tears to my eyes. He was a hero and yes, Pooch was the second reason Mama had wanted me to come home. She said that he acted depressed when Bobby and I left home to move into the dorm. He was lonesome—poor, old Pooch. He was graying around his mouth and eyes and he had become so arthritic that he could only manage to stand and wag his tail when I walked in. He could walk a bit if he had to, but I could tell that it must have been very painful. I had to lift him up on my bed where he always slept when I came home. I ran his golden ears through my fingers, knowing how love in Braille felt to the blind.

I slowed down my rushing when I turned down McNeese Street, drove a couple of more blocks and pulled into the vet's office parking lot. I gathered Pooch on his pillow and carried him in feeling the weight of my wanting—wanting him to live forever. I was saddened when I thought that all the people that I ever loved were transients on a road to God only knows where, stopping to pick a dandelion and blowing the flighty seeds to the wind. I was that dandelion blown to bits of loss. I walked into the fluorescent light like I was delivering a tiara. Pooch knew where he was and started trembling.

"It's okay, boy," I said.

I turned my attention to the counter where I signed my name on a ledger. A girl with a perky flip to her brown hair stood with her back to the glass that separated the waiting room from the office. She talked on the phone while I stood at the counter waiting, conscious of only my name on the page and Pooch's pain. I glanced around the room. A healthy sunlight warmed the pallid walls. A sign hung on the wall that stated "We speak meow" engaged my thoughts. It was more like a language of observation—press here and there and look for a reaction. I looked at Pooch—poor Pooch. Poor animals: frustrated, scared patients that can't say how and where it hurts. Others threaten with a growl that warns, I hiss, I claw, I bite, so there! Our lower nature is to hurt those who hurt us. I drummed my fingers on the counter. A chart on the wall displaying a limner of the cycle of a heartworm: the parasitic miles of loopy thread that settle in the heart like a hairball. I ran my fingers over the spiral notebook—that coiling, wire, worm that binds the page that claimed my name. Walt was here.

The girl behind the desk became aware of my presence and slowly turned around. She wrote a telephone number on a slip of paper.

"Yes, sir, I will give him the message," she said.

I jerked my head up. Her voice sounded familiar. She looked up, and I saw sheets flapping in the wind and the greenest eyes that I had ever seen; I saw my baseball cards fluttering across the tops of the Johnson grass, and I didn't care; I let go of Yogi Berra, Ted Williams, and all my heroes because she gave me the courage to put my hope in her. She was incredibly beautiful, looking at me, who was incredibly ordinary. She stood perfectly still while holding the phone to her ear, speaking—a voice from long ago, a voice in my dreams, a voice that I would remember all of my life.

"Yes, we close at noon today," her voice trailed off.

She stood there, never taking her eyes off me, lifting her left hand and pressing it against the glass.

"Okay, thank you for calling," she said.

I was mesmerized, putting my hand against the glass on the other side, praying that this would be the last barrier of our love, knowing full well that people change, and that there had been many years under that bridge.

She lowered the phone slowly and stared at me, that fraction of a moment when the electricity of love penetrated the glass. She ran around the desk to the door of the waiting room and threw her arms around me.

"Boy," she cried looking up at me. "It's so good to see you. It's been so long."

"Snukie, Snukie, Snukie," I said squeezing her and smelling the sunshine warmth of her hair.

Me with all my fancy words, I couldn't think of a thing to say. I just felt the vibration of her name in my mouth. Dr. Marlow rounded the corner and adjusted his glasses.

"Rayna? Who's Snukie?" he asked looking around the room.

"Oh, Dr. Marlow," she said. "That was my nickname when I was a kid growing up in Cameron. This is my friend, Boy LaCour."

I shook hands with Dr. Marlow.

"*Boy* was my nickname when I was a kid. Now everyone calls me by my real name, *Walt*—Walt LaCour."

"Of course, Walt. I recognize the name. Good to see you. I'll be with you in a minute. I've got to wipe down the table. We are a little short-handed around here."

I was grateful for those few minutes. Rayna giggled, I laughed, and we just stared at each other.

"Oh," she gasped. "Pooch is getting old. Poor baby."

She walked over to him. I watched her move, her slender frame bending over with gentleness. She was filled with the gift of a life-force love for all creatures.

"Yeah. He doesn't move so hot anymore," I said. Snukie stooped down eye level with Pooch and ran her fingers through his soft coat.

"I hear you can't steal bras anymore," she said.

Pooch licked her hand, thumped his tail against the pillow and smiled his happy grin. I laughed, remembering my declaration of love for Snukie and Pooch's role in our embarrassment.

"I thought you moved to Beaumont for all of these years," I said.

"We did. Daddy got transferred to Lake Charles a couple of years ago," she said.

"So, what have you been up to? Are you married?" I said too quickly.

I winced to myself. I certainly didn't want to appear overly eager.

"Not even close. I go to McNeese and work here part time. What about you?" she said.

I saw her glance at my hand to see if I had a ring on. That gave me confidence to go for it.

"No, I'm not married either. After this year, I should have enough hours to be a senior at McNeese. I'm not in a hurry though. Just trying to stay in school. Trying to stay out of 'Nam. I joined the advanced ROTC, so when I graduate, I'll go into the service as an Army Officer for at least two years. Maybe the war will end by then. I live on campus in the Blue Dorm. Bobby started McNeese this semester. You remember my brother Bobby, right?" I cringed at my non-stop monologue. I wondered what had gotten into me. I had known Snukie all of my life, and I was acting like an angst-ridden teenager.

"Of course. How can anyone forget Bobby? How is he?" she said.

"Oh, Bobby, lover boy. He always has a date. He turned out to be a good-looking guy according to the girls. His head finally grew in proportion to his eyes. All the girls in high school mooned over his big, black eyes. Half a dozen of them claimed the song 'I Want to be Bobby's Girl.'"

I shifted my weight and berated myself for being nervous and giving too much information.

"Anyway, so much for Bobby. How is your brother, Al, ole Potted Meat? I haven't heard from him in a long time," I said.

"Al was drafted this summer. He is in boot camp at Fort Polk right now. He will probably be sent to Vietnam," she said and cringed.

"Gee, that's too bad. I hate to hear that."

"Mama is really upset, but what can you do but pray?"

"I'll let Mama know. If you ever need any prayers, she's the one to go to," I said.

"I remember that. Your mom was always in Mass," she said. "When Al gets leave, I'll tell him to give you a call. Maybe you guys can catch up."

"Yeah, that would be great. Be sure and tell him *hello* for me."

I paused. By the way, would you like to go to the football game with me tonight?" I asked. "I have to drive Pooch back to Cameron, but I could be back to pick you up around 5:30. Maybe grab a bite to eat before the game?"

"That sounds great. That will give us some time to catch up," she said. "I still live with my parents. Mama and Daddy will be glad to see you."

She wrote her address and telephone number on a piece of paper and handed it to me.

"I included the phone number in case you get lost," she said.

I put the piece of paper in my shirt pocket over my heart as a reminder to guard it with my life. The door opened and an average looking guy about six feet tall walked in carrying a book. He was average looking until he looked at you. His eyes were the color of clear, blue mountain lakes that I had only seen in pictures. They looked as if they had read a thousand faces or seen a million minutes, if any of that made any sense. I was taken aback. He was more aware than most people—very calm as if he could feel the flow of water through the gills of a fish, or as if he felt the exchange of oxygen and carbon dioxide in my lungs. He was astute in a casual way. He was familiar and unfamiliar, someone aware of nothing and something, one and the same. I wanted to kick myself for always analyzing, always surfing for meaning.

"Hi, John," Rayna said.

"Hi, Rayna."

"John Williams, this is Walt LaCour," Rayna said. "John and I are in Dr. Carlisle's speech class."

I shook his hand and nodded politely. I was surprised that he was in school because he looked older than most students. I figured he had served in the military and was now out and going to school on the GI bill.

"Pleased to meet you," I said, trying to sound cordial.

"Likewise," he said.

"*LaCour* means heart, right?" he said to me. I nodded. "Like in 'get to the heart of the matter'? That reminds me of one of the reasons I stopped by."

He turned to Rayna.

"Thanks for letting me borrow your book," he said as he handed it to her.

"Any time."

"Okay then, I'll see you at ten o'clock on Monday morning," he said.

"You bet," she said.

"Can't wait to hear your speech," John said.

"Well I can certainly wait to give it. I'm not looking forward to that. I know I'll be a nervous wreck," Rayna said.

"Nah, you'll do great," John said to her.

He turned to me.

"Good to meet you."

I nodded. "Same here," I said.

He made me uncomfortable. I wondered if I was jealous, but I wasn't the jealous type, I reasoned. John turned toward the door and took a couple of paces. Pooch got off of the sofa and walked to him. John oddly turned around and bent down to greet Pooch before he saw him coming. Maybe he has supersonic hearing, I thought. It was really weird. Pooch could barely walk to me, yet he walked to this stranger like they had been friends for a long time. How could that be? I had Pooch since he was a pup. John petted Pooch.

"Those old joints ache don't they Pooch, old boy?" he said. "It's going to be okay, my friend. It's going to be okay."

Did he call all dogs Pooch? I wondered. There was something mystic about this Williams guy.

"See you Monday," Rayna said.

John opened the door and exited before I could speak. "How did you know my dog's name?" died on my lips.

My two-second suicidal thoughts of Friday afternoon were put on hold. I was euphoric. All the next day, I lived the snippets of Saturday night with Snukie, Rayna that is. By the time I got Pooch back to Cameron, showered, shaved, and dressed, I was running late, and we didn't have time to go to a sit-down place to eat. Snukie suggested going to the A&W drive-in so that we could sit in the car and talk. "Besides," she had said, "the A&W isn't far from the stadium and it would give us more time."

We laughed over old times and dumb jokes. I was mesmerized with the smallest details that stamped themselves on my brain: Rayna eating French fries with catsup; Rayna flashing white teeth; Rayna laughing with root beer foam on her upper lip that reminded me of that summer day when we drank root beer at Uncle Thib's and succumbed to the giggles. She asked about Papa and Baby Faye and how Mama was handling it.

"She's sad. I guess we are all sad, but we're working on it," I said and turned my head away to stare out the window.

Rayna got the message. That was one subject that was buried, also. She didn't bring it up again. I told her that Mama was going to remarry and that I was glad for her. I changed the subject, and we careened with laughter again.

I ran and reran the details of the evening in my mind as if the evening was put through a sieve and only kernels of minutiae were left: Rayna cheering at the game screaming "Allons Cowboys"; Rayna tiptoeing to kiss me when the Cowboys scored; Rayna, standing in the stands with my arm around her, swaying back and forth to "Jolie Blonde"; Rayna slipping her hand in mine, touching fingertips, not knowing where mine ended and hers began, then making a bridge by entwining them. It was the smallest moments of love that made life worth living—that took my breath away.

That night back at the Blue Dorm, Rayna dominated my dreams, but I was still haunted by faces floating up: Cracklin's full-faced grin, Baby Faye's eyes that wanted to jump out of herself, the man they found floating on the refrigerator, and the many faces of Papa. I thought that all that catching up brought out a lot of old memories. I tried to study all day Sunday, but it was just about useless. I went to Mass, but I couldn't focus. Mass was a reminder that I needed to go to confession. I had been to confession before, but only confessing my venial sins. I tried to speak of my guilt and why I didn't reach out to Papa, but I had barely gotten it out when I couldn't take it anymore. I bolted out of the confessional before the priest gave me absolution. I guess it didn't count. I was a basket case. I turned my thoughts back to Rayna and daydreamed.

When I rolled out of bed on Monday morning, I squeezed my head, as I always did, trying to crush the nightmares with my bare hands. I grabbed my shaving gear and stumbled down the hall to the bathroom. I filled the sink with water and glanced in the mirror. I gasped. I thought my reflection was Papa. I must be hallucinating because I didn't even look like Papa. I lathered my face and took a swipe with the razor. I looked down into the sink full of water and saw Papa's dead face floating, staring at me.

"Damn," I said out of breath. I dropped my razor in the water and backed away from the sink. Pete Combs was shaving at the sink next to me. He looked in the sink.

"What the hell's the matter with you, man?" he said. He glanced at my face and saw a trickle of blood. "Oh, cut yourself shaving, huh? That's a bummer. I thought you had too much to drink this weekend, or you were seeing things," he said.

"Yeah. I guess it could be a little of both," I managed to say, trying to be cordial and not come across as a nut case. I glanced in the mirror and saw the blood. I hadn't even felt the cut. I finished shaving and put a piece of tissue on the cut to stop the bleeding and remembered that I had to hurry to the registrar's office before my class. I dressed hurriedly in a light blue shirt and faded jeans. I took the stairs two at a time.

"You going to breakfast?" Paul said, coming in from his early morning class.

"No. Can't make it this morning. Gotta get to the registrar. I'm switching a class. See you later," I said.

"Must be some hot chick to get your butt moving that fast," he yelled back.

I hustled across campus trying to shake the nightmares and visions that continued to plague me. I'm a rational person, I thought. Why can't I get over this? I knew that was why I was taking psychology classes so that I could figure myself out. Okay, get your mind off of this and think of something else. Rayna. Good choice, I answered myself. At first, Rayna made me think of the past with all the catching up, but now I felt myself thinking of the future, a future that included Rayna. I heard the distant sound of thunder and thought I could detect a slight, crisp smell of the promise of cooler weather in the air. I couldn't wait to walk with Rayna in the crisp air of a colorful fall; the leaves of the tallow trees would be turning to red and gold, even though so many people referred to tallows as trash trees because they proliferated so much; anything plentiful did not seem to have value, but they were beautiful in the fall. No tree was a trash tree to me, even a scrawny gum tree saved lives in Hurricane Audrey. I reached the registrar's building, took the steps two at a time, plowed my way through the door and to the drop/add window. *Mrs. Lackey*, as her nametag read, pursed her lips that were sunken in a fleshy face. She looked over her cat-eyeglasses at me and shuffled some papers around. I knew she was going to be a tough nut to crack because she had been employed at McNeese for a long time and had probably heard every possible excuse.

"Good morning," I said politely hoping to win her cooperation.

"Good morning to you, too. I see you cut yourself shaving this morning. What can I do for you?"

"Oh," I said and peeled the tissue off my face and stuffed it in my pocket. "My name is Walter LaCour, and I'd like to drop my 2:00 p.m. Speech 102 class with Dr. Carlisle on Monday, Wednesday, and Friday and add his 10:00 a.m. class on Monday, Wednesday, and Friday," I explained.

"A good-looking boy like you? There must be some girl in that class," she said peering over her bifocals.

She was a veteran registrar and not easily convinced.

"I see it all the time, and we just can't change classes for those kinds of reasons."

"You mean you would stand in the way of someone's future happiness and the generations of kids and grandkids that are yet to come?" I said with a laugh.

"Yeah, you're full of bull like the rest of them," she said.

I noticed a picture of her hugging two Irish setters and the words just popped out of my mouth.

"Actually, I was just kidding. I'm applying for a job to work in the afternoons at Dr. Marlow's Veterinary Clinic. I've loved animals all of my life. I grew up with a golden retriever named, Pooch," I said. I rambled on. "This seemed like the perfect part time job for me, so I needed to make the switch."

Man, I thought to myself, love sure can make you lie in a hurry. But it's not a bad idea. Didn't Dr. Marlow say he was short-handed?

"I'm partial to animals myself," she said. "In that case, let me take a look at the availability of space in that class. Dr. Carlisle is very popular, and his classes are generally full."

I cocked my head so that I could look at the names on the list. I started from the A's to the M's. There she was, Rayna Kay Miller, aka Snukie. Then I looked back down the list to the W's and didn't see John Williams' name on the list. Maybe he dropped the class. At least I didn't have to put up with someone who made me feel uncomfortable or jealous. Good, I thought. Mrs. Lackey counted the names on the list.

"It looks like it's full," she said.

"Please, if you would be so kind to count one more time—please?" I said with my most believable and endearing whine.

Mrs. Lackey counted again and to her surprise, she came up with a space. She counted a third time to make sure.

"Hmm," she said, "I guess I missed one the first time that I counted. Lucky for you. Okay, Walter Manley?" She lifted her voice in a question.

"Yeah, named after my father—you know, a family name," I said. She wrote out my name saying it out loud.

"Walter Manley LaCour, you are officially enrolled in Dr. Carlisle's 10:00 a.m. class and dropped from the 2:00 p.m. class." She signed her signature and stamped it. "Give this add/drop slip to Dr. Carlisle," she said.

"Thank you, Mrs. Lackey," I said chivalrously.

I pretended to take off a hat and bowed deeply to her.

"My future children and grandchildren thank you, too."

She looked at me in surprise.

"Just kidding, just kidding," I laughed and headed toward class. If she only knew.

Dr. Carlisle meticulously meted out minutes.

"Being on time demonstrates one's interest in class, one's responsibility and most of all one's character. I expect each of you to practice excellence," he had said on the first day of class.

He hated interruptions. I saw him walking across campus in his trademark, tweed jacket with elbow patches, even though the weather wasn't quite cool enough to warrant a jacket. He never went anywhere without an umbrella under his arm. He was known for his old-school formality. He entered the building several yards ahead of me. I broke out in a full run and raced up the steps to catch up. I was determined not to be late and have the door shut in my face. I had to see Rayna. I entered the classroom just as Dr. Carlisle dropped his worn, leather satchel and his umbrella on the desk and turned to walk back to the door to close it. I gave him the add/drop slip, and he wrote my name on the roll. I glanced around the room and saw Rayna sitting in the middle row. I slipped into the empty seat behind her, much to her surprise. I smelled her perfume, *Chantilly* she had told me.

"I switched my 2 o'clock speech class to this one," I said lowering my voice to a whisper. She smiled and gave me the thumbs up sign and turned her attention back to Dr. Carlisle. Dr. Carlisle gave a stack of handouts to everyone on the first row.

"Please pass the handouts back," he said. Dr. Carlisle was known for his politeness. He addressed everyone as Mr., Mrs., or Miss, as the case may be, in a boarding school, gentlemanly fashion. Rayna took one and passed it on to me. I took one and turned to give it to the person behind me. To my surprise, there sat John Williams. I hadn't noticed him when he came in because my eyes were riveted on Snukie. John smiled and nodded. I nodded and turned forward hoping he didn't notice the puzzled look on my face. Maybe he transferred to this class too. No—that wasn't right. It can't be. He had returned Rayna's book the other day and they talked about the class. Gee, he's strange, I thought. This whole situation was strange. Dr. Carlisle went to his desk and put away the extra papers and cleared his throat.

"Before we begin our introductory speeches, I want you to become familiar with the grading chart," Dr. Carlisle began. He looked over at me and said, "Mr. LaCour, this is the same assignment that I gave the 2 o'clock class last week."

"Yes, sir," I said dutifully and nodded in acknowledgement.

"These speeches are merely ice-breakers," he continued. "They won't be graded by me. They will be graded by each of you. Notice the checklist on the handout. These are self-explanatory such as: Did the speaker make eye contact with the audience? Was there any unnecessary movement of the hands or shifting of weight? How many unnecessary words such as *uh, hmm, you know,* etc. were used? At the bottom of the page is a section for comments. Please be constructive and respectful. As you know, the assignment was to talk about an experience that you have had, good or bad. It can be in any form you wish, epistolary, a poem, an essay. You can be as creative as you wish. The idea is simply to get you up here and relieve a little tension and fear of speaking in front of people. Next to death, the most feared experience for the majority of Americans is speaking in public; therefore, I would ask your utmost respect and attention to each speaker."

Dr. Carlisle sat down at the desk while everyone read the grading chart and he concentrated on each student, looking back and forth from his roll book to the student. It took a long time, but there was an unbelievable payoff. His mind recorded the face of each student to the name, another one of his trademarks. That's why everyone liked him. It was rumored that by the third class meeting he could remember everyone's name in all of his classes, and he could greet you by name not only in the classroom, but also anywhere on campus. That type of attentiveness to every soul that crossed his path was truly a gift. When asked about it in the 2 o'clock class, he simply said. "A gift is what you make of it. You have to be diligent and practice. It also demands that you respect each soul that you encounter as unique. Then you commit that uniqueness to memory."

It was such a beautiful comment that I thought that one day it would probably be engraved in brass under a bust of Dr. Carlisle displayed in the Theater building because he also taught drama.

"Okay," he said, "shall we begin? Who would like to go first?"

No one offered. The sounds of shifting weight, rustling paper, and shuffling feet could be heard as everyone squirmed in their seats. No one wanted to go first. I slumped in my chair.

"Going once, going twice. Well then, since we have no brave souls, shall we go by the roll?"

He started to pick up the roll book when Rayna raised her hand.

"I'll go, sir," she said.

"Indeed, we do have a brave soul. Very well, Miss Rayna Miller."

Rayna got up, and I held my breath for her. I wasn't sure if it was from watching her legs and the swish of her skirt or that I was nervous just because she was nervous.

"If anyone hears knocking, it's just my knees," she began with a nervous laugh. We laughed nervously for her. She began.

Faith of 'Fifty-Seven

I don't know what happens when I'm so afraid.
Words deflate.
My lungs are powerless to bring them back to life.
We huddled in the living room on that June day.
Winds razed the most recalcitrant root.
My rabbit cage torqued across the yard.
Grandpa sat forward, arms on his knees,
squinting through his glasses, listening.
Grandma strained a handkerchief in and out of her fingers,
Mama held her ripe belly,
Sister hugged her knees, the other hid behind the sofa.

Daddy was out there somewhere.

I sat on the piano bench, a concerto at my fingertips.

Grandpa said to stop. It distracted him from his fear,

the keening banshee at our door.

I don't know what happens when I'm so afraid.

I pray words limp as washed up clothes and carcasses

hanging on barbed wire fences.

No amount of meaning holds death.

No amount of intensity brings back life.

I said them anyway. I made boats out of them

with wings for sails.

I let them go in the breath of the banshee.

Somehow, I knew they would survive.

My rabbit's cage torqued across the yard.

Daddy was at the door, arms holding.

Everyone sat quietly absorbing the images.

"Very fine poem and presentation, Miss Miller," Dr. Carlisle said, "An interesting perspective. Was that the hurricane of '57?"

"Yes, sir," Rayna said. "Audrey."

"Audrey, of course," he said. "I wasn't living here then, but the storm made a major impact on the residents, I understand."

"Yes, sir," Rayna said.

"I'll give everyone a moment to check your grading charts and make comments. When you are finished please pass them on to Miss Miller."

Rayna sat back down, and I gave her a squeeze on her shoulder. She glanced at me quickly. Her cheeks flushed a warm red, and I remembered how her eyes turned greener when she got flustered. I filled out the chart and wrote on the comment section, "weight was evenly balanced on feet attached to very nice legs. Beautiful smile and a touching poem."

I passed it to her, and she looked back and grinned.

"Okay, who will be next?" Dr. Carlisle said peering over his glasses and looking at us.

I prayed that Dr. Carlisle would not call on me because I had planned on writing my speech before my 2 o'clock class, but with this class change, I didn't have a chance. I slid down in my chair. Someone else volunteered, and I fell into a slump with the soft hum of speeches. I doodled. A guy in a madras shirt gave a speech about going to court for something like a traffic ticket. I couldn't remember. I wasn't paying attention. I was thinking about the clothes and carcasses hanging on the barbed wire fences of Rayna's poem. Anyway, at the end of the speech, the guy took a gavel and hit the podium saying,

"Guilty!"

I nearly jumped out of my chair. The whole class jumped. That woke us all up and got everyone's attention. I sat up in the chair and thought about guilt, my guilt. I was a prisoner of my own guilt. At last, we were dismissed. I took my time fumbling with my papers and books so that I could talk with Rayna. John got up and gave me a folded sheet of paper and walked out of the room. I opened it up. It read, *GUILTY?* I gasped. Was he referring to the guy that gave the speech or to me? I wondered if he had read my mind. Rayna turned around.

"What's the matter?" she asked. "You look pale."

"Oh nothing," I said trying to be nonchalant, trying to be cool and casual, but it bothered the hell out of me. What was John talking about? She turned back to get her books. I wadded the paper up in a ball, stood up, and made a jump shot to the trash basket. It was a ringer. Dr. Carlisle witnessed the shot.

"Nice shot, Mr. LaCour, but this is not a gymnasium," he said.

"Yes, sir," I said. "Just practicing excellence, sir."

"Ya, Ya," Dr. Carlisle said in a brogue that he had picked up from years of teaching in South Africa.

Rayna and I gathered our books and walked out together.

"Don't you think your friend John is a little strange?" I asked when we were in the hall.

"You mean John Williams?" she said.

"Yeah, he's different. I can't pinpoint it."

"His eyes are penetrating," she said. "I don't know him very well, though. I've only known him since this class. Why?"

"Nothing. Just curious."

They descended the steps of the building.

"Wanna come over after I get off work? It's spaghetti night at our house," she said.

"Yeah, that would be great. Your mom doesn't mind?"

"No, of course not."

"Great then. I'll be there around 6:00 o'clock?"

"Perfect. See you then," she said.

She walked in the direction of the parking lot, and I headed toward the Blue dorm, but not before admiring her legs. I watched her until she was out of sight.

"Hey, brother," I heard a familiar voice say. I looked over my shoulder.

"Hi, Bobby," I said.

I waited for him to catch up. His dark hair bounced in the breeze. Jaunty he was, I thought. Yes, jaunty was a good word to describe him.

"What's cooking?" he said.

"A lot."

Bobby looked at me.

"Circles under your eyes. You look like crap," he said.

"Thanks."

"That's what brothers are for. You're not sleeping. Having nightmares again?"

"Yeah."

Three girls in miniskirts walked by and gave Bobby the eye.

"Hi, Bobby," they chorused in a high, female lilt.

"Hi ladies," he said admiringly and turned around walking backwards to watch them walk by. The blonde turned around.

"Caught you looking," she said.

Bobby continued to walk backwards and held his hands up.

"Guilty as charged! I just couldn't help myself, Cher," he said smiling his gregarious smile.

Just like Uncle Baby, I thought. He would have to use the *guilt* word; I brooded. Third time I heard that today. God, are you trying to tell me something?

"Boy," Bobby began, "you've got to get out of this funk. Do what I do. Anesthetize yourself with women."

"Yeah, and how are your grades? It would kill Mama if you got shot up in 'Nam," I said. I thought about the nightly report of war casualties on the TV at the Ranch where I hung out after eating in the cafeteria.

"Hey, don't worry about me. I can handle it," he said. "Life's like surfing. You've got to catch the wave first. Then the trick is to keep it balanced."

"Didn't know that you were so philosophical," I said.

"Beach boy philosophy. I ain't as smart as you, brother, but I'm a hellava lot happier."

"You have a point there," I said. "I went home this weekend. Mama called and wanted to see me."

"Yeah?"

"She wanted to see you too, but I told her you had a date. Was I right?"

"You're right about that brother. I had a date with that cute new cheer-leader, Carla."

Bobby paused. "She is fine. I mean fine. By the way, what did Mama want?"

"You're going to drop your drawers," I said.

"Judge Clarence Chevalier asked Mama to marry him, and she's gonna do it."

"No way!" Bobby said and stopped in his tracks.

"Yeah, he's a little old for her, don't you think?"

We resumed walking.

"Nah," he said. "Love doesn't have an age. Look at me. I like younger women. I like older women."

"Yeah, yeah. I know, Bobby. But love and like are two different things. Face it. You just like women. Just keep your head on straight, okay, man?"

"Will do, 'Captain my Captain,'" he said and veered off across the grassy field.

"Didn't know you knew Whitman," I said.

"Surprise, surprise," he said.

"You're getting more like Uncle Baby every day. See ya," I said and waved.

I was a wine decanted, as if I knew anything about wine, except Mad Dog Twenty-Twenty or Tokay. The only thing I knew about wine was from what I read. Sediment and sludge settled in the back of my brain—not for discussion, but I had a million questions from the sublime to the stupid, the rhetorical to the practical. Rayna laughed, fielded, and fended the majority of them. She was quick-witted and came up with her share of crazy questions. We were inseparable. When we weren't together, and she wasn't working, we talked on the phone. Our conversations closed the gap of years of separation. We became reacquainted with each other. I had not confided in her about my nightmares. Not yet. There were some secrets not worth telling. Maybe, later—years later. I did have to write something personal for my speech. I doodled around most of the night before Dr. Carlisle's class trying to get something on paper. I wasn't going to get too personal. I was going to write about something very benign about my dog, Pooch, but then Éli would be a good subject, too. Later that night, I had the usual nightmares again.

At the next Speech class, Rayna asked me if I had stayed up late.

"Yeah," I said when I took my seat. "Had to work on my speech, although I don't want to give it today."

Dr. Carlisle started out his usual way of asking for volunteers.

"Hmm, no brave souls." He picked up his roll book. "I'll start at the bottom of the roll book this time," he said. "Mr. John Williams."

I wondered how he got his name on Dr. Carlisle's roll. There was a failure in the system somewhere. John approached the podium with no speech in hand.

"Where is your speech, Mr. Williams?" Dr. Carlisle said.

"I don't need it, sir," he said.

"Very well. Proceed," Dr. Carlisle said.

John looked at everyone, and the class became silent. He had an arresting quality about his eyes that riveted your attention. He began.

"I have known the sea. I have known the out-stretched hand of Civil Defense rescuers. I have known the welcomed sandwich and shirt from Red Cross workers. June 27, 1957 Hurricane Audrey hit. It was disaster day for all of us who lived in the Southwest corner of Louisiana. That evening brought the first breaking news to the nation. By the next day, the people from New York to California paused over their morning coffee and watched the aftermath of destruction on their TVs. 'May God, help them,' they probably said, and took the last bite of their toast and rolled the morning paper and tucked it under their arms. They hurried out of the door rushing to get to their subways on time, hoping to sit next to the woman with the breasts that tautly stretched her embroidered blouse and whose sea-colored eyes could drown you with one gaze and baptize you with another. Their world had not been shaken enough to understand. 'Life goes on' clichéd across their lips."

John paused and looked at me. I dropped my eyes and moved nervously. Old wounds began to ooze. John continued.

"I was in that madness. Our house shook from the fury that broke it apart when a tidal wave twenty feet high slammed into it. I heard the joists pulling apart. My family and I rode the roof like a raft, until my baby sister was wrenched from my mother's arms."

I jerked my head up. He was telling my story, but how could he possibly have known? John continued,

"My father jumped in after her, but he couldn't reach her. He made his way back to the section of roof we were on and put his hand out to me—to me—reaching for me, reaching for me to pull him to safety."

I wiped the perspiration from my forehead. I braced my head with my hand shielding my eyes and looked down trying to hide my feelings that I was sure my face betrayed. I felt the blood pounding in my head. I listened to the flap of a hundred wings in my ears. John paused slightly and continued to speak,

"I hesitated," he said. "I thought of all the times my father had beaten me, berated me, and belittled me. I froze. Time was suspended. I tried to make up for that split-second hesitation and jumped in the turbulent waves to save him. A telephone pole hit him, and he went under and drowned. I went under and nearly drowned, too. While I was under water, I felt an infinite, changeless reality beneath this world of madness and change. I was propelled up breaking the skin of the water and I was born into a life of regret. More than anything, I want my father's love and forgiveness. I want to love myself again. Yes, I have known the sea."

No one moved and no one breathed when John walked back to his seat. I also sat frozen in time, filled with overwhelming sorrow. Dr. Carlisle, eyes glistening, sat for a few moments honoring the strength of emotion that John's speech had elicited in all of us—especially me. Standing up, Dr. Carlisle broke the silence and put his roll book in his satchel.

"Masterfully done, Mr. Williams. My heartfelt sorrow goes out to you and your family. I hope you find peace," he said. Then he addressed the rest of the class.

"When you have passed your grading charts to Mr. Williams, you may leave. I don't think anyone would want to follow that speech. Until next time, I bid you *adieu*," Dr. Carlisle said as he put on his hat, picked up his satchel and umbrella, and left the room.

John grabbed his backpack and hurried out of the room without picking up his critique papers. The room filled with the sibilant sounds of the other students whispering. Rayna turned to me and noticed the angst that must have been apparent on my face.

"Are you okay?" she asked.

"Yeah, yeah, I'll be okay," I lied.

"Dredged up unwelcome thoughts, huh?" she asked.

"Yeah, not too fun."

"If he lived in Cameron, I've never heard of him. Do you suppose he was from Creole or Grand Chenier?" she asked.

"I don't know. I haven't ever heard of him either. I think I'll try to catch up with him. I'll call you later, okay?" I said and grabbed my backpack.

I headed for the door.

"Sure," she said watching my face closely.

When I got into the hall, I saw John turning left and exiting at the other end of the building. I exited from the left side entrance and sprinted down the sidewalk to the end of the building. I looked to the left and the right, but John wasn't there. I asked a couple of students sitting on the handrails of the steps if they had seen a guy come out carrying a navy backpack. They shook their heads. I went back into the building and walked up and down the hall and looked in every classroom. John was nowhere to be found. I entered the last classroom and bumped into a few chairs while weaving in and out of the desks to make my way to the tall windows. I leaned my arms against the windowsill and cursed my luck.

"Damn, damn, damn," I said.

I raised my head and looked out of the window. There was John crossing Ryan Street. I tried to raise the window, but it wouldn't budge. I tried to raise another window. No luck. I ran out of the classroom and down the hall dodging students and colliding with another, scattering her books, papers and contents of her purse all over the floor. She was rather explicit on how she felt about me.

"Sorry, so sorry," I yelled.

I slid around the corner and bounded out the front of the building. I stopped briefly to look for John. There he was in the parking lot of Gordon's Drug Store. I took the steps three at a time and ran as if I were the one pursued. I ran across the streets to the heralding cry of screeching brakes, blowing horns, and an occasional "asshole" yelled from a car window. I saw that jerk, John enter the glass doors of the drugstore, and I knew I could slow down and not get myself killed over that weirdo. I opened the door of the drugstore and entered to the jangle of the overhead bells. I looked down the cosmetic aisle, then the laxative and antacid aisle. No John. I got down to the candy display and ran the length of the building looking down all the aisles. No luck.

"May I help you?" the brunette at the register asked.

"I was just trying to catch up with a buddy of mine," I said trying to catch my breath. "I saw him come in here. His name is John. About six feet tall, blond hair. He had a navy backpack."

"You're the first one that has come in the front door for the past half hour," she said.

"It can't be," I said glancing around. "I just saw him walk in here. Is there a back door?"

"I'm sorry, sir. I would have heard the bells on the door jingle. And yes, we have a backdoor, but it's for employees only," the young woman said. I walked to the backdoor next to the employee's time clock and looked around. No John.

"Excuse me," I heard the clerk say. "That area is for employees only."

I opened the employee door and looked out in all directions. Not a trace of John. I thought that I was going crazy or having a nervous breakdown.

"Sir," she called again, and I reappeared.

"Thanks. Sorry, so sorry, I bothered you," I said feeling sheepish over my apparent stupidity.

CHAPTER TWENTY-THREE

I wanted to disappear as John had seemingly disappeared. Where the hell did the jerk go?

I was folding into myself the way my fingers folded into a fist. I would like John's face to fold around my fist. I leisurely walked back across Ryan Street and trudged back through the campus. Each foot slogged in quicksand and sucked my energy. I was oblivious to the people I passed. A distant thunder rumbled and expressed my mood. Mrs. Lackey walked up from behind.

"Looks like you have the weight of the world on your shoulders," she said in her straightforward speech. I tried to brighten up a bit. I hated for people to know the real circumstances of my mood. I hated for anyone to read me so quickly.

"Hi, Mrs. Lackey."

"What's wrong, no future children and grandchildren? No Posterity?" she asked.

While walking across campus with Mrs. Lackey, a spark of an idea struck my mind and ignited the closer we got to the building of the registrar's office. Maybe she could help me.

"No, No, it's not that. I'm kind of sad because of my dog, Pooch. He's twelve years old and in a bad way. His arthritis is so bad that he can hardly walk," I said.

That was an honest statement, I thought, even though manipulation was at the core.

"Oh, I'm sorry. I've experienced firsthand the sorrow of watching a pet age and die," she said. "It's not pleasant."

"No, it's not. It breaks your heart."

"How's your class with Dr. Carlisle coming?" she asked.

"Oh, it's great. He's remarkable at learning everyone's names."

"Yeah, he's a living legend around here," she said.

"Did you add another student to our class? I noticed that when we were counting the list of students there were twenty-nine in the class, and I was the thirtieth. When I went to class there were thirty-one."

"You were the last one that I added in that class. That's strange," she said. "I counted it three times. I know I was accurate."

"Also, when we were counting, I happened to glance at the bottom of the list starting with the Ws and noticed only one, a Walker. But in class, there was a John Williams, a John S. Williams. Can a student audit a class?" I asked as innocently as possible.

"Not in Dr. Carlisle's class," she said. "Now you've got me curious. Let's check it out."

We climbed the steps, and I opened the door for her, and we went to her office. She dropped her purse on the desk and walked to the filing cabinet where she thumbed through several records. She pulled out the file and flipped through the forms.

"Let's see," she said. "That's Dr. Carlisle's 10 a.m. class? John S. Williams, right?"

"That's right."

"Okay, here we go. There are thirty students in that class, and there is no John S. Williams, she said her voice trailing off. She paused to think.

"Well, he's in the class because we graded a speech he gave today."

I showed her the handout and checklist with John's name typed out at the top. I'm glad I had not given it to him.

"Okay then, let me check the university enrollment records," she said.

She went to another filing cabinet and flipped through folders and pulled out a master list. She shook her head.

"There is a John A. Williams and a John L. Williams, but not a John S. Williams. This is getting stranger by the minute," she said as she drummed her fingers on the filing cabinet.

I stood by watching and filtering the deepest recesses of my brain, trying to be of some help. She checked the school nurse's records—no luck. She reached for the phone and called the campus police to see if a parking decal had been issued to him.

"Nothing," she said to me. She dialed a number.

"Dr. Carlisle, this is Della Lackey in the registrar's office. Do you have a John S. Williams in your 10:00 a.m. Speech class on Monday, Wednesday, and Fridays?

"Yes? Did you give him permission to audit your class? No? I understand, sir. That's correct; you haven't received the official rolls yet. You will be receiving them soon. I'll get to the bottom of this. Thank you, sir. Bye."

"I'm sorry I brought this up. It looks like I opened up a can of worms. You've gone to so much effort, but I've got to run to class; besides it looks like it's going to rain a river any minute," I said.

"Oh sure, Walt. This isn't really your concern. Thank you for mentioning it. I'll get it figured out. There's got to be an explanation."

I left her brooding over the circumstances of a student who attended class but was not registered. I gathered my books and turned toward the door.

"I can't believe someone could fall through the cracks like this," she said shaking her head slowly, her earrings dangling.

Walking fast, I headed in the direction of the Blue Dorm. I had to talk with Rayna. I had never told her the details of my father's death; in fact, I was reluctant to talk about the events of Hurricane Audrey at all. Those stupid speeches dug all this up again, and I thought for sure that I would start with the night terrors again, as if they weren't bad enough already. Maybe I should call her. No. I had to talk with her in person. I made an immediate about-face and headed for the parking lot. The parking lot was closer than the dorm phone, so I decided to drive over to her house.

Rayna lived on a side street a couple of blocks from the lake. I always took the long way to her house to avoid the road to the port. I didn't want to go near Shed #5—too many memories, too much sadness. I knew some guys who went to an old bar down by the port out of curiosity. They told tales of foreign sailors dancing traditional folk dances and waving handkerchiefs. The owner of the bar mated his Rhodesian ridgeback dogs in the middle of the floor while the sailors cheered. The rowdiness and the sadness were too juxtaposed, too irreverent to even be spoken of in the same sentence.

Rayna's house was in a more genteel section, a couple of blocks behind the mansions that faced the lake on Shell Beach Drive. It was near St. Patrick's Hospital. Memories of finding Mama at St. Pat's and Dr. Andrews flooded my mind. Maybe, I should talk to Doc about these nightmares. Why didn't I think of that before? I may have a worse condition than just nightmares if I didn't get hold of myself. I needed answers. I needed to get to the root of things. This was not the time to talk to Dr. Andrews. I had to get this settled with John. I turned down Rayna's street and passed white houses with porches neatly tucked in between old oak trees and shrubbery. The brilliant, spring blooms of the azaleas were long gone, but the green foliage lingered through October when the leaves would begin to feel the effect of cooler weather. Fall was a month around the corner, waiting to wield its colors of russet, ochre, and orange—but mostly russet.

I pulled into Rayna's driveway next to her green Volkswagen Beetle and put the gear in park. I hesitated, not able to turn the ignition off. I worried that she may not appreciate me dropping in like this, but I would explain to her the whole situation with John. I gripped the steering wheel for a minute and took a deep breath. Was I ready for this? I didn't know. Would she be appalled? Would she hate me? There was a good chance. Would I lose her? That was a possibility. I wanted Rayna more than anything in my life. I didn't want to lose her again, but it wasn't fair to our relationship to keep secrets, especially one like this. I had to open up to her. I turned the ignition off and got out of the truck slowly. I walked toward the front door, running my hands on the neatly topped box hedges. I stood in front of her door and hesitated. I turned around and started back down the steps. I remembered my problem with hesitation and immediately did an about-face and rang the doorbell before I could change my mind. I heard the bong, bong, bong of the sonorous chimes. Rayna came to the door in her bathing suit; her hair was wrapped in a white towel with a large, brilliant blue and yellow parrot perched on her head. Wow! I momentarily forgot my problems. She laughed at the surprised look on my face, and I laughed at the whole comical scene.

"Come in quickly," she said. "I don't want Beethoven to take off."

I laughed out loud again. It felt good to laugh.

"I didn't know you had a parrot," I said

"He's a macaw and he's not mine. Looks like I may have inherited him, though. His owner is a little old lady, a client of Dr. Marlow's. She's in the hospital and may have to go into a nursing home. So, I've been taking care of him. We will see what happens. I was just going to bathe the old bird. Come on, you can help."

I gladly followed her down the hall to the bathroom, admiring her body in a bathing suit. She turned the water on, stepped into the shower and directed the showerhead up so that it would spray on the parrot or more correctly, macaw. Beethoven cawed hoarsely, flapped his wings in the water and seemed to enjoy it. Rayna turned around in a circle so that the water splashed on his back as well. I wasn't looking at the bird. Droplets of water glittered on Rayna's skin. She and I laughed.

"Lucky bird," I said. I stepped into the shower fully clothed and kissed her. She kissed me back: first tentatively, then more passionately. Without taking my mouth from hers, I reached behind my back and turned the water off. I unbuttoned a couple of buttons of my shirt, too much in a hurry to deal with difficult buttons and pulled it over my head and threw it over the shower door.

"I've never kissed a girl with a parrot on her head," I said when we came up for air.

"A macaw," she said and kissed me again.

The steam made me think of the fog of a dream where I was searching for something. I had found what was missing. It was Rayna. I kissed her neck until my lips reached her lips.

"Good boy, good boy," Beethoven said.

Laughter erupted from our kiss. We stepped out of the shower, and Beethoven shook himself dry, and then preened his shiny feathers. Rayna let him fly out of the bathroom and around the house while she dried off. She tossed a towel to me. I followed her back to the kitchen, suppressing the urge to take her into my arms again. She picked up a box of birdseed and sprinkled some in a dish in Beethoven's cage.

"Come on buddy, dinner time. Come eat your food," she called in a singsong voice.

The macaw flew to the cage and walked in.

"Good boy," she said.

"Good boy, good boy," Beethoven repeated.

They laughed.

"Any idea how he got his name?" I said.

"Sure. Listen. Beethoven sing your Fifth Symphony. Sing, bird," she said.

Beethoven responded when he sang in the symphony's rhythm, "da da da dum, da da da dum."

"Maestro Beethoven, I applaud you," I said bowing. "What a bird."

"Make yourself at home, while I change my clothes," she said. "I'll be back in a sec."

"Do you mind if I throw my shirt in the dryer for a few minutes if that's okay," I said feeling kind of foolish half naked, and hoping her mother would not return home any time soon.

"Of course."

My jeans were only damp, so while my shirt was drying, I walked around the Miller's living room and examined the pictures on the mantel: Potted Meat, or Al in his high school graduation cap with a grin on his face; Al in his US Army uniform with no grin on his face; Rayna in her cap and gown with that big, beautiful smile. There was a small black and white picture of Mr. and Mrs. Miller in front of their old house in Cameron, and to my surprise, our old house was in the background. I was elated. I held the picture close and scrutinized it. I stood at the mantel lost in thought when Rayna returned.

"That's our house in the background in this picture. You know we lost all of our pictures in Audrey," I said.

"I suppose you did. I never thought about it," she said. "My mother put all of our pictures in the trunk of the car when we evacuated."

"Smart woman," I said.

"Would your mom mind if I made a copy of this picture, if you still have the negative?"

"Mama wouldn't mind at all. We may have some more. Wait just a sec, and I'll get them."

She returned with a couple of worn albums, and we sat on the sofa flipping the pages and laughing. However, some of them uprooted many buried memories. I turned the page and there was a picture of me, Bobby, and Mama holding Baby Faye. Although the picture was in black and white, Baby Faye was wearing the white dress with the butternut yellow chicks and orange ducks. I recognized the dress because I remembered Mama making it. I choked. I ran my fingers over the glossy photo trying to imprint that shiny moment into my skin. I would have cried if I had been alone. I had almost forgotten what Baby Faye looked like. She was so sweet.

"I remember that day. Your dad had just gotten a new camera and was trying it out," I said trying to make my voice sound casual. Rayna took the picture out of the album and handed it to me.

"Here," she said. "You can have it."

I held the edges of the picture with both hands and was unable to speak for a minute.

"I think I will frame this and give it to Mama for Christmas," I said softly.

My mood spiraled down, and I felt the heaviness of my dilemma. Rayna noticed the shift in my mood and changed the subject.

"Do you want a Coke?" she asked as she got up.

"Sure."

Rayna left and returned shortly with the bottles and sat down next to me. I sipped the Coke and wondered how I should begin. All my ideas of how to tell her flew the coop.

"Something is bothering you," she said. "I hope these pictures haven't upset you."

I took a deep breath and let out a ragged sigh. I nodded *yes*.

"I don't work in a vet's office for nothing. I've learned to watch animals at Dr. Marlow's, and I just apply that to humans. It's more like a sixth sense, though," she said.

"Do you know anyone who knows John Williams?" I asked feeling like I took a plunge in cold water.

"No. Maybe some of our classmates might know him. We could ask around. He used to sit behind me until you transferred to our section," she said.

"I ran into Mrs. Lackey, the lady at the registrar's office, the one who helped me make the class change," I began.

Rayna nodded.

"She looked through the records and John Williams is not registered at McNeese at all."

"So, what does that have to do with anything? Maybe, it's just a mistake," she said.

I jumped up and paced back and forth.

"No," I said hesitatingly.

I opened my mouth and no words came out. I tried again. I sat down next to her and stared at my hands.

"I don't want to lose you," I began. "I can't do this. I've gotta go." I stood up.

"Walt," she said. "You're running away from something. What is it?"

I sat down again. I had to tell her. I had to know if it was going to make a difference in our relationship. If it did, it was better to know now than to invest any more emotional energy into a relationship that would go nowhere.

"The speech John gave was my story," I said in a gravelly voice. "I have never spoken to anyone of what actually happened that day. The first time I've ever written anything about what happened was a couple of days ago, and I burned every page in my trashcan and crushed the ash. It's like he read my mind," I said.

I covered my face and continued.

"It was Baby Faye that was ripped from Mama's arms, and— and it was me that hesitated to help Papa back on the roof. It was me. I didn't reach out for him. It all happened so fast. He was dogpaddling alongside of the roof we were floating on. He looked at me. For once he needed me, and I let him down. I felt this power and anger like he deserved to have it dished out to him because he always dished it out to me, but I didn't know he would drown. It was pure craziness. All that I know is that he drowned because I didn't reach out in time. He's dead because of me. I killed Papa."

I broke down and cried.

"Oh, my God," she said and put her arms around me.

We cried together.

"You didn't intend to. You didn't know he would drown," she said holding me.

I took a deep breath and tried to regain my composure. She took my hands off my face and kissed me gently on the mouth, and I knew I had not lost her.

"I love you, Walt," she whispered in my ear. "I've loved you all of my life. I'll help you through this."

I took her in my arms and kissed her passionately. I felt that drowning would be okay as long as I drowned in her love. The ocean of grief that had paced the shores between us had finally broken down the barrier. We sat in bewilderment over how John could have known.

"Maybe he had heard the story from someone that your Mama had told?" she said.

"I don't think so. For one thing, Mama doesn't even talk about it, and secondly, she was huddled up against the roof with her back to the waves. If she had turned around, she probably would have been washed off. Besides, my head was turned in her direction. I would have seen her. I deliberately turned my head away from Papa for a split second, and the disgusting thing was that I enjoyed that split-second of power," I said.

My shoulders slumped.

"I can understand that because he certainly lorded it over you," she said.

I followed Rayna into the kitchen. She picked up the Lake Charles phone book and looked up Williams.

"There are a lot of Williams, but no John S," she said as she thumbed through the Ws. I wish I knew his father's name. Looks like we're out of luck," she said.

She dug around in a drawer and found an old Cameron phone book.

"There is a Clyde Williams, but we know him. There isn't any more Williams much less a John S. Williams. But that's not to say that there were not any John S. Williams ten years ago," she said. "He has an accent and doesn't sound like he comes from Cameron," she continued.

"I think I will try to talk with him at the next class meeting," I said, "if he shows up."

I took my shirt out of the dryer and put it on. Rayna stood in front of me and started to button the buttons. She ran her hands across my bare chest and shoulders.

"I may never get this shirt buttoned," she said. I kissed her.

CHAPTER TWENTY-FOUR

I slung the gear in reverse and backed out of Rayna's driveway, shifted into first, and listened to the familiar cant of combustion that rose to a shrill whine. I shifted into second and then into the monotonous hum of third. The steady, low hum comforted me. It was just me and my truck rolling along, I thought. I didn't want to go back to the dorm and have to make conversation with my roommate or anyone else who might be around. Paul and I were friends because we were roommates, but I didn't share secrets with him. For that matter, Paul didn't share secrets with me either. I confided my secrets only to Rayna because I trusted her.

I drove down Lake Shore Drive and followed the curve of the lake into town. I turned right on Broad Street just to have the sun to my back and headed east without any real destination in mind. I was glad that I had told Rayna, but I kicked myself for blubbering like a baby. I turned south on Highway 14 to head back in the direction of McNeese, when I saw the sign for the Bamboo Club. I decided to stop and have a beer, which would give me more time to think.

I opened the door of the low-slung building and entered. I blinked my eyes until they adjusted to the dark room. It felt like a cave and it smelled of cigarettes, beer, and sweaty men just off work. The 5 o'clock crowd had just begun to trickle in; otherwise, there were just a few construction workers and pipe fitters that had probably been there since 4. They took deep drags on their cigarettes in between sips of beer and listened to Clint West and The Boogie Kings practice. I sat at the bar on a stool closest to the door and ordered a beer. I listened to the guys gripe about their foreman and their old ladies in between sets of *Ça Fait Chaud* and Rufus Jagneaux's *Opelousas Sostan*. I had grown up around oilfield workers and roughnecks and was used to being around egos and tough talk. Papa had been one of them. I regretted that thought because when I listened to the Cajun music, I had actually forgotten about all the mess that had been going on since yesterday.

I finished my first beer and dug in my pocket to pay for another. I planned to go back to the dorm after I finished the second beer. I had been there about forty-five minutes and had just taken a couple of sips of my second beer when John Williams walked from across the room. I nearly fell off my stool. Had he been there the whole time? I wondered. I didn't see him over there. There was no back door in that direction. He couldn't have come in the front door. He would have had to pass me. What the hell? John walked toward me and nodded.

"You're just the S.O.B. I've been wanting to talk to," I said, my temper rising.

Alcohol always made me lower my guard—made me less of an actor—made my lip lose its civility, so much for alcohol and testosterone.

"Talk away," John said.

"How did you know that stuff, man? What are you some kind of private investigator? But there was no way you could have known. No one knew that except me—and Papa, and he's dead. Are you some kind of psychic?"

I stood up knocking my stool over. The guys on my right moved away.

"You boys better take it outside," the bartender said.

I took a deep breath and bowed my chest.

"I guess that's for you to find out," John said calmly.

"You sick S.O.B., you stole my story. That was my Papa, my baby sister, and my grief. You stole my grief."

"You have a monopoly on grief?" he said and looked away.

I knew that John didn't see my punch coming, but the second before my fist should have plastered his face, he ducked. He backed out the door and into the parking lot with me swinging punches and missing.

"If you want to know, you'll have to follow me," he said and kicked the stand on his motorcycle and revved it up.

He took off with a biting bark of inertia out of the parking lot, turned left and headed south on Highway 14. I revved up my truck and took off after him. He threaded in and out of traffic, neatly, cleanly, with flashes of chrome. He remained just far enough ahead that I could see which direction he was turning. It wasn't long before I realized that we were on Highway 27 heading toward the Gulf—toward Cameron. I was surprised, but I didn't beat myself up over it.

"He knows everything else about me, so why shouldn't he know that I am from Cameron?" I said out loud.

I could still see him way up ahead. I passed the tree-lined ridges leaving Calcasieu Parish and entering Cameron Parish. After I had passed mile after mile of sallow looking marsh grass and bored with the monotony of beige, I began questioning my own sanity. Maybe this wasn't such a good idea to follow him. It's going to cause nothing but trouble. I had enough of that in my life. Maybe I should just let it go, turn around and go back to Rayna. I was glad that I had told Rayna the circumstances of Papa's death. I was happier that she understood. Rayna was the best thing that had happened to me in a long time. I glanced at the picture on the seat next to me. It was a godsend. I decided that I would make another copy and give one to Bobby, too. Mama would especially be thrilled to have a picture of herself and her three kids in front of our old house. Yes, she would really like that. No one ever knew that when Mr. Miller took that picture of Baby Faye, that she would not survive. No one ever knew that the house that we grew up in and held so many memories of my small life, would break apart into nothing more than kindling. No one ever knows his own fate from one minute to the next.

I strained to see up the road. There he was, chrome flashing, a few cars ahead of me. I tried to pass the cars in front of me, but thought better of it and pulled back in. It wasn't worth getting killed or maimed over. Maybe, I should turn around now and forget about it, I rationalized, but something, perhaps it was my own ego, nudged me on. I had to see this to the finish; besides, my curiosity got the best of me, and I kept going. My mind turned to the waves of spartina grass and the bushy bluestem. The bushy bluestem would soon have coppery foliage with chunks of fluffy flowers that looked like cotton candy. The marsh brimmed with the richness of wildlife: the blankets of snowy egrets or glossy ibis settling over the fields and rippling at the slightest threat of danger. I spied roseate spoonbills and brown pelicans and was amazed at the enormous hunger that was necessary for the survival of the wild. The whole world is hungry, I thought. I remembered as a kid the ingenuity of the killdeer. I had walked along a dusty road when a killdeer scuttled along in front of me like it was wounded, limping, with an awkward flap of a broken wing, faking it, drawing me away from its egg. Deceit in the wild was necessary for survival.

My truck leaned into the blacktop curves. Through the open window, I felt the slightest hint of cool air and smelled the heavy, wet earth in the winds off the marsh. I spotted a pied-billed grebe with its characteristic short straggly feathers in a slue. Grebes or *sac-a-plomb* in French were one of my favorite ducks. They outwitted many hunters with their ability to submerge at the flash from a rifle muzzle, and amazingly just before the pellets peppered the water for lack of a target. Most ducks usually lunged headfirst when danger approached, but grebes could sink straight down and at any depth; then, they could swim underwater until out of danger. Wildlife had an amazing intelligence and that was probably one of the reasons for my break from the hunting and trapping culture of my youth. In the heart of me, they were more beautiful alive than dead and hanging on a wall for one family to see. I did not look at them as food, although, I was not a vegetarian by any means. I didn't want to be controlled by a need for power.

The sun lowered in the distant horizon, casting dark shadows over the marsh. The moon would be rising. Should be a full moon tonight, I thought. I loved the cyclical nature of sun rising and moon setting, moon rising and sun setting. I never understood boundless, yet I wanted to understand timeless. In this world, to think of those things was as futile as a dog chasing its tail that it would never catch; however, I loved the dusty circle that it made in the effort. I took comfort in cyclical things: the change of seasons and the migration of the indigo and painted bunting in the spring.

"Oh great," I said sarcastically. "All my wandering thoughts made me forget what I'm doing. I think I lost the snooping S.O.B.," I said out loud.

My temper flared again as I thought of all the grief this guy had caused me. Sure enough, when I got to Cameron, I had lost John. How in the hell can you lose someone in a place as small as Cameron? Mama was home from work by now. Maybe I ought to stop in for some gumbo or étouffee or whatever Nanan may be cooking. There was always food at Nanan's house. Maybe I could shake this lethargy. I headed home which was right next door to Uncle Thib's Éli's Laissez Les Bons Temps Rouler bar. The lights of the bar twinkled in the late afternoon. When I passed the bar, I noticed that a motorcycle was parked in front. I put on my brakes and pulled into the parking lot just to check it out. It looked like John's bike. I hopped out of my truck and barreled up the steps and banged the front door open. The air-conditioned air hit me in the face, and it felt good. Uncle Thib had insisted on an air conditioner when he rebuilt the bar. I glanced around. John was not there. I'm sure that was his motorcycle, I thought. A couple of guys were sitting at the bar watching the news on TV. Uncle Baby was sitting in his usual chair under the replica of Éli's violin. They all turned around to see what the ruckus was about.

"Boy Oh Boy," Uncle Baby said to me while he lifted a spider that had dropped down on his sleeve and put it on the strings of the violin that hung on the wall. Uncle Thib began his usual greeting.

"Mais garde donc ça, Look what the cat done drug in."

"Let me see," Uncle Baby mused. "Yes, he's the raggedy, tag toad, the nose that knows, the neenie, niny, teeny, tiny," Uncle Baby's voice trailed off from amusing himself with his goofy word rhymes.

I had a fierce scowl on my face and was not amused. Uncle Thib and Uncle Baby stopped short.

"What in the hell is the matter, Walt? Looks like you need a beer."

"I'm looking for someone," I said.

"Well, if you tell me his name or what he looks like, I may be able to help," Uncle Thib said sarcastically. He laid his pipe on the counter.

"I'm sorry, Parrain. I'm looking for a guy from my school. He's kind of weird, about six feet tall, really strange eyes. His name is John Williams."

"Sure," Uncle Thib said. "he came in here fifteen minutes ago. He didn't seem too weird to me. His eyes were kind of different, penetrating would be the best word. Said his name was John and that he was a friend of yours."

"Yeah, sure."

"You having a problem with him?" Uncle Thib asked.

"Well sort of."

"He asked for that section of board that they found when they excavated for the new church," Uncle Thib said.

"What board?"

"The one from your Papa's shrimp boat that he had been working on before it was destroyed during Audrey. It's been out in that shed for a long time. That John fellow said he was going to give it to you," Uncle Thib said.

"Where did he go?" I asked.

"Well, I thought you would know. I think he said he was meeting you down the road on that sandy, stretch of beach."

Although Uncle Thib questioned his memory, I knew better. His memory was sharp and one of his best characteristics. It was his job to tend bar and listen to his customers. He prided himself in his ability to recall and inquire about previous conversations, asking guys about their old ladies by name and stuff like that.

"Thanks, Parrain," I said as I banged out the door, my curiosity and anger rising.

I took the steps two at a time and ran across the parking lot, down the street and to the short stretch of beach. Running felt good. John sat on the board and meditatively stared out across the Gulf as the sun began to set and color the water yellow.

"Hey," I yelled and ran toward him ready to beat the crap out of him. "What the hell are you doing messing with me and my family?"

John got up and faced me.

"Glad you could make it," he said. "I knew you would come."

I glared at him. A window had washed up on the beach.

"Look in the window, Walt. Do you see your Papa's face?" John said.

Stunned for a moment, I took a deep breath and barreled at him with a full-forced determination. John stepped aside easily, and I fell headlong in the sand. I felt as if I was all brute and bungle, and John lithe and calculated.

"How did you know about that, I've never written it anywhere or told anyone," I said. "Who are you? Why are you doing this to me?"

"The question is who are you?" John said.

"Why do you care?" I retorted.

"Who do you hate, Walt?"

I rushed at John again and caught him. We wrestled in the sand. Although I was bigger than him, I felt his muscular strength, and he broke away from me. I jumped up, kicking my shoes off and spat out the earthy, salty taste of sand.

"Who do you hate, Walt?" he asked again, egging me on, egging me into an uncontrollable rage.

"I hate you," I said and lunged at him. He stepped aside, and I fell in the sand again. I rolled from my back, jumped up again, and turned around to face him.

"No, you don't. Who do you hate?" John said.

"My father, that's who. Is that what you wanted to hear? My Papa! I killed him because I hated him," I screamed.

I was a maniac; I wasn't afraid. I wiped my mouth with my sleeve.

"Why?" John said.

"Because he hated me first."

We continued to spar as we hurled accusations back and forth.

"Why do you think he hated you?"

"Because he beat me and didn't want me to be a part of his life. I couldn't do anything right and because—"I choked and caught my breath. "Because he probably thought I wasn't his kid!"

"You don't hate your father. You hate your hesitation."

I swung at him and missed. I swung again and John blocked my punch with his forearm.

"How do you know these things?" I said.

"You hate yourself, don't you? You blame yourself for your father's death."

I swung hard at him again and missed and stumbled forward. I bent over with my hands on my knees trying to catch my breath.

"Where's the piece of Papa's boat?"

"What do you care about your Papa's boat?"

"Because it's a part of him."

"I thought you hated him?" John said.

I shook my head and fell forward on to my knees, sobbing.

"We lost everything. I don't even have a picture of him. The only thing I have left of him now are nightmares."

"What makes you think you could have saved him? You were only a kid. Do you think you're God?" he said.

"But I didn't try."

"Yes, you did. You nearly drowned trying."

"I waited too long. A split-second! A split-second between life and death! If only I could take it back. I want to take it back. I want to take it back," I sobbed.

"That second was not yours to give or take. You're in the divine realm there, buddy. It was your Papa's time. You want this piece of his boat?"

John bent over and picked it up and held it up for me to read: 'Heart of the Sea' was printed in what was once bold red letters that were now faded from exposure to saltwater and time. Underneath the boat's name was printed, "Walter 'Man' LaCour Jr."

"Junior?" I asked and dropped my arms by my side.

"Yes. It was going to be a gift for you," John said. "He didn't have money for college. It was all he could offer you, the work of his hands, his life's occupation, and his name. He wanted you to learn the shrimping business and be his partner. The boat was going to be yours when you got a little older to do as you pleased."

I stood up slowly, shocked by the revelation.

"Why didn't Uncle Thib give it to me?" I said.

"You're a good actor, Walt. No one knew you were hurting so much inside. You were killing yourself."

John held up the board.

"If you still want it, you'll have to go get it," he said, and he slung the board as far out into the Gulf as he could.

In less than a split-second, I ran into the surf and dove into the dark water determined to retrieve it. The moon had come up and glinted on the board ahead. I swam hard against the waves until I reached it. I grabbed it and clung to it spitting out the salty water. I turned back to swim to shore and rubbed the sting of salt from my eyes. I saw the beautiful lady with the long, black hair that had given me the courage to swim for the tree when I was drowning. John stood next to her. They watched me swim toward shore until my feet touched the sandy bottom of the ocean, and I stood up.

"Take care of your mother," John said.

He and the beautiful lady turned and walked into the evening air. I wiped my eyes, straining to see where they had gone. I looked up and down the short expanse of beach. They were no longer there. They simply disappeared. I realized that she looked like Mary, Queen of the Angels, that had hung in my bedroom when I was a kid. A wave knocked me down and washed me onto the shore. I crawled up on the beach dragging the sign with me. I rolled over on my back and laid the board across my chest. I thought I heard Papa kneeling next to me asking,

"Are you okay, son?"

"I'm okay, Papa," I said out loud. "Papa, I never told you that I loved you, but I'm saying it now. I love you." My voice escalated in pitch. "I love you! I love you!!" I screamed. "Please forgive me; may God forgive me," I said into the big sky.

The sea washed over me in whispers. I was called from the tomb. I stretched my arms wide to embrace a galaxy of stars. I lay on the beach for a while allowing the sand to imprint my back and the water to wash over me. At last, I arose. I stood erect. I felt naked like the first man who didn't know he was naked. I lifted my head and shoulders and the weight fell from me. I was no longer curled inward. I was Homo Sapien; I was man of the twenty-first century. I had a brain and a heart that acted like a sieve to filter good from evil, honesty from ego. I was giver and gift. I was single. I was collective. I was one mind and all minds. I was boundary and boundless, but most of all I was fearless and at peace. I knew. I was comfortable and grateful in the knowing that none of us are alone. I surmised that we are presented with two belief systems in life: one positive, the other negative. The first one is that everything is a miracle like the leaf with its webbing of delicate veins that I remembered when I was drowning. The other is that nothing is a miracle. Your choice. I chose the first, the miraculous. If the leaf is a miracle, then what am I?

Mama had told me later that she had worked late preparing documents needed for court the next day and had just locked up and walked over to the bar from the office. She felt an inexplicable nudging to see her brother. She ran her fingers through her windblown hair, opened the door to the bar and stepped in.

"*Comment ça va, mon soeur,*" Uncle Thib said.

"Hello, Alcide," she said. "I'm okay. It looks like it's going to be a wonderful sunset over the water."

"Light and water always makes for a beautiful show. No?"

"Umm hmm," she nodded absently.

"Plop yourself down, cher."

Uncle Thib dried the last of the beer mugs and sat it down. He poured a glass of Coke and handed it to her. She sipped quietly and thought.

"I haven't heard from Walt in a while," she said.

"Boy? He came in here not too long ago. Met a friend way down there at the beach. I told him to slow his hurry down."

"I wonder what that was all about."

"You never know about these young people nowadays. This blond-haired guy comes in here asking for the board we found from Man's boat. Said he was a friend of Walt's, and he was going to meet him down at the beach. The guy kind of looked familiar. Seemed like I've seen him before, but I can't put my finger on it. Then Walt comes in here and asks about this guy with the blue eyes. He said his eyes were strange. Me, I didn't think they were strange. They did look like water and sky mixed together. Different.

You know the kind that can look right through you and see your heart? He kinda looked familiar, but I can't place him."

"Uh huh," Mary Effie said remembering Johann's eyes. She sipped her Coke.

"What was his name?"

"If I ain't forgot my remember again, it was John Williams."

She paused and purposely put her Coke down.

"I think I'll walk down there and see what's going on. I need a little exercise after sitting all day. I'll see you later."

Mama walked toward the beach. The evening breeze blew her skirt and her hair floated behind her. Yes indeed, she agreed with her brother that light and water made a beautiful show. The moon was rising. I was carrying the board when I saw her walking toward me. I was wet and sandy.

"Walt are you okay?" she said.

I nodded my head.

"My friend and this lady seemed to vanish before my eyes," I said, too tired for further conversation. I kept on walking toward the bar. Mama looked at me as I walked by. Out of curiosity she walked toward the beach. John was standing with his back to her looking out at the last glimmer of light on the water.

"John Williams?" she said, and he turned slowly around. Mama gasped.

"Mary Effie," he said.

"Johann!" she said and held her breath. "I don't understand, the telegram said that," her voice trailed off. "I've missed you so."

Johann nodded his head.

"I told you on the train that I would come back to you, and I kept my promise. I'm more alive now than ever. Love is the secret. It makes you live forever. I'll always love you, Mary Effie."

They stared into each other's eyes.

"Take care of our boy," he said.

Johann turned and faded into the dusk.

I carried the board and walked through the sand to the dim lights of Uncle Thib's bar. Rayna sat on the top step, waiting for me. I was surprised. Just when I needed her the most, there she was. She gasped and ran to me and hugged me. I looked over her shoulder and saw a violin case laying on the step. The Star of David and a Christian Cross dangled from the handle. My eyes went from the violin and then back to her with a quizzical look.

"Your Mama gave Éli's violin to my Mom when we were packing to evacuate during Audrey. Mom found it and thought you might want it. She had been saving it for you all along, but as time went by, she forgot."

I was so surprised that I couldn't speak. Tears welled in my eyes. I nodded.

"Go on in," I said. "I just need a moment."

Rayna went into the bar, and I sat on the step and buried my face in my hands and wept. When the rush of emotion settled, I dried my eyes, stood up, and opened the door of the bar.

JUNE—2010

I was running late, but I slowed down my hurry as Uncle Thib used to say. I looked at the neon sign, Éli's Laissez Les Bon Temps Rouler and thought of Éli and his Stradivarius violin. After Rayna gave the violin to me, I gave it to Uncle Thib for safe keeping. Uncle Thib cried. "I thought it was gone forever," he said wiping his eyes. Uncle Thib asked me to research the violin, its origin and worth since those guys had tried so hard to steal it. I spent many hours in the McNeese Library and was stunned by its potential worth, *if* it was real. I wrote letters to experts and arranged for Uncle Thib and myself to fly to New York City to authenticate the violin. It was the first time that I had flown in a plane and the first time that I left the state of Louisiana. Indeed, it was authentic! Yes, indeed, it was made by Antonio Stradivari from Cremona, Italy.

The experts were curious as to how we came to have it, and we told him about how Uncle Thib became Éli's guardian and how Jacob Leitz, Éli's dad, brought it from Germany after he escaped a Nazi concentration camp. They were intrigued with the story of an idiot savant being a master violinist and playing one of the rarest and treasured violins in the world. They were both treasures to this world. A rare violin and an idiot savant who was a master violinist were a phenomena of two geniuses colliding in a moment of time. The science of it all was inexplicable, but the Master Carver put the maple tree through an ice age that stunted its growth and made the wood dense, or perhaps the wood was waterlogged that made the silvery sound of the violin. He made Éli with extreme focus who understood that the sound came from the openness of the violin and from the cracks of his own broken heart. Was this extreme beauty wasted on simple folks? No. We knew we were in the presence of the Divine, and joyous we were. Éli knew that the music changed people because it softened their hearts so that they could love again.

I looked at the night sky and I was incredibly grateful. I had lived and relived the storm throughout my whole life, but now I held the published book of my memoirs of Hurricane Audrey in my hand. I had finally finished it, specifically, for my wife Rayna, my Snuki, our three children Maurice Walter (named in honor of Cracklin and my father) Mary Rose and Callie Faye, their husbands, and our nine grandchildren who waited inside to celebrate my life story. I wanted them to know about the miracles, and that Mary, the mother of our beloved Jesus, Queen of Angels, Star of the Sea, appeared to this old Cajun boy. I wanted them to believe, and I wanted them to know about my real father.

I put my hand on the doorknob and opened the door of Éli's Laissez Les Bon Temps Rouler bar. Rayna was sitting at the bar and slowly turned to me. She was still beautiful, even with wrinkles around her eyes and streaks of gray in her hair. Time had been good to her. I saw my reflection in the mirror over the bar. I was an old man, starkly gray, a little paunchy, but I stood erect. Rayna, my Snukie, looked at me with love in her beautiful, green eyes. I took a deep breath and thought of all those lives that were changed. Hurricane Audrey changed the lenses of everything we had known. We were in that earth's carving. We were the microbes that were sloughed off the magnificent sculpture that remembered ancient and pristine beaches, crystal water that captured light. But we felt assaulted by the change. Our times, our lives, our loves were rearranged in different dimensions. I was that granite being carved, and I was not impenetrable for the Carver. Audrey was a hurricane that hit one time long ago, but time had been the hurricane that ravaged us all. Time was giver and taker. For me, time was the gift I received from the miracle of surviving the drowning. I had so much to show for that time.

Rayna came to me as our kids and grandkids gathered around us. The band played the song that Mama and Papa had danced to in Uncle Thib's bar so long ago, but in my mind, I heard Éli playing that song at the fais-dodo on that windswept night. I heard Mama talking to me about living a life of goodness and grace—a rightly life as I had put it. I remembered how she told me that love changed people. I remembered Uncle Thib telling me to never leave this world hating anyone and that we would be judged by the measure of our love. I remembered the trembling hug of love that Papa had given to me when I jumped overboard to save Pooch. I remembered running my fingers through the hair on Pooch's ears and thinking that this was how love felt in braille. Pooch, my unspoken hero, saved me from drowning in the tidal waves. I remembered Johann's words in his speech, 'More than anything, I want my father's love and forgiveness. I want to love myself again. Yes, I have known the sea.' On the beach that night, I fought the fight of my life, for my soul and my sanity. Johann helped me face my guilt, and later through the sacrament of reconciliation, I could love myself again. I remembered Éli, how special he was, and I knew that God didn't make mistakes. He was a special kind of angel. I remembered my Snuki saying, 'I love you Walt. I have loved you all of my life. I will help you through this.' I remembered that Uncle Thib sold the violin which raised our family out of poverty. By the grace of God, the money did not change us. It made us more generous. Uncle Thib and Mama were long gone, having lived a full life and passing away peacefully. The music slowed down as everyone turned toward me. My brother Bobby, good old Bobby, was in the crowd and remembered Uncle Thib's favorite greeting and spoke out in a big booming voice.

"Mais garde donc ça. Look what the cat done drug in."

GLOSSARY

Allons y: Let's go

Beaucoup: Much or many. A great deal

Bébette: Fool, idiot (children, colloquial)

Bien: To be in good health.

Bonjour: Good day

Bonne nuit: Good night

Bonsoir: Good evening

Ça va bien: Things are going well.

C'est la vie: That's life.

Cher [Sha]: A term of endearment, dear or sweetheart

Cocodrie: Crocodile

Comment ça va: How are you?

Comment ça va, mon soeur: How are you my sister?

Cré boucane: Holy smoke

Couche-couche: A breakfast dish made with cornmeal mush, often served with milk or syrup.

Envie: Desire, or hunger to eat something

Fais-dodo: A Cajun dance party

Grandmère: Grandmother

Grandpère: Grandfather

Grand tétons: Big mountains, or big breasts

Je m'en fichu: I don't care, or I don't give a damn

Jolie Blonde: pretty blonde. The song is a Cajun waltz.

Joie de vivre: Joy of living

La fin du monde: The end of the world

Laissez Les Bons Temps Rouler: Let the good times roll.

Le Grand Dérangement: The Great Expulsion, the removal of the French colonists from Acadia by the British. (1755-1764)

L'oeuvre du paresseux: The work of the lazy.

Loup Garou: Werewolf

Mais garde donc ça: But, look at that.

Maman: Mama

Méli-mélange: jumble, hodge podge

Merci, Mon Dieu: Thanks, my God.

Moi, j'ai pris le grand chemin de fer avec le coeur aussi cassé: I took the train with such a broken heart.

Mon neveu: My nephew

Oui: Yes

Parrain: Godfather

Pauve tete bete: Poor little thing.

Poo Yie: Word used for excitement or something awesome.

Poule d'eau: Moorhen

Voilà: There it is

ABOUT THE AUTHOR

Linda S. Cunningham grew up in Lake Charles, Louisiana where she experienced firsthand accounts of the 1957 Hurricane Audrey that killed nearly five hundred people in Cameron, Louisiana. She and her family watched the devastation from their picture window when the hurricane hit. Her father served as Director of Civil Defense for Calcasieu Parish from whom she heard the many survival stories and saw the coroner's pictures that lend authenticity to the novel. Ms. Cunningham has a B.A. in English and Creative Writing from the University of Houston. She also has a B.S. and M.Ed. in Health and Physical Education from McNeese State University in Lake Charles, Louisiana. She has won awards for screenwriting. She currently resides in Kingwood, Texas.